美国亚裔文学研究丛书
总主编　郭英剑

An Anthology of Vietnamese American Literature
美国越南裔文学作品选

主编　郭英剑　冯元元

本研究受中国人民大学科学研究基金资助，系2017年度重大规划项目"美国亚裔文学研究"（编号：17XNLG10）阶段性成果。

中国人民大学出版社
·北京·

图书在版编目（CIP）数据

美国越南裔文学作品选：英文、汉文 / 郭英剑，冯元元主编. -- 北京：中国人民大学出版社，2022.10
（美国亚裔文学研究丛书 / 郭英剑总主编）
ISBN 978-7-300-31089-3

Ⅰ.①美… Ⅱ.①郭… ②冯… Ⅲ.①文学－作品综合集－美国－英、汉 Ⅳ.① I712.11

中国版本图书馆 CIP 数据核字（2022）第 184120 号

美国亚裔文学研究丛书
美国越南裔文学作品选
总主编　郭英剑
主　编　郭英剑　冯元元
Meiguo Yuenanyi Wenxue Zuopinxuan

出版发行	中国人民大学出版社	
社　　址	北京中关村大街 31 号	邮政编码　100080
电　　话	010-62511242（总编室）	010-62511770（质管部）
	010-82501766（邮购部）	010-62514148（门市部）
	010-62515195（发行公司）	010-62515275（盗版举报）
网　　址	http://www.crup.com.cn	
经　　销	新华书店	
印　　刷	唐山玺诚印务有限公司	
规　　格	170 mm × 240 mm　16 开本	版　次　2022 年 10 月第 1 版
印　　张	14.5	印　次　2022 年 10 月第 2 次印刷
字　　数	273 000	定　价　68.00 元

版权所有　　侵权必究　　印装差错　　负责调换

总 序

美国亚裔文学的历史、现状与未来

郭英剑

一、何谓"美国亚裔文学"?

"美国亚裔文学"(Asian American Literature),简言之,是指由美国社会中的亚裔群体作家所创作的文学。也有人称之为"亚裔美国文学"。

然而,"美国亚裔文学"这个由两个核心词汇——"美国亚裔"和"文学"——所组成的术语,远没有它看上去那么简单。说它极其复杂,一点也不为过。因此,要想对"美国亚裔文学"有基本的了解,就需要从其中的两个关键词入手。

首先,"美国亚裔"中的"亚裔",是指具有亚裔血统的美国人,但其所指并非一个单一的族裔,其组成包括美国来自亚洲各国(或者与亚洲各国有关联)的人员群体及其后裔,比如美国华裔(Chinese Americans)、日裔(Japanese Americans)、菲律宾裔(Filipino Americans)、韩裔(Korean Americans)、越南裔(Vietnamese Americans)、印度裔(Indian Americans)、泰国裔(Thai Americans)等等。

根据联合国的统计,亚洲总计有48个国家。因此,所谓"美国亚裔"自然包括在美国的所有这48个亚洲国家的后裔,或者有其血统的人员。由此所涉及的各国(以及地区)迥异的语言、不同的文化、独特的人生体验,以及群体交叉所产生的多样性,包括亚洲各国由于战争交恶所带给后裔及其有关人员的深刻影响,就构成了"美国亚裔"这一群体具有的极端复杂性。在美国统计局的定义中,美国亚裔是细分为"东亚"(East Asia)、"东南亚"(Southeast Asia)和南亚(South Asia)。[1] 当然,也正由于其复杂性,到现在有些亚洲国家在美国的后裔或者移民,尚未形成一个相对固定的族裔群体。

---

1 参见: Karen R. Humes, Nicholas A. Jones, Roberto R. Ramirez (March 2011). "Overview of Race and Hispanic Origin: 2010" (PDF). United States Census Bureau. U.S. Department of Commerce.

其次，文学主要由作家创作而成，由于"美国亚裔"群体的复杂性，自然导致"美国亚裔"的"作家"群体同样处于极其复杂的状态，但也因此使这一群体的概念具有相当大的包容性。凡是身在美国的亚裔后裔、具有亚洲血统或者后来移民美国的亚裔作家，都可以称之为"美国亚裔作家"。

由于亚裔群体的语言众多，加上一些移民作家的母语并非英语，因此，"美国亚裔文学"一般指的是美国亚裔作家使用英语所创作的文学作品。但由于历史的原因，学术界也把最早进入美国时，亚裔用本国语言所创作的文学作品，无论是口头作品还是文字作品——比如19世纪中期，华人进入美国遭到拘禁时所创作的诗句，也都纳入"美国亚裔文学"的范畴之内。同时，随着全球化时代的到来，各国之间的文学与文化交流日益加强，加之移民日渐增加，因此，也将部分发表时为亚洲各国语言，但后来被翻译成英语的文学作品，同样纳入"美国亚裔文学"的范畴。

最后，"美国亚裔"的划分，除了语言、历史、文化之外，还有一个地理的因素需要考虑。随着时间的推移与学术界研究【特别是离散研究（Diaspora Studies）】的进一步深化，"美国亚裔"中的"美国"（America），也不单单指"the United States"了。我们知道，由于全球化时代所带来的人口流动性的极度增加，国与国之间的界限有时候变得模糊起来，人们的身份也变得日益具有多样性和流动性。比如，由于经济全球化的原因，美国已不单单是一个地理概念上的美国。经济与文化的构成，造就了可口可乐、麦当劳等商业品牌，它们都已经变成了流动的美国的概念。这样的美国不断在"侵入"其他国家，并对其他国家产生了巨大的影响。当然，一个作家的流动性，也无形中扩大了"美国"的概念。比如，一个亚洲作家可能移民到美国，但一个美国亚裔作家也可能移民到其他国家。这样的流动性拓展了"美国亚裔"的定义与范畴。

为此，"美国亚裔文学"这一概念，有时候也包括一些身在美洲地区，但与美国有关联的作家，他们用英语进行创作；或者被翻译成英语的文学作品，也会被纳入这一范畴之内。

应该指出的是，由于"亚裔"群体进入美国的时间早晚不同，加上"亚裔"群体的复杂性，那么，每一个"亚裔"群体，都有其独有的美国族裔特征，比如华裔与日裔有所不同，印度裔与日裔也有所不同。如此一来，正如一些学者所认为那样，各个族裔的特征最好应该分开来叙述和加以研究。[2]

2　参见：Chin, Frank, et al. 1991. "Preface" to *Aiiieeeee! An Anthology of Asian American Writers*. Edited by Frank China, Jeffery Paul Chan, Lawson Fusao Inada, and Shawn Wong. A Mentor Book. p.xi.

二、为何要研究"美国亚裔文学"?

虽然上文中提出,"美国亚裔"是个复杂而多元的群体,"美国亚裔文学"包含了极具多样化的亚裔群体作家,但是我们还是要把"美国亚裔文学"当作一个整体来进行研究。理由有三:

首先,"美国亚裔文学"与"美国亚裔作家"(Asian American Writers)最早出现时,即是作为一个统一的概念而提出的。1974年,赵健秀(Frank Chin)等学者出版了《哎咿!美国亚裔作家选集》。[3] 作为首部划时代的"美国亚裔作家"的文学作品选集,该书通过发现和挖掘此前50年中被遗忘的华裔、日裔与菲律宾裔中的重要作家,选取其代表性作品,进而提出要建立作为独立的研究领域的"美国亚裔文学"(Asian American Literature)。[4]

其次,在亚裔崛起的过程中,无论是亚裔的无心之为,还是美国主流社会与其他族裔的有意为之,亚裔都是作为一个整体被安置在一起的。因此,亚裔文学也是作为一个整体而存在的。近年来,我国的"美国华裔文学"研究成为美国文学研究学界的一个热点。但在美国,虽然有"美国华裔文学"(Chinese American Literature)的说法,但真正作为学科存在的,则是"美国亚裔文学"(Asian American Literature),甚至更多的则是"美国亚裔研究"(Asian American Studies)。

再次,1970年代之后,"美国亚裔文学"的发展在美国学术界逐渐成为研究的热点,引发了研究者的广泛关注,为此,包括耶鲁大学、哥伦比亚大学、布朗大学、宾夕法尼亚大学等常青藤盟校以及斯坦福大学、加州大学系统的伯克利分校、洛杉矶分校等美国众多高校,都设置了"美国亚裔研究"(Asian American Studies)专业,也设置了"美国亚裔学系"(Department of Asian American Studies)或者"亚裔研究中心",开设了丰富多彩的亚裔文学与亚裔研究方面的课程。包括哈佛大学在内的众多高校也都陆续开设了众多的美国亚裔研究以及美国亚裔文学的课程,学术研究成果丰富多彩。

那么,我们需要提出的一个问题是,在中国语境下,研究"美国亚裔文学"的意义与价值究竟何在?我的看法如下:

第一,"美国亚裔文学"是"美国文学"的重要组成部分。不研究亚裔文学或者忽视甚至贬低亚裔文学,学术界对于美国文学的研究就是不完整的。如上文所说,亚裔文学的真正兴起是在20世纪六七十年代。美国六七十年代特殊的时代背景极大促进了亚裔文学发展,自此,亚裔文学作品层出不穷,包括小说、戏

---

[3] Chin, Frank, Chan, Jeffery Paul, Inada, Lawson Fusao, et al. 1974. *Aiiieeeee! An Anthology of Asian-American Writers*. Howard University Press.

[4] 参见:Chin, Frank, et al. 1991. "Preface" to *Aiiieeeee! An Anthology of Asian American Writers*. Edited by Frank China, Jeffery Paul Chan, Lawson Fusao Inada, and Shawn Wong. A Mentor Book. pp.xi–xxii.

剧、传记、短篇小说、诗歌等各种文学形式。在当下的美国，亚裔文学及其研究与亚裔的整体生存状态息息相关；种族、历史、人口以及政治诉求等因素促使被总称为"亚裔"的各个少数族裔联合发声，以期在美国政治领域和主流社会达到最大的影响力与辐射度。对此，学术界不能视而不见。

第二，我国现有的"美国华裔文学"研究，无法替代更不能取代"美国亚裔文学"研究。自从1980年代开始译介美国亚裔文学以来，我国国内的研究就主要集中在华裔文学领域，研究对象也仅为少数知名华裔作家及长篇小说创作领域。相较于当代国外亚裔文学研究的全面与广博，国内对于亚裔的其他族裔作家的作品关注太少。即使是那些亚裔文学的经典之作，如菲律宾裔作家卡罗斯·布鲁桑（Carlos Bulosan）的《美国在我心中》（*America Is in the Heart*，1946），日裔女作家山本久惠（Hisaye Yamamoto）的《第十七个音节及其他故事》（*Seventeen Syllables and Other Stories*，1949）、日裔约翰·冈田（John Okada）的《不－不仔》（*NO-NO Boy*，1959），以及如今在美国文学界如日中天的青年印度裔作家裘帕·拉希莉（Jhumpa Lahiri）的作品，专题研究均十分少见。即便是像华裔作家任璧莲（Gish Jen）这样已经受到学者很大关注和研究的作家，其长篇小说之外体裁的作品同样没有得到足够的重视，更遑论国内学术界对亚裔文学在诗歌、戏剧方面的研究了。换句话说，我国学术界对于整个"美国亚裔文学"的研究来说还很匮乏，属于亟待开发的领域。实际上，在我看来，不研究"美国亚裔文学"，也无法真正理解"美国华裔文学"。

第三，在中国"一带一路"倡议与中国文化走出去的今天，作为美国文学研究的新型增长点，大力开展"美国亚裔文学"研究，特别是研究中国的亚洲周边国家如韩国、日本、印度等国在美国移民状况的文学表现，以及与华裔在美国的文学再现，使之与美国和世界其他国家的"美国亚裔文学"保持同步发展，具有较大的理论意义与学术价值。

三、"美国亚裔文学"及其研究：历史与现状

历史上看，来自亚洲国家的移民进入美国，可以追溯到18世纪。但真正开始较大规模的移民则是到了19世纪中后期。然而，亚裔从进入美国一开始，就遭遇到来自美国社会与官方的阻力与法律限制。从1880年代到1940年代这半个多世纪的岁月中，为了保护美国本土而出台的一系列移民法，都将亚洲各国人民排除在外，禁止他们当中的大部分人进入美国大陆地区。直到20世纪40至60年代移民法有所改革时，这种状况才有所改观。其中的改革措施之一就是取消了国家配额。如此一来，亚洲移民人数才开始大规模上升。2010年的美国国家统

计局分析显示，亚裔是美国社会移民人数增长最快的少数族裔。[5]

"美国亚裔"实际是个新兴词汇。这个词汇的创立与诞生实际上已经到了1960年代后期。在此之前，亚洲人或者具有亚洲血统者通常被称为"Oriental"（东方人）、"Asiatic"（亚洲人）和"Mongoloid"（蒙古人、黄种人）。[6]美国历史学家市冈裕次（Yuji Ichioka）在1960年代末期，开创性地开始使用Asian American这个术语，[7]从此，这一词汇开始被人普遍接受和广泛使用。

与此时间同步，"美国亚裔文学"在随后的1970年代作为一个文学类别开始出现并逐步产生影响。1974年，有两部著作几乎同时出版，都以美国亚裔命名。一部是《美国亚裔传统：散文与诗歌选集》,[8]另外一部则是前面提到过的《哎咿！美国亚裔作家选集》。[9]这两部著作，将过去长期被人遗忘的亚裔文学带到了聚光灯下，让人们仿佛看到了一种新的文学形式。其后，新的亚裔作家不断涌现，文学作品层出不穷。

最初亚裔文学的主要主题与主要内容为种族（race）、身份（identity）、亚洲文化传统、亚洲与美国或者西方国家之间的文化冲突，当然也少不了性别（sexuality）、社会性别（gender）、性别歧视、社会歧视等。后来，随着移民作家的大规模出现，离散文学的兴起，亚裔文学也开始关注移民、语言、家国、想象、全球化、劳工、战争、帝国主义、殖民主义等问题。

如果说，上述1974年的两部著作代表着亚裔文学进入美国文学的世界版图之中，那么，1982年著名美国亚裔研究专家金惠经（Elaine Kim）的《美国亚裔文学的创作及其社会语境》[10]的出版，作为第一部学术著作，则代表着美国亚裔文学研究正式登上美国学术界的舞台。自此以后，不仅亚裔文学创作兴盛起来，而且亚裔文学研究也逐渐成为热点，成果不断推陈出新。

同时，人们对于如何界定"美国亚裔文学"等众多问题进行了深入的探讨，进一步推动了这一学科向前发展。相关问题包括：究竟谁可以说自己是美国亚

---

5 参见：Wikipedia依据"U.S. Census Show Asians Are Fastest Growing Racial Group"（NPR.org）所得出的数据统计。https://en.wikipedia.org/wiki/Asian_Americans。

6 Mio, Jeffrey Scott, ed. 1999. *Key Words in Multicultural Interventions: A Dictionary*. ABC-Clio ebook. Greenwood Publishing Group, p. 20.

7 K. Connie Kang, "Yuji Ichioka, 66; Led Way in Studying Lives of Asian Americans," *Los Angeles Times*, September 7, 2002. Reproduced at ucla.edu by the Asian American Studies Center.

8 Wand, David Hsin-fu, ed. 1974. *Asian American Heritage: An Anthology of Prose and Poetry*. New York: Pocket Books.

9 Chin, Frank, Chan, Jeffery, Paul, Inada, Lawson Fusao, et al. 1974. *Aiiieeeee! An Anthology of Asian-American Writers*. Howard University Press.

10 Kim, Elaine. 1982. *Asian American Literature: An Introduction to the Writings and Their Social Context*. Philadelphia: Temple University Press.

裔（an Asian America）？这里的 America 是不是就是单指"美国"（the United States）？是否可以包括"美洲"（Americas）？如果亚裔作家所写的内容与亚裔无关，能否算是"亚裔文学"？如果不是亚裔作家，但所写内容与亚裔有关，能否算在"亚裔文学"之内？

总体上看，早期的亚裔文学研究专注于美国身份的建构，即界定亚裔文学的范畴，以及争取其在美国文化与美国文学中应得的席位，是 20 世纪七八十年代亚裔民权运动的前沿阵地。早期学者如赵健秀、徐忠雄（Shawn Wong）等为领军人物。随后出现的金惠经、张敬珏（King-Kok Cheung）、骆里山（Lisa Lowe）等人均成为了亚裔文学研究领域的权威学者，他/她们的著作影响并造就了第二代美国亚裔文学研究者。20 世纪 90 年代之后的亚裔文学研究逐渐淡化了早期研究中对于意识形态的侧重，开始向传统的学科分支、研究方法以及研究理论靠拢，研究视角多集中在学术马克思主义（academic Marxism）、后结构主义、后殖民、女权主义以及心理分析等。

进入 21 世纪以来，"美国亚裔文学"研究开始向多元化、全球化与跨学科方向发展。随着亚裔文学作品爆炸式的增长，来自阿富汗、印度、巴基斯坦、越南等族裔作家的作品开始受到关注，极大丰富与拓展了亚裔文学研究的领域。当代"美国亚裔文学"研究的视角与方法也不断创新，战争研究、帝国研究、跨国研究、视觉文化理论、空间理论、身体研究、环境理论等层出不穷。新的理论与常规性研究交叉进行，不但开创了新的研究领域，对于经典问题（例如身份建构）的研究也提供了新的解读方式与方法。

四、作为课题的"美国亚裔文学"研究及其丛书

"美国亚裔文学"研究，是由我担任课题负责人的 2017 年度中国人民大学科学研究基金重大规划项目。"美国亚裔文学研究丛书"，即是该项课题的结题成果。作为"美国亚裔文学"方面的系列丛书，将由文学史、文学作品选、文学评论集、学术论著等组成，由我担任该丛书的总主编。

"美国亚裔文学"研究在 2017 年 4 月立项。随后，该丛书的论证计划，得到了国内外专家的一致认可。2017 年 5 月 27 日，中国人民大学科学研究基金重大规划项目"美国亚裔文学研究"开题报告会暨"美国亚裔文学研究高端论坛"在中国人民大学隆重召开。参加此次会议的专家学者全部为美国亚裔文学研究领域中的顶尖学者，包括美国加州大学洛杉矶分校的张敬珏教授、南京大学海外教育学院前院长程爱民教授、南京大学海外教育学院院长赵文书教授、北京语言大学应用外语学院院长陆薇教授、北京外国语大学潘志明教授、解放军外国语学院石

平萍教授等。在此次会议上，我向与会专家介绍了该项目的基本情况、未来研究方向与预计出版成果。与会专家对该项目的设立给予高度评价，强调在当今时代加强"美国亚裔文学"研究的必要性，针对该项目的预计研究及其成果，也提出了一些很好的建议。

根据最初的计划，这套丛书将包括文学史2部：《美国亚裔文学史》和《美国华裔文学史》；文学选集2部：《美国亚裔文学作品选》和《美国华裔文学作品选》；批评文选2部：《美国亚裔文学评论集》和《美国华裔文学评论集》；访谈录1部：《美国亚裔作家访谈录》；学术论著3部，包括美国学者张敬珏教授的《静默留声》和《文心无界》。总计10部著作。

根据我的基本设想，《美国亚裔文学史》和《美国华裔文学史》的撰写，将力图体现研究者对美国亚裔文学的研究进入到了较为深入的阶段。由于文学史是建立在研究者对该研究领域发展变化的总体认识上，涉及文学流派、创作方式、文学与社会变化的关系、作家间的关联等各方面的问题，我们试图通过对亚裔文学发展进行总结和评价，旨在为当前亚裔文学和华裔文学的研究和推广做出一定贡献。

《美国亚裔文学作品选》和《美国华裔文学作品选》，除了记录、介绍等基本功能，还将在一定程度上发挥形成民族认同、促进意识形态整合等功能。作品选编是民族共同体想象性构建的重要途径，也是作为文学经典得以确立和修正的最基本方式之一。因此，这样的作品选编，也要对美国亚裔文学的研究起到重要的促进作用。

《美国亚裔文学评论集》和《美国华裔文学评论集》，将主要选编美国、中国以及世界上最有学术价值的学术论文，虽然有些可能因为版权问题而不得不舍弃，但我们努力使之成为中国学术界研究"美国亚裔文学"和"美国华裔文学"的重要参考书目。

《美国亚裔作家访谈录》、美国学者的著作汉译、中国学者的美国亚裔文学学术专著等，将力图促使中美两国学者之间的学术对话，特别是希望中国的"美国亚裔文学"研究，既在中国的美国文学研究界，也要在美国和世界上的美国文学研究界发出中国学者的声音。"一带一路"倡议的实施，使得文学研究的关注发生了转变，从过分关注西方话语，到逐步转向关注中国（亚洲）话语，我们的美国亚裔（华裔）文学研究，正是从全球化视角切入，思考美国亚裔（华裔）文学的世界性。

2018年，我们按照原计划出版了《美国亚裔文学作品选》《美国华裔文学作品选》《美国亚裔文学评论集》《美国华裔文学评论集》。2022年上半年，我们出版了学术专著《文心无界——不拘性别、文类与形式的华美文学》。2022 年下半年，还将出版《美国日裔文学作品选》《美国韩裔文学作品选》《美国越南裔文学作品选》《美国西亚裔文学作品选》《美国南亚裔文学作品选》等 5 部文学选集。

需要说明的是，这 5 部选集是在原有计划之外的产物。之所以在《美国亚裔文学作品选》之外又专门将其中最主要的国家与区域的文学作品结集出版，是因为在研究过程中我发现，现有的《美国亚裔文学作品选》已经无法涵盖丰富多彩的亚裔文学。更重要的是，无论是在国内还是在美国，像这样将美国亚裔按照国别与区域划分后的文学作品选全部是空白，国内外学术界对这些国别与区域的文学创作的整体关注也较少，可以说它们都属于亟待开垦的新研究领域。通过这 5 部选集，可以让国内对于美国亚裔文学有更为完整的了解。我也希望借此填补国内外在这个领域的空白。

等到丛书全部完成出版，将会成为一套由 15 部著作所组成的系列丛书。2018 年的时候，我曾经把这套丛书界定为"国内第一套较为完整的美国亚裔文学方面的系列丛书"。现在，时隔 4 年之后，特别是在有了这新出版的 5 部选集之后，我可以说这套丛书将是"国内外第一套最为完整的美国亚裔文学方面的系列丛书"。

那么，我们为什么要对"美国亚裔文学"进行深入研究，并要编辑、撰写和翻译这套丛书呢？

首先，虽然"美国亚裔文学"在国外已有较大的影响，学术界也对此具有相当规模的研究，但在国内学术界，出于对"美国华裔文学"的偏爱与关注，"美国亚裔文学"相对还是一个较为陌生的领域。因此，本课题首次以"亚裔"集体的形式标示亚裔文学的存在，旨在介绍"美国亚裔文学"，推介具有族裔特色和代表性的作家作品。

其次，选择"美国亚裔文学"为研究对象，其中也有对"美国华裔文学"的研究，希望能够体现我们对全球化视野中华裔文学的关注，也体现试图融合亚裔、深入亚裔文学研究的学术自觉。同时，在多元化多种族的美国社会语境中，我们力主打破国内长久以来专注"美国华裔文学"研究的固有模式，转而关注包括华裔作家在内的亚裔作家所具有的世界性眼光。

最后，顺应美国亚裔文学发展的趋势，对美国亚裔文学的研究不仅是文学研究界的关注热点，还是我国外语与文学教育的关注焦点。我们希望为高校未来"美国亚裔文学"的课程教学，提供一套高水平的参考丛书。

五、"美国亚裔文学"及其研究的未来

如前所述,"美国亚裔文学"在20世纪70年代逐渐崛起后,使得亚裔文学从沉默走向了发声。到21世纪,亚裔文学呈现出多元化的发展特征,更重要的是,许多新生代作家开始崭露头角。单就这些新的亚裔作家群体,就有许多值得我们关注的话题。

2018年6月23日,"2018美国亚裔文学高端论坛——跨界:21世纪的美国亚裔文学"在中国人民大学隆重召开。参加会议的专家学者将近150人。

在此次会议上,我提出来:今天,为什么要研究美国亚裔文学?我们要研究什么?

正如我们在会议通知上所说,美国亚裔文学在一百多年的风雨沧桑中历经"沉默""觉醒",走向"发声",见证了美国亚裔族群的沉浮兴衰。21世纪以来,美国亚裔文学在全球冷战思维升温和战火硝烟不断的时空背景下,不囿于狭隘的种族主义藩篱,以"众声合奏"与"兼容并蓄"之势构筑出一道跨洋、跨国、跨种族、跨语言、跨文化、跨媒介、跨学科的文学景观,呈现出鲜明的世界主义意识。为此,我们拟定了一些主要议题。包括:1.美国亚裔文学中的跨洋书写;2.美国亚裔文学中的跨国书写;3.美国亚裔文学中的跨种族书写;4.美国亚裔文学中的跨语言书写;5.美国亚裔文学中的跨文化书写;6.美国亚裔文学的翻译跨界研究;7.美国亚裔文学的跨媒介研究;8.美国亚裔文学的跨学科研究等。

2019年6月22日,"2019美国亚裔文学高端论坛"在中国人民大学举行,会议的主题是"战争与和平:美国亚裔文学研究中的生命书写"。那次会议,依旧有来自中国的近80所高校的150余位教师和硕博研究生参加我们的论坛。

2020年年初,全球疫情大暴发,我们的"2020美国亚裔文学高端论坛"一直往后推迟,直到2020年12月5日在延边大学举行,会议的主题是"疫情之思:变局中的美国亚裔文学"。因为疫情原因,我们劝阻了很多愿意来参会的学者,但即便如此,也有近百位来自各地的专家学者与研究生前来参会。

2021年6月26—27日,"相遇与融合:2021首届华文/华裔文学研讨会"在西北师范大学举行。这次会议是由我在延边大学的会议上提出倡议,得到了中国社会科学院文学所赵稀方教授的积极响应,由他和我一起联合发起并主办,由西北师范大学外国语学院承办。我们知道,长期以来,华裔文学和华文文学分属不同的学科和研究领域,其研究对象、传统和范式都有所不同,但血脉相承的天然联系终究会让两者相遇、走向融合。从时下的研究看,虽然两者的研究范式自成体系、独树一帜,但都面临着华裔作家用中文创作和华人作家用外文创作的新趋势,这给双方的学科发展与研究领域都带来了新的挑战,也带来了新的学科发

展机遇。我们都相信,在学科交叉融合已成为实现创新发展必然趋势的当下语境中,华裔/华文文学走到了相遇与融合的最佳时机。为此,我们倡议并搭建平台,希望两个领域的学者同台进行学术交流与对话,探讨文学研究的新发展,以求实现华裔文学和华文文学的跨界融通。

事实上,21 世纪以来,亚裔群体、亚裔所面临的问题、亚裔研究都发生了巨大的变化。从过去较为单纯的亚裔走向了跨越太平洋(transpacific);从过去的彰显美国身份(claiming America)到今天的批评美国身份(critiquing America);过去单一的 America,现在变成了复数的 Americas,这些变化都值得引起我们的高度重视。由此所引发的诸多问题,也需要我们去认真对待。比如:如何在"21世纪"这个特殊的时间区间内去理解"美国亚裔文学"这一概念?有关"美国亚裔文学"的概念构建,是否本身就存在着作家的身份焦虑与书写的界限划分?如何把握"美国亚裔文学"的整体性与区域性?"亚裔"身份是否是作家在表达过程中去主动拥抱的归属之地?等等。

2021 年年底,国家社会科学基金重大招标课题揭晓,我申请的"美国族裔文学中的文化共同体思想研究"喜获中标。这将进一步推动我目前所从事的美国亚裔文学研究,并在未来由现在的美国亚裔文学研究走向美国的整个族裔文学研究。

展望未来,"美国亚裔文学"呈现出更加生机勃勃的生命力,"美国亚裔文学"的研究也将迎来更加光明的前途。

2018 年 8 月 28 日定稿于哈佛大学
2022 年 8 月 28 日修改于北京

前　言

"美国亚裔文学"研究，是由中国人民大学"杰出学者"特聘教授郭英剑先生担任课题负责人的2017年度中国人民大学科学研究基金重大规划项目。"美国亚裔文学研究丛书"，是该项课题的结题成果，由郭英剑教授担任该套丛书的总主编。这是国内第一套最为完整的"美国亚裔文学"方面的系列丛书，由文学史、文学作品选、文学评论集、学术论著等所组成。

所谓"美国越南裔文学"，是指具有越南血统的美国人用英语创作的文学作品。这里的美国越南裔作家主要由美国越南裔第一代、1.5代（年幼的越南难民）作家，以及在美国出生的越南裔第二代作家组成。三代作家有不同的成长背景、文化诉求和身份认同，这些因素促成了美国越南裔文学主题、体裁与风格的多元化。

"美国越南裔文学"无疑是"美国亚裔文学"版图中不可或缺的一部分，它在短时间内取得了引人注目的成绩，成为美国少数族裔文学中的佼佼者。与华裔文学和日裔文学等美国亚裔文学相比，"美国越南裔文学"发展起步较晚、历史较短，文学作品相对较少，但随着1.5代越南裔和第二代越南裔作家的崛起，越南裔文学发展迅猛，影响力逐渐扩大，逐步得到美国与其他国家学者的追捧研究。通过"美国越南裔文学"，人们可以观察美国与越南的战争历史和现实处境，同时作为观照，促使我们反思亚裔的发展历史和进行自我文化探索。

20世纪60年代，越南的殖民历史启发了越南裔对战争和历史的思考，为美国越南裔文学的发展奠定了基础。陈文颖的《船上无乘客》（1965）是其中的杰出代表。随着1975年越南战争的结束，大批越南难民涌入美国，在黎莉·海思利浦和梅·艾略特等第一代作家的努力下，美国越南裔文学开始发轫。

从20世纪90年代开始，随着越南裔1.5代作家的成长，越南裔文学开始崭露头角，文学作品产出迅猛，阮清越、莫妮卡·张与赖清荷等越南裔作家荣获普利策奖、美国国家图书奖与代顿文学奖等重要奖项，让越南裔文学阔步进入新的发展纪元。

进入新世纪以来，美国越南裔第二代作家在美国文坛崛起。与第一代和 1.5 代作家相比，第二代作家在写作风格、文学特色和问题思考方面变得更加多元化，他们围绕战争，但又不限于历史，创造出颇多优秀的作品，裴施、陈家宝和陈禹申等当属代表性作家。

鉴于越来越多的越南裔作家涌上文坛及其愈加显著的影响力，我们认为需要将"越南裔文学"单独列出来，编写这部《美国越南裔文学作品选》，便于人们领略更多越南裔作家的风采。

《美国越南裔文学作品选》以历史为发展脉络，精选了 22 位美国越南裔作家及其作品，并以作家的出生年代为顺序进行编目排列。选集力图反映美国越南裔文学的整体发展脉络，突出展现美国越南裔文学对战争历史、文化冲突和身份建构的关注。作品选自美国越南裔第一代、1.5 代和第二代作家，作品出版时间从 20 世纪 80 年代持续到 2021 年，试图展现美国越南裔文学的发展和变迁，以及它的"整体"特征。在体裁方面，本选集涵盖回忆录、小说、漫画回忆录、散体诗与诗歌等，努力体现越南裔文学的新发展和新现象。

遗憾的是，由于篇幅所限，《美国越南裔文学作品选》中的部分作品只是节选片段，而且由于各种历史与现实的原因，还有一些作家的作品未能囊括其中。但通过本作品选所展现出的冰山一角，大家可以根据兴趣继续挖掘，探寻越南裔文学的广袤空间。

无论如何，我们都希望《美国越南裔文学作品选》能够成为学术界研究"美国亚裔文学"特别是"美国越南裔文学"的重要参考书目。

编者
2022 年 8 月 28 日

目 录

1. 陈文颖 (Tran Van Dinh, 1923—2011) ·· 1
   Blue Dragon White Tiger: A Tet Story ·· 2
2. 梅·艾略特 (Duong Van Mai Elliott, 1941—) ································ 7
   The Sacred Willow ·· 8
3. 黎莉·海斯利浦 (Le Ly Hayslip, 1949—) ···································· 16
   When Heaven and Earth Changed Places ································· 17
   Child of War, Woman of Peace ··· 22
4. 黄玉光 (Jade Ngoc Quang Huynh, 1957—) ································ 27
   South Wind Changing ·· 28
5. 阮奎德 (Nguyen Qui Duc, 1958—) ·· 40
   Where the Ashes Are: The Odyssey of a Vietnamese Family ········· 41
6. 高兰 (Lan Cao, 1961—) ·· 47
   Monkey Bridge ··· 48
   The Lotus and the Storm ·· 52
7. 丁令 (Linh Dinh, 1963—) ·· 57
   Love Like Hate ··· 58
   Fake House ··· 60
8. 安德鲁·林 (Andrew Lam, 1964—) ·· 66
   Perfume Dreams ··· 67
   East Eats West ··· 71
9. 阮坚 (Kien Nguyen, 1967—) ·· 74
   The Unwanted ·· 75
   The Tapestries ··· 79
10. 赖清荷 (Thanhha Lai, 1965—) ·· 85
    Inside Out & Back Again ·· 86
    Listen, Slowly ·· 87

11. 安德鲁·X. 范 (Andrew X. Pham, 1967—) ·· 94
　　Catfish and Mandala ··· 95
　　The Eaves of Heaven ·· 101

12. 莫妮卡·张 (Monique Truong, 1968—) ··· 107
　　The Book of Salt ·· 108
　　Bitter in the Mouth ··· 114

13. 阮清越 (Viet Thanh Nguyen, 1971—) ··· 118
　　Nothing Ever Dies: Vietnam and The Memory of War ································· 119
　　The Refugees ··· 124

14. 黎氏艳翠 (Le Thi Diem Thuy, 1972—) ·· 128
　　The Gangsters We Are All Looking For ··· 129

15. 姚·斯托洛姆 (Dao Strom, 1973—) ··· 133
　　Grass Roof, Tin Roof ··· 134
　　The Gentle Order of Girls and Boys ··· 135

16. 阮碧铭 (Bich Minh Nguyen, 1974—) ·· 139
　　Stealing Buddha's Dinner ··· 140
　　Short Girls ··· 145

17. 裴施 (Thi Bui, 1975—) ··· 148
　　The Best We Could Do ·· 149

18. 陈禹申 (Vu Hoang Tran, 1975—) ·· 163
　　Dragonfish ··· 164

19. 陈家宝 (GB Tran, 1976—) ··· 173
　　Vietnamerica ·· 174

20. 艾米·潘 (Aimee Phan, 1977—) ··· 190
　　We Should Never Meet ·· 191
　　The Reeducation of Cherry Truong ·· 197

21. 王洋 (Ocean Vuong, 1988—) ··· 201
　　On Earth We're Briefly Gorgeous ··· 202
　　Night Sky With Exit Wounds ··· 205

22. 维奥莱特·库伯史密斯 (Violet Kupersmith, 1989—) ····························· 207
　　The Frangipani Hotel ·· 208
　　Build Your House Around My Body ··· 211

1

(Tran Van Dinh, 1923—2011)
陈文颖

作者简介

陈文颖（Tran Van Dinh, 1923—2011），美国越南裔作家，美国天普大学（Temple University）教授，曾任越南外交官。他出生于越南顺化(Hue)一个上层阶级家庭，家族中多人曾活跃于越南政界、军事与文化领域。陈文颖曾随父率兵攻打法国侵略者，为国家立下赫赫战功。从1951年开始，他作为南越驻外大使在泰国、缅甸、美国、阿根廷与墨西哥等地工作，还参与过美国民权运动。1963年，他辞去外交官一职，专心投入教学工作，先后在纽约州立大学（State University of New York）与天普大学任教。

他的著作包括专著《独立、解放与革命：理解第三世界的方法》(*Independence Liberation Revolution: An Approach to the Understanding of The Third World*, 1987)与《变化世界里的交流与外交》(*Communication and Diplomacy in a Changing World*, 1987)；两部越南战争小说分别是《船上无乘客》(*No Passenger on the River*, 1965)与《青龙白虎：一个新春故事》(*Blue Dragon White Tiger: A Tet Story*, 1983)。此外，他还写了数百篇文章和随笔，登刊于《纽约时报》、《国家》、《国家地理》与《基督教科学箴言报》等美国影响力较大的期刊杂志。

《青龙白虎》是陈文颖在1983年出版的小说，被誉为"第一部美国越南裔用英语写作的有关越南战争的自传体小说"。选段出自《青龙白虎》的结尾部分，讲述了陈文颖离开越南返回美国的经历，表达了作者对殖民侵略、越南战争与越南历史斗争的反思。

作品选读

Blue Dragon White Tiger: A Tet Story

(XII Tiger's Jaws, Serpent's Fangs)
By Tran Van Dinh

Late the next afternoon Trang called the passengers together.

"My friends," he said, "despite our misfortune we have reached our goal. We'll be in Chantaburi no later than five o'clock. I have told you that the Prime Minister of Thailand is an old friend of our dear friend and brother, Doctor Minh. With your approval, I shall ask him to be our representative to the Thai authorities. We can celebrate the Tet's eve in Chantaburi, but I think it would be proper that we do so on our boat which is, according to international law, Vietnamese territory."

With the end of their journey in sight, the passengers seemed to have forgotten the nightmarish incident that had engulfed them in sorrow and despair the day before. They applauded Trang's announcement, and Minh was asked to speak.

"I shall never forget, as long as I live, our boat family. I shall do everything I can to help all of you settle in the new lands of freedom, either in Thailand or America. Obviously, the situation here is very favorable to us because of my connection with the Prime Minister, but one always has to be careful about politics in Thailand. The Prime Minister reached power through a *coup d'etat*, and there could be a counter-coup at any time. When we arrive there, I'll contact the Prime Minister and see what his attitude to us will be." His short speech ended with several rounds of applause.

Early in the evening the junk lowered its anchor off Chantaburi. Operation New Spring had come to an end. A police motorboat met the refugees. In Thai Minh asked the police officer to take him to the local army commander. Within half an hour, Minh and the police lieutenant were at the office of Colonel Amneuy Luksanand, commanding officer of the 25th Royal Thai Infantry Regiment. Minh explained the situation, reported the bandits attack, and requested that he be allowed to contact the Prime Minister, his old friend Chamni. The colonel politely invited Minh to wait while he phoned Bangkok.

Minh was admiring a pot of blooming orchids when the colonel entered the living room.

"Professor, the Prime Minister is on the line. You can use the phone in my office."

Minh picked up the receiver. "Hello, Mr. Prime Minister. Congratulations."

"Stop it, Minh, I'm still Chamni, your old friend."

"But I'm now a boat person without a country, a wandering soul, as we say in Vietnamese."

"Forget about your boat and your wandering soul. You can stay in Thailand as long as you wish, as my government's guest. Thailand is now your country. Buddha will protect you. I'll have the colonel bring you to Bangkok tonight so you can have a good rest and we can meet for breakfast tomorrow. As for your compatriot boat people, how many of them are there?"

"Nineteen, including me."

"They'll be given special consideration by the Ministry of Interior, but in the meantime they'll have to stay in a refugees camp. I'm sorry about that, but I can't change all the laws even as a Prime Minister. I have to leave for a meeting now. I'll see you tomorrow. Sleep well, my dear friend."

"Thank you and goodnight, Mr. Prime Minister."

The colonel invited Minh to have dinner with him before his trip to Bangkok by helicopter. Minh explained that because it was Tet's eve, he preferred to eat with his compatriots. The colonel quickly proposed that the whole group be invited along to a Chinese restaurant. They accepted the invitation but they had no appetite: Minh had warned them before dinner that they would be temporarily sent to a refugee camp.

Minh slept soundly in his spacious room at the Royal Thai Army guest house, the same one he'd slept in before when he'd passed through Bangkok on his return to Vietnam from the States. He woke refreshed and relaxed. A hot shower, a luxury he'd almost forgotten, in a large marble bathroom in a foreign residence in a foreign land, brought back to him memories of the night he'd spent with Jennifer at the Statler Hilton in New York ten years before. He vividly recalled the passage from *Markings* that had come to him so suddenly that morning as he'd watched her sleeping beside him:

> As she lies stretched out on the riverbank—beyond all human nakedness in the inaccessible solitude of death, her firm breasts are lifted to the sunlight—a heroic torso of marble-blond stone in the soft grass.

Minh had feared then that she would die. And now she was dead, killed by a bomb. But her actual death didn't frighten him as he had imagined it would. He was almost grateful that she had passed away. With her, his innocence, their innocence, was gone. He now had to face life in all its about realities, without illusion, without the benevolent protection of the Blue Dragon, by himself and for himself; and only as a lonely individual, outside the North Vietnamese Party discipline of collectivism, could he fully develop and maintain his integrity as a writer. Will the White Tiger leave me alone, he wondered?

He sank into a blue velvet sofa and lit his pipe, following the spiralling smoke with his dreamy eyes. Pulling *the Tao Te Ching* from his knapsack, he read Chapter 42: "One gains by losing and loses by gaining."

He smiled at these wise words of Lao Tsu. "Indeed," he said to himself. "I've lost everything, but at the same time, I'm gaining everything back. I'm reclaiming myself. Thank you, Jennifer, and you too, Xuan and Loc. Thank you, Vietnam, thank you, North Vietnamese Party. Thank you all. I've lost all of you in different ways in different circumstances, but I've gained everything. I've regained myself."

There was a knock on the door. A soldier stood at attention and announced, "Sir, the Prime Minister is in the living room."

Minh hurried downstairs.

"*Swasdi*, my good friend Minh. Welcome to Thailand. Make yourself at home." Prime Minister Chamras Panyakupta, in a dark blue civilian suit, greeted him, his arms opened wide in a welcoming gesture.

"Thank you, Mr. Prime Minister. Thank you for everything you've done for me," Minh said, his eyes wet with gratitude.

"As I've always said, we were friends, we are friends, and we'll always be friends, regardless of our personal situations."

"Yes, I know, and again, congratulations on your new position."

"Well, it makes little difference. I had to stage *a coup d'état* to protect the monarchy and to cleanse the country of corrupt and opportunistic elements. Now, I simply have to work harder and longer hours at the office and be a little more careful about my private life."

They laughed and went into the dining room for breakfast.

"Mr. Prime Minister."

"You can still call me Chamni in private."

"Chamni, you don't know how grateful I am for your inviting me to stay in Thailand as your government's guest for an indefinite period. But I've thought it over, and no matter how much I'd like to accept your kind offer, I still feel I must decline it, at least at this particular moment in my life. I plan to return to America as soon as possible. Really, I don't know exactly why I want to. I hope you understand. Perhaps when I settle in America, I'll write and explain everything."

"You don't need to explain anything to me. But to be honest, I don't quite understand why you want to go to the United States. There, you'll always be a stranger. Here, you're among people of the same color skin, the same religion. Still, it's your decision. But you can rest assured that if and when you change your mind you can always count on me. I'm sorry we don't have much time to talk the way we did in the good old days, but I deeply sympathize with what has happened to you."

"Someday, Chamni, you'll know why, perhaps when I write a book about my own experiences. But for the time being I'm numb with gratitude and affection for you and I can't say much about anything."

Chamni pulled an envelope from his breast pocket and handed it to Minh. "Take this. It's just a little something for your needs while you're in Bangkok. If you need more, don't hesitate to contact my aide-de-camp and tell him what you want. He's the same officer who greeted you at Dong Muang Airport when you passed through here ten years ago."

"Thank you so much, Chamni. You're very kind and thoughtful."

"And now that I know of your plan to leave for the U.S., I'll ask my office to get a first-class open ticket for you on the Royal Thai Airways. There's a direct flight now once a week from Bangkok to New York City, with a stopover in Paris. Minh, I'm sorry I have so little time to spend with you. I must go now."

At the door Chamni stopped and put his arm on Minh's shoulder. "Goodbye, my friend. Be happy. Life is for living, and not to be worried about or even understood. Remember our Buddhist doctrine of the impermanence of all things." He paused. "By the way, I've asked my secretary to pack some of my new clothes for you, we wear about the same size, and other things you might need. It's up in your room now, I'm sure."

"Thank you, Chamni, thank you, Mr. Prime Minister," Minh murmured to himself as Chamni's black Mercedes sped away flanked by an escort of police motorbikes.

. . .

Minh tried each of the three brand-new suits and found that they all fit him perfectly. He thought mockingly to himself, "The North Vietnamese Party haven't treated me badly after all. I still keep my shape and my mind in order."

Dressed in a light brown Manchester cotton suit and a striped dark blue Thai silk tie, Minh walked slowly to the American Embassy on Wireless Road, six blocks away. The morning was still cool. The noise, the dirt, the smell, the chaotic traffic on the crowded narrow streets didn't bother or annoy him as they had the last time he was here. He even liked them now. They were, he believed, part of the necessary, insignificant price one had to pay for individual liberty. And after all, he thought, smiling, "I can always go back to the clean, air-conditioned suite at the Royal Thai Army guest house."

Minh asked a Thai woman clerk in the consular section of the American Embassy for an application form for an immigrant visa to the United States of America. He glanced at it and discovered that he didn't have all the necessary information to fill it out properly. He had no passport to prove his citizenship, he'd forgotten the number of his green card, (the permanent resident identification issued to him fourteen years ago by the U.S.

authorities), he didn't have five passport-sized pictures, he didn't have a job. He decided to fill in only his name, place and date of birth, skipping other items, with the exception of two: respondent in Thailand—the Royal Thai Army guest house; and actual and former professions—one of the boat people, formerly professor of political science, Thomas Paine College, Amherst Massachusetts, U.S.A.

He gave the form back to the clerk who couldn't hide her surprise at so many unanswered items. She politely asked him, "Sir, are you sure that the address of your respondent in Thailand is given correctly?"

"Yes, Madam," he answered softly and added, "May I see the viceconsul?"

"Yes sir. I think so. I'll give him the form. Please wait."

To Minhs amazement the interview with the vice-consul went without a hitch. He was questioned about his credentials and his past, a quick phone call was made to Chamni's office to confirm his identity, and he was issued a temporary entrance permit. When he arrived in the States, he was told, he must go to an immigration office, where his status as a permanent resident would be promptly restored.

Minh decided to leave Thailand on the seventh day of the lunar New Year. Officially, it would be the last day of the Tet holiday, the day when the Vietnamese took down the traditional *Cay Neu*, the bamboo tree they planted in front of their homes before Tet to ward off bad spirits. On that day, on the wings of a Royal Thai plane, he would fly to New York. He would kneel at the foot of the Statue of Liberty. He would leave behind all the Tets of the past with their thousand-year old ceremonials and traditions. From then on, he would spend his Tets in the cold and snow of the United States, deprived of all the perfumes and tastes of his native Vietnam. He would surely miss them. But, he hoped, he would have gained something new, Something he had never quite understood before: the real meaning and essence of Tet, the spirit of Tet, the moment of truce between the Blue Dragon and the White Tiger, the harmonization of Tinh, feeling, and *ly,* reason, among his fellow men and women, among the living and dead, between tradition and revolution, among the past, the present, and the future. But it would be henceforward the spirit of the historic Vietnam that he held in his heart, not the political one—the mystic Vietnam, not the vulgar and brutal one.

He would live and work in New York City. Jennifer would have liked him to do so. For the first time in many days, he thought of Loc, no longer in admiration and gratitude, only with compassion. He felt liberated.

Suddenly, vivid details of the last night he spent on the soil of Vietnam and in the bed of Madame Luu surged back into his memory. He burst into a prolonged and tearful laughter. He knew he was laughing at his own laughter.

2

(Duong Van Mai Elliott, 1941—)
梅·艾略特

作者简介

梅·艾略特（Mai Elliott, 1941— ），全名董文梅·艾略特（Duong Van Mai Elliott），越南裔作家和翻译家。1941年出生于越南一个中产阶级家庭，她的祖父是大学士，精通儒家经典，曾是越南朝廷官员。她的父亲自幼饱读诗书，曾前往法国留学，回国后在法国殖民的南越政府担任海防知事。第二次世界大战结束，在越南复杂的政治环境下，梅的家庭里出现了政治信仰上的分歧。父母在政治上持中立态度，妹妹加入了北越，两位兄长也应征加入了越南自由联盟（Viet Minh），一家人经历了诸多波折与坎坷。这些经历促成了她的回忆录《圣柳：越南一家四代人的生活》(*The Sacred Willow: Four Generations in the Life of a Vietnamese Family*, 1999)。这本书被提名2000年普利策奖。1960年，梅申请到美国政府的奖学金，开启了赴美求学之路。1963年，梅从乔治城大学（Georgetown University）外交学院毕业，并回西贡任职。在那里，梅结识了她的美国丈夫大卫·艾略特（David Elliott），夫妻二人婚后在一家美国智库公司工作，他们负责采访北越战俘和叛逃者。1975年，越南战争结束后，艾略特夫妇回到美国定居。

选段出自《圣柳》中的《深夜葬礼》("A Burial in the Night")，讲述了有关梅家族运气的神话故事，表达了梅对家族历史的骄傲和越南文化的敬仰。

作品选读

The Sacred Willow

(A Burial in the Night)
By Duong Van Mai Elliott

A Burial in the Night

My family owes its good fortune to a mysterious man. What he did one night changed my ancestors' destiny, leading them from poverty to social prominence.

When this enigmatic figure appeared in my family's story toward the end of the eighteenth century, Vietnam was still in the throes of a civil war that would erupt intermittently and last over 200 years. It was an unsettled time, with several clans backed by armies vying for domination. After their province in the central region of the country had turned into a raging battlefield, my ancestors fled. But there was no safe haven in the next province, or the next, as the opposing armies swept swept back and forth destroying everything in their path. So, along with thousands of other desperate peasants, my ancestors kept moving further and further north, trying to escape warfare, drought, and hunger. The trek finally took them to Van Dinh, where they settled down. This village is located on the bank of the Day River, about forty kilometers south of Hanoi. People here earned their livelihood by growing rice. They also grew vegetables in the soil along the bank of the river and sugarcane on higher ground. For extra food, they caught fish, shrimp, and freshwater clams, as well as crabs and snails that became plentiful in the flooded rice fields during the rainy season. The industrious villagers also sold bricks, cooking pots, and toys that they made by using clay scooped from the riverbank.

The Day is a branch of the mighty Red River, which irrigates and nourishes the delta of northern Vietnam with its rich silt. From its source in the mountain range in southern China, the Red River flows for hundreds of miles before pouring into the sea. As it penetrated into the flat delta, this river, enlarged by tributaries, began to course in a bed that was higher than the surrounding plain. During the monsoon, especially in July and August, the river would become menacing. Swollen by the incessant and torrential rainfall, it raged its way to the sea, frequently overflowing its banks and threatening to drown the surrounding land. To tame the floodwaters, an elaborate network of dikes had been constructed centuries before.

But the dikes, built with wooden pillars, bamboo poles, and compacted earth, could not always contain the river and its branches. Inundations continued to occur almost every year, killing people and animals, and destroying crops and houses. Bandits usually emerged after the most disastrous inundations, as destitute peasants resorted to armed robbery for survival.

For villages like Van Dinh, the Day River was both a blessing and a bane, providing water to irrigate their lands, but also threatening them with flooding. The river drew the villagers to its rich alluvial soil, but also compelled them to keep their distance, shielded by the dike or safely perched on the higher ground near the market place. The thirteen-foot-tall dike, whose flat and wide top also served as the main road into the village, dominated Van Dinh's landscape. When my ancestors arrived, all the desirable housing spots had been taken, so they built their hut near the river's edge, on the "wrong side" of the dike. Whenever the water level rose, the river overflowed into their back yard and occasionally even into their house. As outsiders, my ancestors were viewed with suspicion and discriminated against by the clannish villagers. Most of the rice fields were the communal property of the village and were distributed only to the indigenous residents for cultivation. Migrants who came to settle like my ancestors were not entitled to a part of the land, and so were deprived of this main source of income. Some of the migrants earned their living by making clay pots, while others survived by doing odd jobs, fishing in the river, and by catching crabs and snails in the rice fields. The only hope for them to escape their lowly status and poverty was to produce sons who could become mandarins—officials in the imperial bureaucracy and the elite of society at the time.

Scholars who aspired to become mandarins had to spend years mastering classical Chinese, introduced when China ruled the country from 111 B.C. to A.D. 939, and thereafter retained by the royal court, even after independence had been achieved, as the official language for all its documents. In addition, these scholars had to digest a daunting body of Chinese writings, learn how to compose elegant prose and poetry, and memorize Vietnamese and Chinese history, in order to pass a series of progressively more difficult exams. The goal of this education was not to encourage original thinking, but to produce men of culture who could master the wisdom of Confucius and his disciples and apply it to protect the welfare of the people. The higher the degree earned, the higher the potential appointment would be within the imperial bureaucracy and the faster the rise to the top. Only a relatively small number of people had the ambition and the persistence to pursue this career path.

My ancestors, who descended from scholars, were determined to continue their family's tradition, in spite of their poverty. The men focused on their studies and did odd jobs on the side. They survived mainly because their wives were able to contribute to the meager income by buying and selling goods at the various local markets. Every three years, the men tried their chances at the civil service exams, hoping to pass and to earn a position in the bureaucracy. If they succeeded, they would have power and prestige, though they certainly would not become rich, as the court paid mandarins only a low salary, supplemented with a rice ration sufficient to feed their families. Joining the imperial bureaucracy was, in fact, like joining the priesthood, as mandarins were expected to dedicate themselves to a life of virtue and duty and to accept a standard of living that was only slightly above that of the people they governed. In the view of the court, when it made a scholar a mandarin, it gave him such an honor—anointing him as one of the country's most wise, most educated, and most virtuous men—that it did not need to pay him generously as well.

The mysterious man's connection with my family began with his friendship with Duc Thang, my ancestor of six generations ago. By this time, my family had lived in Van Dinh for about a hundred years. Three generations had come and gone, without achieving any noticeable success. The family had escaped poverty at one point, when one of the men married into a rich household. But by Duc Thang's generation, the family had once again fallen into abject poverty, victimized by the bandits that were taking advantage of the unsettled situation in the countryside. In their forays into Van Dinh, they had ransacked and burned down Duc Thang's hut—not once, but several times. Instead of destroying his spirit, this motivated him to study harder to pass his exam and escape his predicament.

At this time, most people could not read or write. Whenever illiterate people needed to have something recorded, they would go to students, scholars, or retired mandarins for help. In exchange, they would pay them a small sum or, since barter was common, give them betel leaves, areca nuts, rice wine, tea, or a combination of these. Duc Thang used to sit outside the gate of a pagoda near his village and hire himself out to the faithful, writing prayers in Chinese characters in exchange for a small fee. When worshipers had a big favor to ask of the deities, they would burn such messages in a special trough inside the pagoda courtyard to convey their pleas to the...

It was at this pagoda that the mysterious man met Duc Thang, and liked him immediately. They became friends, but after Duc Thang stopped visiting the pagoda, the man lost contact with him. Several years later, he decided to look for him in Van Dinh. When he arrived, disguised as a poor traveler, he learned that the scholar had been dead for many years. He found Duc Thang's house as evening fell. The poverty he saw was appalling. Without telling her who he was, he asked Duc Thang's widow for some water to wash his dusty feet. Although he looked poor, she greeted him with kindness and hospitality. He thought she was worthy of help and revealed that he was a geomancer, someone who could read signs in the earth and identify auspicious spots for burial sites to ensure the good fortune of future generations. He said, "I can show you where to put your husband's grave so that your descendants will have a better life. But you must tell me first whether you want them to be rich or to become successful scholars and mandarins." She answered, "I want them to have success and prestige, not wealth." Her choice made sense because, during the time in which she lived, scholars and mandarins were the most respected social classes. The wealthy, on the other hand, were despised because people believed that commerce, the usual source of money for the rich, was a parasitic—if not dishonest—occupation. Over time, as social values changed, my relatives would come to regret the widow's selection. In my generation, many of my relatives would rather have traded their academic successes and poorly paid government jobs for wealth. And in my family, whenever we had money problems, my siblings and I would half-jokingly condemn Duc Thang's widow for her bad judgment.

After the widow told him what she wanted, the man said, "I'll help you get your wish. I know of a very good location for a grave in the village. I want you to dig up your husband's bones and rebury them there." But she protested. Exhumation was out of the question: she did not have the money to buy a clay pot in which to put the bones for reburial, as required by custom. The stranger reassured her, "Don't worry, just use a bamboo basket, if you can't afford to buy a clay pot." At exactly midnight, the man asked Duc Thang's widow and son to take him to the grave. After the bones had been dug up and placed in the basket, he told them to follow him. Guided only by starlight, they made their way to the new site the man had chosen. It turned out to be located in the middle of a common graveyard, where only wretched people without relatives or descendants to take care of their graves were buried. Wandering souls resided here, forever disconsolate because no one was burning joss sticks or making offerings to their spirits. Duc Thang's widow wept with disappointment and clung to the basket, refusing to bury the bones here. The stranger soothed her, "Don't worry. This is an auspicious site. In three years, all the other graves will be relocated. With them gone, the earth's currents will be unblocked and will flow directly into your husband's grave." Before leaving, he told the widow not to build a tomb over the grave. He also wrote a cryptic poem predicting the successes of future generations:

> First, a member of the Royal Academy
> Second, two governors
> Every twenty years, a generation of scholars
> Every twenty years, a generation of mandarins

Earth termites later built up the mound so that the grave, unrestricted by construction, kept growing year by year, an encouraging sign that it had been placed in powerful earth currents. It is said that if you stood on high ground and looked down at the grave, you would see that the contours of the earth around it formed the shape of an ink slab and a brush, the writing implements used by a scholar. You would also see the shape of a horse, the animal that a scholar rode on his triumphant return to his village, after winning the *tien si*, or doctorate degree—the pinnacle of academic achievement and a door-opener to a high position in the government. When I visited Duc Thang's grave in October 1993, I was astonished to find that, after almost 200 years, the mound had not been leveled by the passage of time. While all the old graves in the vicinity had disappeared, Duc Thang's burial site could still be seen protruding over the rice fields surrounding it. The ink slab and the brush had, unfortunately, been turned into rice fields, and the horse had had his left foot clipped when a nearby road was built. Because of this injury to the horse's left foot, people in my clan have become prone to accidents involving the left leg. When I fell and broke my left kneecap in 1981, I became another casualty of the carelessness of those road builders.

For about a hundred years after he first appeared in our history, we did not know who the mysterious stranger was. Then, one night, my great-grandfather spoke to the... of Tan Vien Mountain, Vietnam's most sacred peak, through a medium. This spirit, a mythical figure associated with the origins of our people, told him that this enigmatic person was a monk who had taken the ordained name of Thanh Tinh Thien Su, or Master of Purity and Serenity. From that day onward, my great-grandfather began to worship the monk as if he were one of our ancestors. On the anniversaries of their deaths and at Tet, our lunar new year, when he prayed to their departed souls, he would also thank this holy man for his deed. This became a tradition for my clan. The predictions came true one by one. Duc Thang's son received the honorific title of royal academician upon his retirement as the mandarin in charge of education for Son Tay Province, and launched the family on the path of success and better fortune. The two governors foretold by the monk, Duong Lam and Duong Khue, my great-grandfather and great-granduncle, did not appear until three generations later. Every twenty years—or so runs my family's belief—one or several relatives should achieve prominence in government service or as scholars, just as the monk predicted.

Duong Lam, my great-grandfather, was born in 1851, the third year of Emperor Tu Duc's reign during the Nguyen dynasty, the one that had emerged triumphant from the long civil war and that would be the last to exist. Considering the tradition in Duong Lam's family, there was no question that he would train to become a scholar and an official. So he immersed himself for years in the study of philosophy, history, and poetry, under his father's tutelage. He wanted success for himself, to earn fame as a scholar and prestige as a mandarin. But he also wanted success for his parents, who had great hopes for him, and whom he wanted to repay with the honor that society would bestow on them if he triumphed. He excelled in his studies, and mastered the art of writing prose and poetry. But scholastic brilliance could not always guarantee success. As is the case with any exam anywhere in the world, luck—or fate—has much to do with passing or failing. The Vietnamese also believed that justice beyond the grave was at work during exams. The souls of those that had been wronged would come back to seek revenge against the perpetrators, while those that owed a debt to those still living would return to help their benefactors.

The first-level examination consisted of three to four sessions. Candidates who passed all of them received what can be called a master's degree—or *cu nhan*—and those who passed all but one earned a *tutai*—or a bachelor's degree—the lowest in the system. The examination was extremely competitive, and only a few candidates were chosen out of a field of thousands, with usually twenty to twenty-five master's degrees and seventy to seventy-five bachelor's degrees at each site. Seven major categories of complex if not incomprehensible rules governed all the exams, and an infraction could result in disqualification or even imprisonment, depending on the seriousness of the oversight or offense. A careful juxtaposition of words unintentionally implying a criticism of the throne was considered *lèse-majesti*é and could land the candidate in jail.

The exam tested not only a candidate's intellect, but also his mental and physical endurance. Due to the huge number of candidates at each site, there were no permanent exam rooms. Instead, each candidate had to bring his own tent, a portable bamboo couch that also served as a writing table, paper, brushes, ink, water, and food, as each session lasted all day and candidates were not allowed to leave the site. On exam day, the candidates had to arrive before daybreak and submit themselves to a thorough search by the guards before being allowed inside, to make sure they were not smuggling in any written materials along with their paraphernalia.

Strict measures were taken to prevent cheating. Sentinels standing guard in watchtowers and soldiers patrolling on horseback kept vigil to prevent candidates from sneaking into one another's tent and offering help. To make sure that the papers submitted by the candidate had been composed at the site and not prepared beforehand and smuggled in, the first ten or so pages used by each candidate were stamped with an official seal, and the manuscript had to be stamped again at noon on the exam day. An elaborate procedure for selecting the examiners and for grading was observed to prevent cheating. Mandarins appointed as examiners were chosen from outside the region where the exam was to be held. At the site, they were put in cramped quarters, and held virtually like prisoners until the sessions were over, completely cut off from the outside world, and even unable to communicate among themselves. The manuscripts submitted to them for grading were anonymous, with the candidates' names removed and bearing only coded numbers. Two sets of examiners independently graded each manuscript, and the cumulative grade stood as the final grade, to ensure objectivity and avoid favoritism or cheating. As an added precaution, a military mandarin with no ties to the examiners was put in charge of keeping watch over them and enforcing order at the site.

In his first try at the regional examination, in 1867 at age sixteen, my great-grandfather did not succeed completely, getting only the bachelor's degree. If he was disappointed, he would also have felt comforted by the fact that he had done better than thousands of other scholars who never managed to earn even this degree, and spent their youth making repeated but fruitless attempts. Brilliant scholars who failed were not despised but simply pitied because fate did not reward their talent, and *hoc tai thi phan*—"learning depends on one's ability, but succeeding at the exams depends on one's fate"—became the common lament for those cursed with bad luck at the exam site.

In normal times, my great-grandfather would have focused his energy only on succeeding in the next exam. But he was not living in normal times. In 1873, French troops bombarded and stormed Hanoi's citadel. This attack was France's first salvo in its war to take over the northern part of Vietnam following its conquest of the southern region in 1867. Outgunned, the governor of Hanoi felt he had only one honorable response. Wounded and taken prisoner, he ripped off his bandages and committed suicide by starving himself to death. After taking over Hanoi, French forces moved out to conquer the surrounding area. The campaign gave my great-grandfather the opportunity to prove himself. He recruited and trained militiamen to defend a citadel in his native district that stood in the way of the French advance. Under his leadership, the citadel resisted the enemy siege for two months. It was ultimately spared when the invaders withdrew from the north following their commander's death in a skirmish in Hanoi. For his achievement, Duong Lam was later cited by the court in its official account of those events.

With the departure of the French, things returned to normal. In 1878, Duong Lam took the mandarin exam again and not only earned the *cu nhan* degree, but took the highest honor as the valedictorian. In a country that revered learning, Duong Lam's success won him instant fame. After that, there was only one thing left for him to do: pursue the most prized degree—the *tien si*, equivalent to the doctorate. But first, he would have to make the arduous trip to Hue, the imperial capital, where this series of exams was held. Hundreds of miles lay between Van Dinh and Hue. He would have to get there and back on foot and by boat, sailing along the shore of the South China Sea, then making his way by land through jungles and mountains. The trip took over a month.

The imperial exam, held every three years, was extremely competitive. Each time, only ten scholars out of a field of 150 to 200 candidates would be chosen. The exam would begin with three rigorous sessions. Those that passed would sit for a fourth, held in the Imperial Palace, with subjects chosen by the emperor himself. Sometimes, an emperor would even grade the exams personally. If the candidates succeeded, they would earn the doctorate degree. If not, they would become "Candidate doctors." My great-grandfather entered the first round of exams with great confidence. But although he turned in brilliant papers, he was disqualified because of a minor infraction. For the rest of his life, this twist of fate would nag at him. When his oldest son, my grandfather, also failed the same exam years later, it was like rubbing salt in the wound. The family was finally vindicated in 1919 when my oldest uncle Tuong earned the doctorate degree, in the last *tien si* exam to be held in Vietnam.

The failure rankled even more because Duong Lam's older brother Duong Khue, whom he measured himself against, had taken and passed this exam in 1868, and had received many honors. My great-granduncle could easily have failed as well. When Duong Khue sat for the palace exam, he and the other candidates were asked to write an essay on a topic Emperor Tu Duc had chosen himself: "Make War or Make Peace." The imperial Council of Ministers was then hotly debating this issue. The court was split. On one side were those that wanted to make peace with the French. On the other side were those that wanted to go to war to get back the southern provinces that the emperor had been forced to cede to France. The emperor took the opportunity of the exam to test the best minds in the country on this issue. For the candidates, it was a loaded topic, because they had no way of knowing what the emperor himself was thinking. However they came down on the issue, they might run the risk of offending the throne.

Duong Khue couched his essay in such diplomatic language that the emperor did not take offense. In it, my great-granduncle opposed the concession the emperor had made, but avoided criticizing the throne directly. He said simply that as a loyal subject he had wept upon reading the royal edict announcing the loss of territory to the French. Then he went on to recommend that the court go to war to expel the foreigners. The emperor liked the composition, but did not agree with this suggestion, and wrote the comment "Not appropriate to the situation" in vermillion ink in the margin. That was not the last time my great-granduncle recommended going to war. He would do this two more times in petitions he addressed to the throne. This audacity could have cost him his career, if not his freedom or even his head.

If my great-grandfather had passed the *tien si* exam, he would have enjoyed the many honors that his older brother had experienced. After earning the doctorate degree, Duong Khue was granted an audience with the emperor, entertained at a royal banquet, given a robe and a hat adorned with a silver flower design of his own choosing, and invited to stroll the imperial garden. The emperor also gave Duong Khue a gift of precious cinnamon bark that had been presented to the court as tribute, observing, "We notice that *tien si* Duong Khue does not look well. We instruct him to take care of his health so that he can serve the country." This was great honor, since this cinnamon—a kind found on only a few trees out of thousands growing in a cinnamon forest—was believed to be a wonder drug, capable of curing innumerable diseases, and even of bringing the dying back to life.

3

(Le Ly Hayslip, 1949—)
黎莉·海斯利浦

作者简介

黎莉·海斯利浦（Le Ly Hayslip, 1949— ），越南名"Phùng Thị Lệ Lý"，美国越南裔作家和慈善家，生于越南中部的一个农村家庭。她年轻时命运多舛。在越南战争期间加入北越地下工作，身份暴露后遭受南越政府的牢狱之灾，之后又被北越政府怀疑"叛变"而判处死刑。侥幸逃脱后，她逃到西贡从事底层工作，一度靠出卖身体赚取生活费。后来，她结识了一位年长的美国兵，与其结婚后定居美国。

《天翻地覆》（*When Heaven and Earth Changed Places*, 1989）是海斯利浦的第一部回忆录，系与美国越南裔作家杰伊·伍尔茨（Jay Wurts）合作创作。这本书在美国一度风靡市场，还被拍成了好莱坞电影。它成就了海斯利浦美国越南裔作家的名望和地位，也促使她在1988年创立了慈善基金"东遇西基金"（East Meets West Foundation），为亚洲和非洲的贫困地区儿童提供健康、饮水、卫生和教育方面的资助。第二部回忆录《战争之子，和平之母》（*Child of War, Woman of Peace*, 1993）是第一部回忆录的续篇，讲述了海斯利浦在美国的生活经历与奋斗历史。

选段分别出自《天翻地覆》与《战争之子，和平之母》。前一选段讲述了海斯利浦首次返回越南的情形，穿插了她曾经在越南的艰苦经历，表达了作者对战争、历史与现实的反思。后一选段讲述了她在美国的创业经历，表达了她对待失败和挫折的乐观态度。

作品选读（一）

When Heaven and Earth Changed Places

(Seven: A Different View)
By Le Ly Hayslip & Jay Wurts

  With the sickening feeling that I was now a stranger in my own homeland, I crossed the last few yards to my house with a lump in my throat and a growing sense of dread. Houses could be rebuilt and damaged dikes repaired—but the loss of our temples and shrines meant the death of our culture itself. It meant that a generation of children would grow up without fathers to teach them about their ancestors or the rituals of worship. Families would lose records of their lineage and with them the umbilicals to the very root of our society—not just old buildings and books, but people who once lived and loved like them. Our ties to our past were being severed, setting us adrift on a sea of borrowed Western materialism, disrespect for the elderly, and selfishness. The war no longer seemed like a fight to see which view would prevail. Instead, it had become a fight to see just how much and how far the Vietnam of my ancestors would be transformed. It was as if I was standing by the cradle of a dying child and speculating with its aunts and uncles on what the doomed baby would have looked like had it grown up. By tugging on their baby so brutally, both parents had wound up killing it. Even worse, the war now attacked Mother Earth—the seedbed of us all. This, to me, was the highest crime—the frenzied suicide of cannibals. How shall one mourn a lifeless planet?

  Inside, the neat, clean home of my childhood was a hovel. What few furnishings and tools were left after the battles had been looted or burned for fuel. Our household shrine, which always greeted new arrivals as the centerpiece of our family's pride, was in shambles. Immediately I saw the bag of bones and torn sinew that was my father lying in his bed. Our eyes met briefly but there was no sign of recognition in his dull face. Instead, he rolled away from me and asked:

  "Where is your son?"

  I crossed the room and knelt by his bed. I was afraid to touch him for fear of disturbing his wounds or tormenting his aching soul even more. He clutched his side as if his ribs hurt badly and I could see that his face was bruised and swollen.

"I am alone," I answered, swallowing back my tears. "Who did this to you?"

"Dich"(The enemy.) It was a peasant's standard answer.

I went to the kitchen and made some tea from a few dried leaves. It was as if my father knew he was dying and did not wish the house or its stores to survive him. If one must die alone, it should be in an empty place without wasting a thing.

When I returned, he was on his back. I held his poor, scabbed head and helped him drink some tea. I could see he was dehydrated, being unable to draw water from the well or get up to drink it even when neighbors brought some to the house.

"Where were you taken? What was the charge?" I asked.

"It doesn't matter." My father drank gratefully and lay back on the bed. "The Americans came to examine our family bunker. Because it was so big, they thought Viet Cong might be hiding inside and ordered me to go in first. When I came out and told them no one was there, they didn't believe me and threw in some grenades. One of them didn't go off right away and the two Americans who went in afterward were killed. They were just boys—" My father coughed up blood. "I don't blame them for being angry. That's what war is all about, isn't it? Bad luck. Bad karma."

"So they beat you up?"

"They pinned a paper on my back that said 'VC' and took me to Hoa Cam District for interrogation. I don't have to tell you what happened after that. I'm just lucky to be alive."

As sad as I felt about my father's misfortune, growing fury now burned inside me. There was no reason to beat this poor man almost to death because of a soldier's tragic mistake.

I made my father as comfortable as possible and climbed the hill to the American fortress with my bucket of merchandise, intent on making a different kind of sale.

"Honcho?" I asked the first soldier I saw on the trail. I didn't understand his answer, but eventually I made myself understood well enough to impress him with my harmlessness: "You buy? Very nice? No bum—bum! See captain. Where honcho?"

Eventually I made my way to an officer who poked around my bucket, which by now had been searched four or five times by Americans for explosives. When he finally understood I wanted to talk to him about more than the price of bracelets, he called for the camp's Vietnamese translator.

"Thank..." I said, bowing politely to the frowning Republican soldier who was not from the Central Coast. I explained the situation quickly to him in Vietnamese. I told him there had been a terrible mistake and that my father lay badly wounded in our house down the hill. I told him I wanted the Americans to take him to a hospital where he would be cared for and to help repair his house when he came back. I told him I knew the Americans were required to do all these things by their own regulations.

The Republican translator only laughed at me. "Look, missy," he said, "the Americans do what they damn well please around here. They don't take orders from anybody, especially little Vietnamese girls. Now, if you're smart, you'll take your father and get the hell out of here!"

"But you didn't even translate what I said to the captain!" I protested. "Come on—give the American a chance to speak for himself!"

"Look—" the translator exploded. "You'd better get out of here now or I'll denounce you as VC! If you have a complaint, go to district headquarters like everyone else! Put your request through channels—and be prepared to spend some money. Now run along before I get mad!"

I gathered my things and went back down the hill. Although some GIs tried to wave me over, I was too upset to make a sale. I just wanted to help my father and keep things from getting worse.

Because the Americans so dominated the area, I felt comparatively safe staying near my house and tending to my father. Unlike the Republicans, who commandeered civilian houses for their quarters, the Americans kept their distance and so managed to avoid a lot of friction with the peasants. I no longer tried to sell anything (the villagers still hated anyone who dealt with the invaders) and pretended I didn't speak English when their troops stopped me from time to time. Although people going to the toilet or gathering firewood were still shot occasionally by jumpy soldiers, things remained blessedly quiet. It had been months since a major Viet Cong attack and a new, if smaller, generation of children now played in Ky La's streets. More dangerous were the Koreans who now patrolled the American sector. Because a child from our village once walked into their camp and exploded a Viet Cong bomb wired to his body, the Koreans took terrible retribution against the children themselves (whom they saw simply as little Viet Cong). After the incident, some Korean soldiers went to a school, snatched up some boys, threw them into a well, and tossed a grenade in afterward as an example to the others. To the villagers, these Koreans were like the Moroccans—tougher and meaner than the white soldiers they supported. Like the Japanese of World War II, they seemed to have no conscience and went about their duties as ruthless killing machines. No wonder they found my country a perfect place to ply their terrible trade.

I discovered that most of the kids I grew up with (those who had not been killed in the fighting) had married or moved away. Girls my age, if they had not yet married, were considered burdens on their family—old maids who consumed food without producing children. They also attracted the unsavory attention of soldiers, which always led to trouble. One reason so many of our young women wound up in the cities was because the shortage of available men made them liabilities to their families. At least a dutiful grown—up daughter could work as a housekeeper, nanny, hostess, or prostitute and send back money to the family who no longer wanted her. Many families, too, had been uprooted—like the refugees from Bai Gian or those who had been moved so that their houses could be bulldozed to provide a better fire zone for the Americans. For every soldier who went to battle, a hundred civilians moved ahead of him—to get out of the way; or behind him—following in his wake the way leaves are pulled along in a cyclone, hoping to live off his garbage, his money, and when all else failed, his mercy.

    This is not to say that rubble and refugees were the only by—products of our war. Hundreds of thousands of tons of rice and countless motorbikes, luxury cars, TVs, stereos, refrigerators, air conditioners, and crates of cigarettes, liquor, and cosmetics were imported for the Vietnamese elite and the Americans who supported them. This created a new class of privileged people—wealthy young officers, officials, and war profiteers—who supplanted the elderly as objects of veneration. Consequently, displaced farmers—old people, now, as well as young—became their servants, working as maids to the madams or bootblacks for fuzz—cheeked GIs. It was a common sight to see old people prostrate themselves before these young... crying lay ong—I beg you, sir!—where before such elderly people paid homage to no one but their ancestors. It was a world turned on its head.

    Of those villagers who remained in Ky La, many were disfigured from the war, suffering amputated limbs, jagged scars, or the diseases that followed malnutrition or took over a body no longer inhabited by a happy human spirit.

    Saddest of all these, perhaps, was Ong Xa Quang, a once—wealthy man who had been like a second father to me in the village. Quang was a handsome, good—natured man who sent two sons north in 1954. Of his two remaining sons, one was drafted by the Republican army and the other, much later, joined the Viet Cong. His two daughters married men who also went north, and so were left widows for at least the duration of the war. When I went to visit Quang I found his home and his life in ruins. He had lost both legs to an American mine, and every last son had been killed in battle. His wife now neglected him (she wasn't home when I called) because he was so much trouble to care for and he looked malnourished and on the verge of starvation. Still, he counted himself lucky. Fate had spared his life while it took the lives of so many others around him. All his suffering was part of his life's education—but for what purpose, he admitted he was still not wise enough to know. Nonetheless, Quang said I should remember everything he told me, and to forget none of the details of the tragedies I myself had seen and was yet to see. I gave him a daughter's tearful hug and left, knowing I would probably never see him alive again.

I walked to the hill behind my house where my father had taken me when I was a little girl—the hill where he told me about my destiny and duty as a Phung Thi woman. I surveyed the broken dikes and battered crops and empty animal pens of my once flourishing village. I saw the ghosts of my friends and relatives going about their work and a generation of children who would never be born playing in the muddy fields and dusty streets. I wondered about the martyrs and heroes of our ancient legends—shouldn't they be here to throw back the invaders and punish the Vietnamese on both sides who were making our country not just a graveyard, but a sewer of corruption and prison of fear? Could a... who made such saints as well as ordinary people truly be a god if he couldn't feel our suffering with us? For that matter, what use was... at all when people, not deities, seemed to cause our problems on earth?

I shut my eyes and called on my spirit sense to answer but I heard no reply. It was as if life's cycle was no longer birth, growth, and death but only endless dying brought about by endless war. I realized that I, along with so many of my countrymen, had been born into war and that my soul knew nothing else. I tried to imagine people somewhere who knew only peace—what a paradise! How many souls in that world were blessed with the simple privilege of saying good—bye to their loved ones before they died? And how many of those loved ones died with the smile of a life well lived on their lips—knowing that their existence added up to something more than a number in a "body count" or another human brick on a towering wall of corpses? Perhaps such a place was America, although American wives and mothers, too, were losing husbands and sons every day in the evil vortex between heaven and hell that my country had become.

I sat on the hill for a very long time, like a vessel waiting to be filled up with rain-soft wisdom from heaven—but the sun simply drifted lower in the west and the insects buzzed and the tin roofs of the American camp shimmered in the heat and my village and the war sat heavily—unmoved and unmovable like an oppressive gravestone—on my land and in my heart. I got up and dusted off my pants. It was time to feed my father.

Back home, I told him about my visit to "our hilltop." I said I now regretted fleeing Ky La. Perhaps it would have been better to stay and fight—to fight the Americans with the Viet Cong or the Viet Cong with the Republicans or to fight both together by myself and with anyone else who would join me.

作品选读（二）

Child of War, Woman of Peace

(ELEVEN: Two Halves Make a Whole)
By *Le Ly Hayslip & Jay Wurts*

Crossing the checkerboard rice paddies on the dikes with the setting sun warm on my face was like moving back in time. As we splashed through a shallow causeway onto the island, my legs felt younger and a song popped into my head—one I remembered hearing my mother and sister Hai sing during the war with the French. It's about a Viet Minh fighter returning home after being too long at the front. I sang it softly:

> So long ago I left this place
> Of home—cooked meals,
> Rau muon soup and purple eggplant,
> And villagers toiling in the fields
> Under hot noon sun or foggy morning,
> They carry buckets and plant new rice
> I must return to this sacred spot:
> The motherland that gave me life
> Back I've come now to my farm
> I'll plant crops and take
> One meal in the morning and one at night,
> From the land, all that she gives
> Vietnam gives rain
> To wash away death and make plants grow;
> And from the draught inside my heart
> Make rivers of happiness overflow

When the song ended, we were standing in a clearing just big enough for a couple of kids to kick around a ball. Near a line of brush a few yards away was a shallow indentation, barely perceptible, and its sister pile of dirt eroded by twenty years of wind and rain—yin and yang of what this nightmare playground and those years had been all about. I think the crew was a little disappointed at this pint—sized "killing field." It was not a graveyard or even a place of execution, but an area set aside by the Viet Cong to make its victims think it so. Still, at the time, it had been enough to do its job. I always felt very uncomfortable thinking about this place and now I realized why. It was not just the unfair trial and threatened execution or even my rape—as horrible as those things were—that tormented me. What I hated and feared most about this place was that, for at least a little while during my stay on earth, other humans had taken away my spirit—my will to love. I had talked and written a lot in the last few years about forgiveness. I had been able to forgive the two VC guards, Loi and Tau, for the terrible things they did to me, but that was easy compared to what the cosmic god was now calling on me to do. I now had to forgive myself for the biggest sin of all from those years: turning my back on life. I now knew why coming back to this place, and starting the clinic nearby, was so important. Others may call it charity, but I was really saving my soul.

In the vans going back to the hotel, I asked the boys what they thought about the place where their mom grew up.

"Is it always this hot?" Jimmy asked.

"This is a nice day," I laughed. "Wait for the summer monsoon!"

"We had enough trouble carrying all that video gear in shorts and T-shirts," Tommy added. "I can't imagine GIs patrolling the paddies in fatigues and backpacks. Even if you got up the energy to move, you'd sink in the mud up to your knees. Unbelievable! I wonder why they never dressed for the occasion?"

"At least I got to ride on a water buffalo," Jimmy said.

"You mean that dinky little cow I saw you sitting on when we got back?" I teased.

"Well—it's a lot bigger when you get close up."

"It was just a small cow!"

"Let's just tell people I rode a water buffalo, okay? And leave it at that."

The next day, after seeing the television crew off, Tommy met some girls who invited him to a concert in Danang. When he returned, the other boys teased him to death.

"Hey, Tom," Jimmy said, "you want Mom to call the village matchmaker?"

"You're just jealous 'cause they're cuter than that cow you dated in Ky La."

Bathroom towels, wrapped into whips, snapped like gunfire and I thought they would wreck the hotel room.

"Okay, okay, that's enough!" I shouted. "Of course, Jimmy, Grandma Phung is right. You're a young man now. Pretty soon you'll be finished with college and ready to settle down. I can have Ba Ngoai start looking for a nice Vietnamese girl for you."

"Whoaa—hold it! Time out!" Jimmy made a T with his hands. "Vietnamese girls are too shy. Tom says you can't even hold their hands while you're dancing. All they want to do is practice their English and talk about school."

"Of course," I said proudly. "These are village girls! They want to impress you with their seriousness. You have to be patient. In America, finding love is like grabbing a Big

Mac. Here, it's like planting rice. You can't sow and reap in the same evening, for goodness sake!"

"How about just spreading some fertilizer?" Tommy asked.

I belted him with a pillow myself and the other boys jumped on top of him.

"If you talk like that, you'll never find a girlfriend in Vietnam," I said. "These girls are too nice for you!"

I sounded just like my mother. Secretly, though, I could think of nothing better than for my sons to discover the love of their life among the poor girls of Vietnam—I knew what strong hearts and willing hands they could bring to a marriage, to complement and fulfill a good man's life. I also knew, of course, what any rural girl would be up against in America, even though my boys had my example—written down now, like a textbook!—to advise them. But I wouldn't hold my breath. There were some things, in the East and West, each generation insists on learning for itself.

We left Vietnam a slightly different family. In many respects, the trip had brought us closer together. The boys had seen their mother's origin and no longer had to imagine it from books, old photos, and stories. In other ways, though, the hairline gap of age and culture that had always existed between me and my sons now grew into the gulf that always and inevitably separates the generations, especially in the West. I could no longer pretend that my boys were somehow displaced Vietnamese—surrogate villagers provided by... to decorate my life with familiar things. More clearly than I, they saw Vietnam's wretchedness as part of the bigger wretchedness of all mankind. Their perspective was one of globe—straddling, well-educated Americans—businessmen, doctors, lawyers, artists, whatever they would become—not a country girl with a third-grade education trying to heal in a day the wounds of an entire people. Just as each trip instructed me further about my mission, so it caused me to realize that my American sons truly had life missions of their own. Without question, our lives and missions would intersect from time to time, but their karma was their own. Such is the discovery every mother makes and the lesson every child must learn. As for us, we could not have asked for better teachers.

Back in the United States, the movie rights to my book were optioned by Oliver Stone, an Oscar-winning filmmaker who was a Vietnam veteran himself. He saw in my story the third installment of his great Vietnam trilogy, which began with Platoon and continued with Born on the Fourth of July. We met to discuss the project and I found him to be a down-to-earth, creative person who tried unsuccessfully to hide his big heart and generous spirit. Like so many veterans I had worked with, he still held in a lot of anger about the war. But he also had the... given soul of an artist, which allowed him to appreciate his feelings and transform them into compelling, and ultimately healing, images on film. I saw in Oliver a kindred spirit who could help my story touch a much bigger world audience that only movies can reach.

He was also a man who liked to make things happen.

Three days after he had asked to see plans for the Mother's Love Clinic and background information about East Meets West, he donated a check for the amount needed to finish our work. Just as miraculously, as if triggered by this first domino, we received our license from the State Department to build our clinic and our waivers to the 1942 Trading with the Enemy Act. Brick by brick, the wall that had isolated my old from my new country was coming down.

In September 1989, I was back in Vietnam. Several uncles had arrived at Danang and were going to Ky La for the clinic's grand opening two days hence. I hitched a ride with them and appeared at my mother's door shortly after sundown.

"I'm going to spend the night in my village," I announced to my mother and Hai. Once the clinic was opened, the village and its spirits would enter a new life cycle. These would be the last two nights I could recapture the world of my youth.

Hai checked all the windows for eavesdroppers and my mother blew out the lights to discourage visitors. With my uncles, we sat together on the floor like kids telling ghost stories in the dark.

"This reminds me of 1975," Hai said with a laugh, "when the North took over Danang. Everyone ran to the American Army PX at China Beach because they were giving away the food. I grabbed a couple of empty sacks and went down myself. I was a little angry that the Republicans were charging an entry fee, but I paid and filled my bags. When I came out, a Southern soldier took my loot—yes, just grabbed it. They were using the peasants to do their dirty work! I started shouting and punching the soldier when shots rang out. Somebody yelled '*Giai phong, giai phong*!—Liberate the people!'—and quick as a wink, the Republicans had shed their uniforms and hidden their rifles. The man who had just stolen my bag tried to trade it back for some of my clothes—can you believe it? Anyway, the Northern soldiers surrounded the place. They arrested the Republicans and tied them to the heavy bags so they couldn't run away, then let the peasants go. I hated to lose that big bag of loot, but it was good to see those bullies get what they deserved!"

Everyone laughed but my mother. "Tonight reminds me of the night the village psychic told me about Sau Ban—"

I stopped laughing, too. This was news to me.

"Somebody told you what happened to my brother?" I asked.

My mother shifted her tiny body on the mat and looked up, as if she could see the stars through our thatched roof.

"Not long ago, Bon Nghe hired an *ong thay xac dong* down South to locate Sau Ban's remains. He interviewed a lot of villagers and believes he knows what happened. Sau

Ban was serving with a cannon squad in the Dai Loc District just before the Tet Offensive in 1968—just before your father died. He was scouting from a hilltop fort and spotted a column of American tanks. He signaled his gun crew to fire but they missed the lead tank, and a moment later every cannon in the U.S. column had zeroed in on their position. His crew was wiped out in the first salvo, although Sau Ban, who was gravely wounded, was able to crawl away before the American troopers came. He lay in the sun all day until a VC medical team came along and took him to an underground hospital. They arrived about midnight, but it was too late. Your brother died and his body was buried at Dai Hong. Some of the older villagers have corroborated this story. That's where we'll go to find him—someday."

A mosquito buzzed in my ear and I swatted it away. My mother was right. The house—each building in every village—had a spirit separate and apart from the generations of people who inhabited it. That spark of life, granted by Mother Earth, is what animates the world and binds a people to a place. Into this ancient, vibrant web, I was about to introduce a new entity, a place of healing, like a wandering herbalist come to help the sick and give the dying a little comfort. The day after tomorrow, my old world would be gone forever. We could only hope the new one would be better.

After talking a little more about Sau Ban, I turned to my mother, "So, Mama Du, you're happy with your life?"

"What kind of question is that for an old lady? You have to be my age to realize that just being alive is a blessing—a miracle! From the smallest bug to the biggest whale, everything rejoices at being alive. When you stop to think about it, that's all that counts. Hai Ngai and the others talk about independence from invaders and I suppose that's okay. It gives people something to think about from the time they're born and have everything to learn and the time they die and have forgotten it all. To tell you the truth, I'm looking forward to passing over into the spirit world. We have a lot of new ghosts out here in the countryside."

"What do you mean, Mama Du?"

"I mean that a lot of people sacrificed in the war have come back as babies, and many of those are now young men and women. They're dissatisfied with what now passes for peace. They want to make things better and, one way or another, they're going to do it. How do you think your clinic got built? If the old ghosts didn't want it, it wouldn't be here. That's what this country is all about now, Bay Ly—life, not death. Your clinic is just one of its new green shoots."

At eight the next morning, all the honored guests had arrived: officials from the Health Ministry and Red Cross; physicians and nurses from town who would rotate shifts in the clinic; minor functionaries from a variety of provincial departments; and, of course, every villager who could walk and many who could not.

4

(Jade Ngoc Quang Huynh, 1957—)
黄玉光

作者简介

黄玉光（Jade Ngoc Quang Huynh, 1957— ），美国越南裔作家。他出生于湄公河三角洲，1974年考入西贡大学。当时，北越政府统一了南越，作为一名大学生，黄玉光无辜被捕，被送进北越"再教育营"（reeducation camp），经历了生死磨难。1977年获释后，他坐船逃离了越南，几经波折到达美国。在那里，他从事农场劳工、服务员、建筑工人等体力劳动来维持生计。在不懈努力下，他得以继续学业，从本宁顿学院（Bennington College）获得了学士学位，后从布朗大学（Brown University）获得了艺术硕士学位。

回忆录《南风在变》（*South Wind Changing*, 1994）是黄玉光的代表作，讲述了作者在越南遭受的磨难、九死一生的逃难经历以及在美国心酸的奋斗历程。这本书入围美国国家图书奖，登上《时代》杂志图书之榜。

选段出自《南风在变》的第八章，讲述了主人公在"再教育营"的磨难经历，展示了战争对南越人造成的创伤记忆，以及作者面对困境勇往向前的励志经历。

作品选读

South Wind Changing
(Chapter 10—12)
By Jade Ngoc Quang Huynh

Chapter 8

It was sometime in August of 1976, I don't remember the exact day, but there was a half-moon far away in the night sky; a dim light shone through the restless woods. I heard the frogs croaking louder and softer, starting and stopping continuously. Along with this croaking sound crickets were making shrill, chirping noises like they were composing "wild-nature" music. It made me feel like I was at a concert, but this particular one had only one audience—me. I was lost in thought. Then I heard heavy, brisk footsteps running along the bamboo fences, and the clicking of grenades jostling on the belts of the guards. Then the sharp metal sound of the AK-47s being cocked, ready to shoot. I shivered and looked out from the hut. Many shadows were moving in different directions.

"Shoot him, shoot him now, comrade."

"He went this way. Let's go," someone shouted back. There were two guards approaching my hut. One of them came inside the hut, grasped Hung's thin neck and threw him on the ground.

"Come on, move it," the guard shouted, while he used his gun to scramble his belongings.

Hung staggered out of the hut as the guard shoved the gun in his back. I didn't know what was going on, but I had an awful feeling. I wanted to stop Hung from going, but I didn't know what to do. I saw Hung's shadow appear under the unsettled moon, then disappear past the booth. I was frightened. I heard some gun shots vaguely in the distance, violently disturbing the night, and I felt like I had just been shot.

Everyone in the hut was awake, but we stayed quiet. I wondered what had happened to Hung, what would happen to us now. Would anyone know about this after the war was over, or was this the beginning of a new war—the war in which brothers kill brothers? Torture was happening everywhere in the labor camps around the country, but people did not seem to know or care, especially the people who negotiated this kind of "peace" for Vietnam. Happy to celebrate their victory after Saigon fell, the north took over all the southern cities and people called this a "happy reunification." The happier they were the more bitterness I felt. I looked at the heads of my fellow prisoners in the dark and I wondered if anyone else felt like this. Or did they try not to think about it? I didn't hear anything except my own thoughts echoing inside my head: "Am I going to weep? No, I'm going to fight, whatever the circumstances, till the last drop of blood." I bit my lip harder, clenched my fists, stared at the moon going down at the side of the forest. Within myself there were only two things left—impotent hatred and the thirst for revenge.

At last, the wild rooster cried out somewhere in the bamboo bushes for his family. He was our dawn every morning. We got up restlessly to begin a new day. What happened last night stayed with me. "Am I going to die? And how? I have to find a way out!" I mumbled to myself. It was then that I remembered something my grandfather had said: "You are a good fighter and a good fighter has to be a leader himself; a good leader is a leader who doesn't need to show up at the battlefield." Was it true, grandfather? I am at battle right now I must start planning. First: we need to unite, we prisoners. Then what? Rebel, kill them, or escape? If we revolt, some inmates will oppose it. Then what will happen? If we want to kill the guards, how will we go about it? The guards have weapons; we don't. How about scape? I could escape myself I don't need any force from outside or inside. No one is going to get hurt. I only need a knife and a match.

And if they shoot me? Then I die faster than if I were tortured, or starved, or worked to death. I will be happy this way The thought kept drifting through my mind, like a slow-motion picture. I grabbed my latanier leaf hat, placing it on my head. We formed a single line, walked out of the hut, picking up our tools as usual.

"Hey, you! Come here," the guard shouted.

"Are you talking to me?" I asked.

"Yeah, you. Are you deaf?"

I went to him hesitantly and he threw me a shovel.

"Are you in the L-19 group?"

"Yeah."

"Rice field today."

I walked away from him, following the group to the rice field. I noticed there were four guards in the group. One walked in front, two in the middle, and one at the end of the line. We reached the rice field outside of the woods about three kilometers from the clearing where our huts were.

"Build the dike around the rice field in order to retain the water for the rice to grow," the guard said, while he demonstrated with his hands.

The soil was neither dry nor muddy. We stepped down, began to dig.

"Do you understand clearly?" the guard asked.

"Yes, comrade."

He walked toward the woods and sat down beneath a tree, his eyes set on us. We formed a human conveyor belt, digging soil and passing it man to man down to the dike.

"Can you dig less?" I asked the man next to me.

"What's the matter with you? Too much?" he said with a sarcastic look.

"Yes, I can't carry it."

"That's your problem," the man said.

I was angry and yanked the shovel away from him when he was digging in the soil; he lost his balance and splashed into the water. He jumped up, trying to grab me, but I had already stepped away from him. He was furious, having missed his chance at revenge.

"Come on, break it up," a man in the group said.

"If he would dig less I would stop," I said.

"Yeah, do him a favor. He's a new guy, Chung," the group yelled at him. Then the guard appeared.

"What's going on here?" the guard asked.

"Nothing," I said.

"You again?" the guard called to me. "Come here."

I walked up to him. He hit my jaw with his elbow, swung his body around, and jabbed his rifle into my ribs. I tasted salt in my mouth as I fell to the ground. I wiped my face, and there was blood. I looked at Chung, who was glancing at the group with a look that said, "I'm not your enemy, the guard is our enemy." But everybody just turned away.

"Go back to work. If you make any more trouble, you will be at the guillotine," the guard shouted.

I walked back to my work station, already feeling the tight rope around my thumbs and toes. The pain went through my veins, spreading throughout my body. I felt cold and quivery I began to gather the soil, to pass it oil endlessly.

Time went by slowly, from one hour to the next Noon arrived finally; I knew this because the sun was beating down on my head. I didn't know what time we could eat. My stomach was growling, my heart was beating harder, faster every second. My legs were trembling. I had no more energy left. I conveyed a piece of soil to one of the men on the line, but it felt it weighed a ton. My hands moved slower and slower; I felt weaker and weaker.

"Time to cat," the guard yelled.

We all scrubbed our hands and cleaned our faces with the dirty water where we dug. I felt refreshed, even though the water wasn't clean. I learned a good lesson: anything that is dirty has its own purity.

We all lined up, walking along the grassy trail back to the camp.

"Comrade. I found him," comrade Son happily called to the other guard that was walking with us.

"Who?" the tired guard asked.

"The man last night," Son replied.

"Where?" He turned around, and walked with Son toward the forest. We all looked at each other, following the guards like we were robots. There were many trees along the trail, with ferns and green moss on the muddy ground and dew on the grass where the shade was deep. Weeds crawled around, consorting with all the wild crawling plants. The forest was dense. We walked by a couple of ditches. It seemed to me there had been a struggle here some time ago. In the ditch, there were many dead leaves with mud scattered about. Small broken branches and stems from a young tree covered the trail. I saw handprints in the mud and on the tree. It looked like someone had been holding on to the tree, then had fallen down. I noticed the mud spots splattered on the ground. In the distance they grew more uneven. I saw the footprints: it appeared that someone had been limping here. Beneath the tree was a man lying on the grass with his head bent.

Everybody rushed to him. I saw a plastic bag carefully folded beneath the leaves. I picked it up, stuffed it in my pocket. I approached the dead man. One of his eyes was dangling on his check. His other eye stared at the pale blue sky and grey clouds. He was looking at the tall tree, whose shadow covered him like a blanket, as if he was searching for something up there.

There was a small indentation on one side of his forehead, with a big bruise. I knelt, and touched his head there: it was as soft as jello, moving in and out under his messy black hair. It looked like someone had used a hammer to strike his head. He had a broken nose; one side of his cheek was stretched up towards his eye and it made his mouth look a little like a half smile. His skin had turned green and his body was as cold as ice. He looked young—thirty-six. His arms were stretched apart while his legs were crossed together. He looked like he was going to be put on a cross... or had just been taken from one. He was very frail under his dirty white shirt and black trousers. I saw a little red hole on his stomach where the shirt had been torn apart. Around the hole the skin had turned brown. The brown color had streaked down to his thighs. The guard bent down and frisked the dead body but found nothing except the wedding ring on the corpse's finger. The guard took his knife from the holster, cut the finger off and pocketed the ring.

"I knew him. He was in the L-21 hut group near mine," Teo said.

"Are you sure?" the guard asked.

"Yes I'm sure because I was working with his group in the sweet potato garden last week."

"Take him back to the hut," the guard ordered.

Two of us grabbed his legs, two his arms; we heaved him up and walked onto the trail with the guard at our backs, his gun aimed at us. We walked about five hundred meters but the odor of the body was overwhelming. I was gagging. I released his legs, fling to the ground.

"What's wrong with you? You never seen a dead body before?" the guard scolded, his face stern. While I was vomiting, the men constructed a stretcher consisting of branches, which they then tied to the body.

"Move it, I don't have all day!" the guard shouted We elevated the dead body and began walking. It seemed like the trail was getting longer and longer. Finally, we arrived at the security booth.

"Put him down here," the sweating guard said as he walked into the booth.

"What is it, comrade?" the guard in the booth asked

"We found the piece to the puzzle," our boss said, and burst out laughing. "What do you think? Did you get your share yet?"

They winked at each other, with self-satisfied grins. One of them turned to us.

"Go in to eat. Come right back for your next assignment?"

We walked slowly to the usual place to get our food, but everything had been put away except for a small pot. Each of us took a coconut bowl and poured the watery rice from the pot into our bowls. There was more water than rice. I could count each grain in my bowl—plus one cockroach, displaying his belly and looking at me with his innocent eyes. It reminded me of the dead body we had just brought back. I wasn't sure of my feelings at this moment, but I still brought the bowl up to my mouth and swallowed the rice. I felt something tickling in my throat. I started to choke.

Hung never came back and his body was never found. No one knew for sure whether he was dead or alive. We listed him in our collective Missing In Action memory. That evening, I went to our "communication center" to learn what I could. I found that the scene last night had been a setup. Some of the guards were jealous of those who had received bribes from Hung and the man from the L-21 hut; they threatened to call for an investigation. To get rid of the evidence, the bribetakers had terminated their victims—Hung, and the man I found.

Chapter 9

The afternoon slipped by slowly as I finished my lunch. I was still hungry but there was nothing left to eat. I tried to keep my mind off my hunger but my stomach kept torturing me. I got up but had to sit down again because I was dizzy. I cupped my hand over my eyes, held it there for a moment, then opened it slowly. I saw a black cloud appear in the sky; the sun was barely shining, as if it didn't have any more strength. The wind was whispering gently through the trees, then suddenly died down.

"Are you okay?" one of my friends, Thanh, asked.

"I'm all right, just a little dizzy."

He grasped my hand and helped me up. We walked back to the security booth. I was thinking that my situation was getting worse. The guard walked out of the booth and came to us.

"Follow me."

We walked behind him to the meeting place in front of the shack. All of the prisoners were there, sitting in rows of fifteen. Comrade Son stood under the awning of the hut. He started his speech as if he was a general:

"From now on, no one can go out for any reason, even if you have to go to the bathroom. There was an incident last night. I think you all know what I'm talking about. He asked our permission to go out, but he ran away. So we shot him. This is a very good lesson for all of you. I am a good person because I follow the North Vietnamese rules of how to treat prisoners. I follow Uncle Ho's ways. If you don't study hard and become a good citizen, you won't have a chance to appear in front of the people" court and ask them to forgive you of your crime. You betrayed them and your country. You followed the southern puppet government, the U.S. regime. This is the time for you to do something to pay us back, to prove your sincerity to our people. If you don't, you may stay here forever. Make your decision. I want you to write. down your family history, your background and whether you feel guilty or innocent. I want the truth. If you lie we know what to do." He had a low, grating voice. Someone gave him a glass of water. He drank it, continued. "People are the owners, the government is the worker for the people, and the North Vietnamese government manages peoples' businesses. Long live Ho Chi Minh," he yelled.

"Long live Ho Chi Minh," we repeated after him, like a broken record.

He paused for a moment while the guard walked over to the front row to tell them to stand up.

"Come here!" he pointed to a new captive who wore glasses.

The guard shoved the new man in the back with his gun to make him walk up to Son.

"You look handsome with your glasses. You are an intellectual from the south, huh? You know too much. You are the one who had a revolution against us, against our people, against our country for over twenty years and our people had to bleed all that time. You are a traitor, you are an idealist. Am I right, our citizens?" he rasped in his heavy accent full of scorn. Then he grinned.

"Yes, comrade, yes, comrade. He's our traitor!" we all shouted as if we were furious. Many guns were held at our backs ready to fire. I felt so bitter since every bad thing I said about others made my mouth dirty. Did I have any choice? The prisoner wearing glasses said softly:

"No, comrade, I'm not an intellectual person. I'm a mechanic in the army and I never held a gun to anyone. Look, look at my hands. They're all dirty with calluses. I'm not a traitor. Please forgive me!" He raised his voice louder and louder, repeatedly; but the crowd's voices were overpowering his.

"Don't lie to the party," Comrade Son shouted. "I have all your files here. You were working for the secret police. You have to confess to us now!"

The crowd quieted. The prisoner kneeled down and crawled over to him and begged for forgiveness. "I'm not a traitor, please forgive me!" he patted his hands on Son's legs and bowed down; Son pushed him away. He crawled back again, but this time the guard who stood next to Son raised his gun and knocked him down. The blood began to dribble from his mouth.

"Who will volunteer to punish our traitor?" comrade Son asked.

One of the men in the antenna group, the prisoners who spied for the guards, stood up and walked over to him like a dog obeying his maser. Son threw him a rope. He held it, pulled the prisoner's arms to his back and firmly tied the left thumb to the right toe and the left toe to the right thumb. He jerked the man toward the flag pole, dragging him in the dirt like an animal. I didn't know if I was an animal or a human being at this moment. The antenna group man walked over, picked up the glasses and gave them to Son while the captive was moaning, trying to get up on his feet. He couldn't see anything without his glasses, his face was close to the ground. He pushed with his head, trying to sit up, but he didn't succeed. Son walked over to him and pulled him up. The inmate stood silently, his mouth bleeding. Son held his glasses in front of his face.

"Are you trying to act blind? We are the people; we are the justice We know you so well, traitor. Why don't you come and get them?" Son waved the glasses in front of his face and the captive stood still. "You ignore me." Son dropped the glasses into the dirt, lifted his foot, then brought it down grinding glass into the dust. He laughed. The leader of the antenna group walked over to the captive, spit in his face, and kicked his stomach. The man fell down. The guard yanked him up. The next inmate stepped forward to continue the execution. We all lined up in a line, spit on him, and called him traitor. We held our confession papers, giving them to the guard as we walked up.

The guard called on individuals to stand up and make a remark. Abruptly a huge shadow covered the whole area. Rain drip-dropped on my hat. It rained harder every moment. The guard raised his voice louder and louder to lecture about his North Vietnamese theory. He tried to speak over the rain so we could hear him. The louder he spoke the stronger the rain fell. I got wet, but I was happy because I didn't have to listen to him rattle on. Water flooded the ground, running down the side of the hut. We were wet like soaked rats. I looked around the group. Each row of people looked like gravestones in a cemetery. We sat still, thinking to ourselves. Some cold, some hard, and some joyous faces. I didn't know exactly what they were thinking, but felt I could see into their minds. I knew they wished they were home with their families, with their wives and children. How will we get out of this trap? I thought. They just promise, but nothing is done. Look! The rain dropped down in a puddle at my side, making bubbles. The bubbles disappeared. Again, the rain dropped. More bubbles, then gone, so quickly.

"Come on! Let's go back to the hut," Thanh called to me.

I stood up and walked with him.

"What do you think?" I asked.

"Politics, all lies. They make promises but don't keep them," he said.

"What do you plan to do?" I asked.

"Lower your voice," he whispered. We looked around, but nobody was in sight.

"Do you have anything to eat?" I said.

"Yeah, some burned rice," said Thanh.

"Where do you hide it?"

"Close to where I sleep so I can eat at night," he said. "I'll give you some when I go to sleep, but don't let anybody know."

"Sure." He went to his spot; I went to mine.

There was mud all around the hut and we walked barefoot. Footprints were everywhere, some big, some small, in different shapes. Inside, the hut looked like a pigpen. I placed the bamboo frame on the floor, and put some hay over it. I had a nice bed—I felt so happy, like a child who sees his mother coming home from the market. It reminded me of when I was young. I would pretend to build a house with a bed in my father's backyard. I remembered my brothers, sisters, and friends playing together. What had happened to my family? I wanted badly to see them. I wanted to put my head on my mother's chest, feel her warmth and tenderness. I longed for my father's embrace. I wanted to hold my sister's hands, share her happiness and sorrow. When I was in trouble, I ran to my brother. Now, I wanted to sit down with my friend beneath the shadow of a tree, near a creek with a waterfall. I wanted to sit down on the green grass and look at the flowers bloom and smell the freshness of early spring.

My friend and I told each other our stories. Where were my loved ones? Here are my kisses, my embrace, my love, and my prayers. I want to send them all to you, I was thinking. I wanted to bury my head in my pillow—the pillow I used to sleep with, the pillow I used to fight with. Oh, my happiness, my happiness.

"You can borrow my linen bag." Thanh patted me on the shoulder, winked, and handed me the bag. I knew there was some food in the bag, and I looked at him, showing my gratefulness. He turned around and walked away. I lay down on my bed, reached into the bag to get the dried burned rice. I put it in my mouth, chewed it slowly It was soft and mushy with a bittersweet taste. I swallowed it like a sweet drop of water which people in the desert thirst for. I let my happiness soak through all my body tissues, spread out to my veins, to my blood which ran to my heart. I could feel it beating faster and steadily It felt as if my heart was going to jump out of my chest, and so I pressed my hand over it on my shirt pocket.

I felt something hard. I took it out—it was the plastic bag that I had picked up next to the corpse. I opened the bag, and pulled out a photograph of the dead man's family, some documents, and a letter to his wife.

I read:

Em,

What will I say to you now? I don't know if this letter will reach you or not. It would be easy for me to say I'm sorry, but this was unbearable. I couldn't hold onto my lift any more, any longer. I had to run. If they shoot me, I will die faster than by being tortured here. I know I hold the love for you and our children, but what can I do…?Will you understand me? I wish I could share with you and our children…I wanted to take my family there but how could I? I don't want to compare the life of being tortured and the love that is out there for me. 1 don't want to compare the life of being tortured and the love that is out there for me. I don't care to look into these two things because I know it would be impossible for me to escape. Here are my kisses to you, hugs for my little daughter and son. I hope you raise them to be real human beings. Our son to be like me, our daughter to be like you. Send my love to my family and your family. If this letter comes to you, it will be very fortunate for me. If it doesn't come to you it was my acceptance of fate. Whether I come to you through my spirit or body; dead or alive.

Farewell—dear,

Anh

The pencil writing was scattered across the page and to wards the bottom it looked like his hand had been shaking. I looked at his family picture and I saw him standing next to his wife. He was holding his son. His wife was pregnant though she looked very young. I didn't know how old this photograph was, but I could see it was from his youth—the time of triumphs and fighting for victory. What had happened to this generation, all the young, brave men that stood up for our country, tor honor and duty? I looked at myself, felt that I was born at the wrong time. Where was my patriotism? I knew I had it in my blood, but it wouldn't come out. I had to wait to take my chances. I felt I wanted to prove something to myself at this moment—do something for this family. I would hide the nylon bag which

I had just opened. I promised myself I would take it back to his family if I could get out of this place. I prayed that his spirit would help me escape safely so that I could bring his message to his family. Where was his soul wandering? Did he have a place to rest? Did he know how to find his way home? Or was he just one of the wandering souls who have no place to go, no family to love, like a wasted person roaming the city? Or did he just die and that's the end?

Outside, the night stood still, waiting for the new day. The moon was dim, shining through the hut, through the bamboo wall. All kinds of animals were on the prowl, ready for a hunting night, but leaves had folded on the trees for the sleeping night, I could hear animals calling each other to prepare for their journey. They were whispering through the trees, in the thickets. The air was getting cooler. It seemed as if the whole universe was ready for a new beginning of life. How long have I been here? I couldn't remember. I touched the bamboo wall to count the marks on it: more than 350 days. It seemed like my whole life. I couldn't sleep, thinking of the memories now long past.

Suddenly, there was a strange noise outside the hut. My eyes followed the rustling, looked beyond the barbed wire fence at the back of the security booth. I saw a dark shadow crawling towards the dead body which we carried in on our way back to the camp in die afternoon and left near the fence, not having had time to bury it yet. The shadow stopped at the corpse for a moment, then the figure moved back, vanishing beyond the fence. I couldn't figure out what was going on. Were there any guards in the booth? Were they watching us? There wasn't any action. Could it be that the remnants of the South Vietnamese army had invaded the place and the guards had run off? But why was it so quiet then? If they had invaded the area I would have heard shooting. Maybe they attacked using a special force. I had heard of incidents like this lately I was more hopeful.

I raised my head, looked at the booth and beyond the barbed wire fence. Everything was still quiet. The moon hid its face behind the trees. I could hear the birds flapping their wings and flying away. In the distance, the rooster crowed. Above, the North Star shone, mixing together with the dawn which was finally arriving. The sky became brighter and brighter. I had not slept.

The old folks have a saying: If you're awake all night, you know how long the night is. I understood that now. I got up and walked out of the hut to prepare for another working day. I went to the shack to pick up the tools.

"I'm in L-19 group. Where shall I work today?" I asked.

"You cook, but before you begin, call your friend Thanh and get a shovel," Chu Tu ordered. "Come back after."

I went back to my hut to find Thanh but halfway there I saw him coming towards me.

"Thanh, we work together today?"

"What is our job?"

"Chu Tu told me to have yon get a shovel and see him before we cook."

"So we cook today. That's good," Thanh looked at me, smiling while we walked.

"What are you smiling about?" I asked.

"Nothing, really."

We stopped at the shack to get shovels and went to the well to look for Chu Tu. I saw him squatting like a frog at the side of the well.

"What do you want us to do, Chu Tu?"

"Make me some tea first," he said while he was washing his face. We walked to the place where we cooked.

"And don't forget to fill the barrels up with water," Chu Tu yelled at us.

I chopped some wood, then built a fire while Thanh got a kettle, filled it with water and put it over the fire.

"What will we cook for lunch?"

"White rice for our comrades. Leftover rice mixed together with sweet potato and old corn for us as usual?"

"Do we have any sweet potatoes?"

"No, but we have a small bag of old corn left," Thanh said while he was checking the ingredients. I saw steam coming from the spout on the kettle. It began to boil.

"I'm going to Chu Tu's hut to get his cup. I'll be back" I ran out of the place. I came to Chu Tu as he was talking to some of the other comrades. I got his cup and he told me to make some for these other comrades too. I went back to make the tea and carried it to them.

"Would you like sugar in your tea, Chu Tu?" Thanh asked.

"Yes, here is my jar of sugar."

Thanh took it and opened it. He got a spoon to scoop the sugar out of the jar, put some in the cups and stirred them.

"These cups too, Thanh." I gave them to him.

He put more sugar in the cups a second time, but he didn't stir them. I looked at him curiously, opening my eyes wider. I tried to ask him but he looked at me, winking his eye. I remained silent. We handed the tea to the hut. We came to the well, dropped the bucket of water into the barrel until it was full.

"Why did you do that before with the sugar?"

He didn't say a word but gave me a smile, you are learning, I thought.

"You and Thanh come here," Chu Tu called us.

We ran over to him.

"What do you want us to do?"

"Clean the cups and get your shovels," said Chu Tu. "Come to the security booth after you're done."

We brought the cups to the well to wash I hem. Thanh put a little water in the cup, drank it. I looked into the cups, and saw there was some sugar left on the bottom. Now I knew his purpose. I hadn't tested sugar in a long time. I used my finger to scoop the sugar, placed it on my tongue, and slowly let it melt. I didn't want to swallow it. I just wanted to let it soak in my mouth, I wanted to see what the taste was, as if I had never tasted it before in my life. I smiled to myself.

"Are you dreaming?" Thanh called me. "Let's go."

I felt invigorated. I didn't know where all this energy was coming from. I felt like I was a new person. I got up.

"Yes, let's go."

We walked to the security booth to see Chu Tu. He walked out of the booth to the gate. He waited at the gate till we arrived.

"Go dig a hole to bury the body you brought back yesterday," he said, and pointed to the side of the gate.

We began to chop the weeds and surrounding grass away. Afterwards, we dug.

"When you're finished, come and get me," Chu Tu said.

He walked back to the booth to talk to the other guard. "Thank you for the sugar, Thanh," I said.

"What are you thanking me for? Are we friends or what?" "Yeah, we are friends."

5

(Nguyen Qui Duc, 1958—)
阮奎德

作者简介

  阮奎德（Nguyen Qui Duc, 1958— ），越南名"Nguyễn Quí Đức"，美国越南裔作家、编辑和翻译。他出生于越南大叻（Đà Lạt），父亲曾是南越政府高官，母亲曾在学校任职。1975年越南战争后，阮奎德父亲被关进劳改营，母亲带着残疾的姐姐四处奔波，维持生计。1975年越南战争结束前夕，阮奎德逃难到美国。他曾在伦敦英国广播公司（British Broadcasting Corporation）工作，担任过美国国家公共广播电台（National Public Radio）的评论员。2006年的秋天，他返回越南并定居河内（Hà Nội）。

  阮奎德是一个才华横溢的作家，最具代表性的作品是《落叶归根：一个越南家庭的奥德赛》(*Where the Ashes Are: The Odyssey of a Vietnamese Family*, 1993)。他创作了诸多散文、诗歌和短篇小说。他的文章发表在《亚洲华尔街日报周刊》(*The Asian Wall Street Journal Weekly*)、《纽约时报杂志》(*The New York Times Magazine*)、《旧金山考官》(*The San Francisco Examiner*)、《圣何塞水星新闻》(*The San Jose Mercury News*) 等重要刊物上。他还创作了有关中国青年的纪录片《上海之夜》(*Shanghai Nights*)，荣获2004年美国海外新闻俱乐部（Overseas Press Club of America）颁发的爱德华·R.玛洛（Edward R. Murrow）电视纪录片优秀奖。同年，他获得了亚历山大·格博德基金会（Alexander Gerbode Foundation）的"杰出成就奖"。2006年获得专业记者协会（The Society of Professional Journalists）颁发的"杰出服务奖"。他还被"A-Media"提名为"30位最具影响力的美国亚裔"。

  选段选自《落叶归根》中的"胖男归家"（"Fat Man's Come Home"），讲述了作者在时隔多年后回到越南与家人团聚的场景，表达了阮奎德对战争历史的反思，以及对文化寻根的探索。

作品选读

Where the Ashes Are: The Odyssey of a Vietnamese Family

(Fat Man's Come Home)

By Nguyen Qui Duc

TWELVE

Fat Man's Come Home

HỒ CHÍ MINH CITY

"Ô, vÔ đây, vÔ đây!" "Oh, come in, come in!"

Aunt Diệu-Mai hadn't changed much, her hair still smooth and long, her eyes sad yet sparkling. She grabbed my arms and sobbed as we hugged. Her dog barked at us: Peter Breslow, Arthur Laurent, the Foreign Ministry guide, and me. We came unannounced, setting up our recording equipment at the entrance to the little alley leading to her house.

She had had to give up her villa, and now lived in a dark apartment in this narrow way. I was concerned about her health; she had had a stroke.

"I'm better now," she said. "How come you're so fat?"

"American food." I laughed.

"Everyone here is so poor, have you noticed?"

"Yes." I didn't know what else to say. "Ma and Cha sent a letter."

"I'll read it later. Have some tea first. Who are these people?"

I explained my assignment. I'd arrived home the day before, on my thirty-first birthday. Anxious about my reunion with Aunt Diệu-Mai after fourteen years, I couldn't sleep that first night. From San Francisco I had written to arrange for her to meet me at my hotel. I feared the curiosity of the police and her neighbors, especially as I would be accompanied by Americans with microphones, tape machines, and other suspicious recording equipment. Once in Hồ Chí Minh City (or Sài Gòn, as it was still known), I became impatient. "Let's just go over there," I said to my guide. I wanted to save Aunt Diệu-Mai the trip to the hotel since I knew she had trouble walking. Peter also preferred capturing on tape our spontaneous reunion.

The ceiling fan at my aunt's didn't do much to cool us; there was barely enough power to make it spin. Sài Gòn was always hot. "You want a hand fan?" Aunt Diệu-Mai asked me. She shuffled away.

"It was hotter than this back in April '75," I yelled after her.

"We should have left then, too," my aunt said when she came back, a purple paper fan in her hand. Like hundreds of thousands of others, her husband, my uncle Hải, had been put in jail—officially a reeducation camp—shortly after the North Vietnamese came. He died in captivity in 1983. I asked about Diệu-Quỳnh's illnesses.

"She just gave up, I think," Aunt Diệu-Mai replied. "Now what about your parents? Are they okay?"

"They're both working," I said.

"Your mom wrote and said you've abandoned her. She doesn't get to see you. Why don't you let them live with you? How come you're not supporting them?"

"But I'm so poor!"

"Poor as the people here?"

It hit home. I couldn't decide whether Aunt Diệu-Mai was joking. "You unfilial son!"

"I'll wait until you get there—then we can all live together."

"If I had to wait for you, Cu Bé, to house me, and to feed me"—she laughed—"I'd die of hunger, or old age." Her using my childhood nickname told me I was home again.

Among my mother's many siblings—my grandfather had had four wives—Aunt Diệu-Mai was the only one still in Việt Nam. She had no children. Soon she might be on her way to America. My uncle Thinh-Anh in Maryland had completed the paperwork to sponsor her.

"Your uncles all live in such cold places! Maryland, Virginia—I'd rather live with your parents in California."

"You should," I replied.

"And who will cook for me? You? Vietnamese food?"

"If you'll teach me," I said. "Hue beef noodle."

"Don't be smart!" She laughed, then said, "Who knows when I'll be able to leave?"

She patted my cheeks. "I'm glad you're home. Of all the people who left, you're the only one to come back. Come to dinner tomorrow! Bring your American friends."

I wondered who would cook. Aunt Diệu-Mai was nearly seventy years old.

At two in the afternoon, my cousins were asleep on the floor when I knocked. Seven people, all living in one room. The cousins had also been primary school classmates. Their mother had worked at my mother's school. I apologized for my unannounced arrival. "I was afraid you might be at work," I said.

They smiled. No one had a job. They warned that the shoes
I left outside the door might get stolen.

"They're cheap," I said. "Just a few dollars." I then looked at the shoes lying haphazardly in the hallway. My white canvas sneakers looked obscenely opulent next to the seven pairs of ragged flip-flops.

Crouched in a corner of the room where he smoked a cigarette, my cousin Bảo avoided my eyes. He directed a remark to his mother. "Cu Bé's so fat, don't you think, Ma?"

I felt obese. My white shirt was soaked in sweat.

"Can you get Vietnamese food in California?" his mother asked.

From across the room, Bảo's sister Lý stared at me. She had been my sister's classmate. "Is Diệu-Hà still beautiful? She must be."

I smiled in the way a Vietnamese smiles to avoid having to answer a question. I had suddenly realized that Bão and his siblings all had extremely dark skin. I glanced at my hand, seeing as if for the first time how pale it was.

"Cu Bé, you have any pictures of your house in America?"

"Oh, I just have a rented flat," I answered.

"Big?"

"No, no, a plain two-bedroom apartment."

"For you and your wife? Why can't your parents live with you?"

My aunt asked to see pictures of my wife. I picked my shoulder bag off the floor and began to rummage through it, looking for the photos. As I did so I pulled out my professional tools. Microphones, cassette recorder, camera—all looked like monstrous objects from outer space, and expensive. The T-shirts I had thought would be good gifts now seemed inadequate. I stuffed everything back in the bag. "I must have forgotten the photos at the hotel," I said.

Looking up, I caught my cousins averting their eyes. The wonderful reunion I had anticipated seemed to have stabbed them with glimpses of a rich world they could never know.

Again I could not sleep in my stuffy hotel room that night, so I wandered out into the street. Gaunt men, young and old, buzzed like flies around the block of hotels near the river, fighting to sell a pedicab tour of Sài Gòn at half past midnight. "*Đi vòng vòng chòi mà—cho mát,*" one driver suggested. "Let's go round and round, for fun—get some breeze."

We went a few blocks along the river, then doubled back on the wide boulevards forming Sài Gòn's downtown. The Continental Hotel had a new coat of paint; its veranda, once a café made famous by Graham Greene and later hordes of foreign correspondents covering the Việt Nam War, was now enclosed in a garish glass structure. The old National Assembly building was again a theater, and across from it the square was no longer covered with grass. The ugly concrete statue of a South Vietnamese marine brandishing a rifle was torn down just after the North Vietnamese arrived; in its place now sat a few sorry benches around a cement fountain with no water. Over on General Uprising Street, once Freedom Street, a row of hotels competed for attention on the only block in the city which had regular, uninterrupted electricity. The whole area had somehow recaptured the gaudiness of days gone by when noisy bars and kiosks selling bootle tapes of Bob Dylan and the Beatles had catered to American soldiers, and those who came to profit from the war. On my first night back I was shocked to see smartly dressed bands of youths as well as entire families circling the area on motorcycles, riding aimlessly as though gasoline were something that had to be used up by the end of the night.

My midnight pedicab turned into a small road. The naked poverty of the neighborhood struck me abruptly. Shadows dragged tattered burlap sacks back and forth across dim streets. Frail, half-dressed boys sang and chewed old bread, pissing on the walls or in the gutters all the while. Rows and rows of people were trying to slee on straw mats on the pavement, surrounded by skeletal dogs too weak to fight over the contents of rubbish heaps. The turning wheels of the pedicab echoed deep in my bones, and in the darkness the scene took on a nightmarish and sinister character.

"Is there anything you won't do for a story, Đức?" I hated Peter's sarcastic tone. Half naked, trousers rolled up to my knees, I was about to slip through a narrow hole into a maze of under-ground tunnels the Việt Cộng had built during the war. The Foreign Ministry had organized this trip to the village of Củ Chi, half an hour from Sài Gòn, where I met Út Nghiệp, a former Việt Cộng soldier whose ideal of life was shaped by war. He had joined the National Liberation Front in 1961, when he was fourteen. He and men like him fought for ten, fifteen years in the war, as their fathers had done against foreign invaders. During the war Nghiệp would live underground for two weeks at a time.

"He's so fat," said a villager, "how's he gonna get through?"

Down below I could neither breathe nor see. Bats flew out of walls of packed earth. I was petrified of getting lost. Gasping, I crouched along inch by inch, fearing Nghiệp might abandon me. I hated the thought that I had trusted a former enemy to guide me through these tunnels.

Waves of late morning breeze softened the heat in Củ Chi when we emerged. Our amiable guide Tien suggested a coconut drink at the thatched-roof local "café." The barefooted owner was a peasant wearing a simple shirt over a pair of loose black pants. Her hair was knotted into a small bundle in back, revealing the wrinkles on her face. Her irregular teeth were dyed black; her hands were rough and calloused.

Nodding toward Peter, she said, "Tell him I used to have a house over there." Her arm made an arc. "The Americans burned it down. My husband died too. Americans killed him."

Tiến and the driver were nervous, smiling the way Asians do when they are embarrassed. I was exact in my translation. Arthur looked away.

Peter asked me to say something back. Anything.

"Ah, it's okay," the old woman laughed. "Why doesn't he just marry my daughter? Take her to America!"

Our van baking in the early afternoon heat, we headed back to the mad mess called Sài Gòn.

It was cloudy the afternoon Peter, Arthur, and I arrived at the pagoda on the outskirts of Sài Gòn. My father's sister Xuân-Liễu and her husband, my uncle Vinh, came with us. Dozens of kids followed us from the main street into the alley leading to the courtyard in front of the pagoda. For some inexplicable reason they wouldn't stop screaming as they surrounded us on the path to the main temple. All eyes were on us. Arthur, not as tall or as thin as the muscular Peter, looked painfully pale. A bright red bag swung from his shoulder along with coils of black wires. His microphones were hooked to a metal pole and encased in a plastic zeppelin the size of a watermelon. My own baggy trousers and canvas shoes were hideously bright and white.

In the principal chamber a man was sitting before an enormous statue of the Buddha. Chanting a monotonous prayer, he dragged out his words, accompanying himself on a wooden bell the size of a skull. I knelt down and prayed as two monks looked on. They had been watching over Diệu-Qùynh's ashes for the last ten years. When the physical and mental illnesses had finally taken their toll, only my mother was still in Sài Gòn. I had now come for my sister's ashes.

It was pouring, Sài Gòn's usual afternoon shower. The man at the altar continued to chant, undisturbed. I was taken around the veranda to a room full of urns. I wandered between the shelves, stopping at the urns bearing names I recognized. The one containing Diệu-Qùynh's ashes was made of ceramic, with blue flowers. A black-and-white photo of Diệu-Qùynh was glued to the outside. I recognized my mother's handwriting on the piece of paper that gave her name and dates: 1950-1979.

For a time I stood before the urn. Soon I was to be on my way again. Like me, my aunt, my cousins, friends, and other relatives still in Việt Nam might all leave one day to create new lives in a place of exile. We'd live there for ten, twelve, fifteen years, perhaps the rest of our lives. But some of us had to come back for the things we had left behind: our childhood home—the place, as the Vietnamese say, where our umbilical cords were cut. We would come back changed, but we would come back, for a loved one, and her ashes.

6

(Lan Cao, 1961—)
高兰

作者简介

　　高兰（Lan Cao, 1961—），美国越南裔小说家、律师和法学教授。她出生于越南西贡（Saigon）（今胡志明市），父亲高文元（Cao Văn Viên）曾是南越一名海军大校。在1975年北越攻陷西贡前，高文元夫妇将14岁的女儿高兰托付给了美国好友，带其到美国生活。在越南战争结束后不久，高兰父母移民美国与女儿重聚。1983年，高兰从曼荷莲学院（Mount Holyoke College）获得学士学位，几年后从耶鲁大学法学院（Yale Law School）获得法学博士学位。毕业后任职于布鲁克林法学院（Brooklyn Law School）、杜克大学法学院（Duke Law School）与密歇根法学院（Michigan Law School）等高校。同时，她也是一位才华横溢的作家。

　　她的文学作品有，小说《猴桥》（*Monkey Bridge*, 1997）与《莲与暴》（*The Lotus and the Storm*, 2014）、回忆录《说六种声调的家庭：一个难民母亲与一个美国女儿》（*Family in Six Tones: A Refugee Mother, an American Daughter*, 2020）以及与赫摩斯·诺瓦斯（Himilce Novas）合著《美国亚裔历史全解》（*Everything You Need to Know About Asian American History*, 2004）。

　　选段分别出自《猴桥》的第2章与《莲与暴》的第29章。前一选段讲述了主人公母亲初到美国"出洋相"的场景，以幽默诙谐的口吻展现了美越文化差异，以及越南裔在美国的生存之苦。后一选段讲述了主人公与创伤历史和解的片段，表达了作者对和平与和解的追寻。

作品选读（一）

Monkey Bridge

（Chapter 2）

By Lan Cao

Despite my mother's multiple good-luck preparations, that, of course, was not how it had turned out. The days he packed me on to a Pan Am flight out of Vietnam alone with Uncle Michael, a few months before the end of the war, she had burned three sticks of incense, added several photographs to the family altar, pasted strips of paper colored a bright, auspicious red on every window and door, and, as if she hadn't summoned enough good luck or done enough to appease our ancestral spirits, invoked yet another icon from her paraphernalia of luck, a plaster Virgin Mary, her "Sainte Vierge" from convent boarding-school days, which she placed on the table by the front door—just in case.

What else could she have done to ensure our return to Vietnam? How could we have known there would be no coming back from America, no tucked wings or perfect landing in Tan Son Nhut Airport?

"You can lose a house, apiece of land, even a country," she had sighed our first night in Virginia after the war, as welay surrounded by a melancholic array of impermanence. We were in bed, on a flabby mattress my mother had had to reinforce with her makeshift box spring, apiece of plywood she bought and lugged from Hechinger lumber yard. She had given me the good side of the mattress, the side without the fat purplish stains that reminded me of those dead, water-logged worms clogged in our drain after every big tropical rain.

We had been separated for almost six months. While I stayed in the safety of Connecticut, my mother, true to her obligation as a daughter, had stayed behind until she could convince Baba Quan to leave before the last U.S. military plane departed from Saigon. But even then, fate, unpropitious and hard, had intervened.

It's not my fault, it's my mother's, I could tell Bobbie.

I blamed my mother for my flawed eye. My mother often said karma means there's always going to be something you'll have to inherit, and I suppose that was how I found myself seeing the world through such an eye that night. My mother was my karma, her eye my inheritance. Through that eye I could see nothing but danger in the phantom landscape ahead. The border, this Canadian border, I felt, contained the unthinkable, more ominous with its terrifying nakedness than all the helmeted men and barbed wire combined.

Danger lurked everywhere, everyday, for my mother. When we first moved into the apartment complex in Falls Church, Virginia, she had insisted I beg the rental manager for another apartment in the building. "How dare he insult us, making us pay for an apartment no one would want?" she fumed and stabbed the air, once, twice, three times, with her three pitchfork fingers aimed in the direction of the rental office. I averted my eyes from her glare and prayed that what-ever plot she was harboring would dissipate. "You tell him we refuse live in a place that's been hexed with a curse, "she screamed and pointed a stern chin t the giant antenna on the building across from our apartment. In the gleaming darkness, the big metallic rod threw a menacing shadow across our window. Aimed straight into our living room, its long wiry spike became a deathly sword that threatened to slash our fortune and health in two.

And so, because our life itself was on the line as far as she was concerned, my mother insisted I apply my halting English to a good cause. "Tell him to give us another apartment, or else tell him to chop down that antenna," she ordered, animal panic in her voice.

I had longed, as we stood staring at the words "Rental Office" suspended over the doorway, for a sudden spurt of courage to defy, but thirteen well-bred years of Confucian ethics had taught me the fine points of family etiquette and coached me into near-automatic obedience. "Tell him we can put several mirrors up to deflect the curse in his direction if he doesn't do something quick," my mother commanded, nudging me inside with her shoulder.

"Please, Ma. He'll think I'm crazy. Nobody believes in curses and counter curses here."

"You tell him, 'My mother said to do it.' He'll know you're just translating. Children," she sniffed.

The manager peered uneasily from beneath a baseball cap, red with "Orioles" stitched in yellow, with curiosity, fascination, and suspicion in his eyes. "Well? C'mon. I haven't got all day." A pair of veins ran along the sides of his prizefighter's neck like electrical wires. "What's Madame Nhu here saying?" he smirked, popping his knuckles and winking at a woman in tight black jeans sitting by his side. The woman chuckled and looked us up and down with her bright-blue eyes.

I concentrated on his face and on my New World tricks. "How do you do," I said in the clearest, most metronomic English I knew. His rubber soles glared from the table, two giant sneakers like two smeared and muddy halves of a yin-yang circle.

"My mother saw a green snake coming out of the drain yesterday and again this morning. There's no way she can set foot in that bathroom again. She has a phobia about snakes," I added, making sure to emphasize the word "phobia." Psychology is the new American religion.Uncle Michael had once said.

"She almost fainted. And ever since, she's been afraid to go into the bathroom. Can we switch to another apartment? There's an empty one on the same floor facing the other side of the building," I squeaked.

"What's that? Come again?"

"A snake. Cliff, that's what she said, isn't that what you said? And now the poor mother can't pee. How'd it get there in the first place?" The woman shuddered. "I don't blame you. I wouldn't want to pee knowing a snake is watching me," she said, turning to my mother. "Don't worry. Cliff here'll get you another apartment." She gave a quick leave-it-to-me look that promised victory.

"This one even had a long forked tongue and rubbery scales and a long body that twisted back and forth," I said for added effect.

"It gives me the creeps just thinking about it. Poor things. Why not, Cliff? What do you say? It's the same thing, same two-bedroom, same floor, same price." She was now on our side. She leaned over and pinched the manager's cheeks, running her hand over his two-day stubble.

"Well..."

My mother sensed uncertainty in the manager's voice and wanted me to finish him off with a threat of our own. "He's insulting the whole family," she coached me. The "whole family" meant not only the two of us and my dead father, but our ancestors going back several generations as well. "Tell him we have to be out today or we'll retaliate with our own hex," my mother ordered.

"My mother says she's sure you can help us, because you're the manager," I translated.

The manager leaned back and sucked on his cigarette, fiddling with the radio knob, pretending to be deep in big, important thoughts. He stacked several quarters on his elbow and flipped them toward the ceiling. "It's all in the wrist," he said with a wink, snapping them up in one swift swoop of the hand.

"Okay. Sure, why not. Whatever Mamasan wants, Mamasan gets," he finally said after a long silent pause, stroking the thick blond hair pushing through his shirt, and squinting at me through threads of yellow smoke expelled from his nose.

"Remember this lesson: you have to stand up to the Americans if you want anything in this country," my mother whispered rapidly, hugging me. Before we moved our things into the new apartment, she had first inspected every room, then burned three sticks of incense in a canon the windowsill to remove all traces of danger.

The antenna's counterpart, in my mother's mind, must have been the colossal black statue of several South Vietnamese soldiers cemented directly opposite the National Assembly in Saigon. On the attack, their brutal guns had pointed straight into the building, the heart and brain of the legislature of the South Vietnamese government itself. "What kind of a way is that to fight a war?" my mother often complained. "Who needs enemies when your own guns are pointed at your head?" And when I shrugged off her peculiar understanding of cause and effect, she would, like a holy woman imparting wisdom, poke me with her finger and insist I hear her advice. "A curse can only be checked by another curse. Did a thousand American bombs succeed in counter-acting a curse as big as that ugly statue?"

The new country must have doubled her sense of impending doom, because my mother began to see danger every where, danger screaming out of the earth and the sky and even the birds—three hoots of an owl made her skin pucker with fright. Yet she remained miraculously unconcerned about crime or kidnappers or busy cross streets. "Two men with guns came into the 7-Eleven yesterday afternoon and held it up," I had once told her. I could have been in there buying Slurpees and Hershey bars on my way home from school. "Good thing I wasn't in there at the time," I added. "Don't go there," she barked. "They charge too much for detergent, almost double the supermarket price, then act insulted—can you believe that?—when you haggle them down."

A defective traffic light, an inadequately marked cross-walk, or a school bus without snow tires in the winter—my mother ignored my embarrassment and left every neighborhood petition unsigned. What troubled her was something much larger, much more mysterious. She believed in the infinite, untouchable forces that made up the hidden universe: hexes and curses, destiny and karma. That was why she thoughts he had to be with me, or at least near me, all the time, to deflect their powers, since I was too ignorant to detect danger myself Only it should really have been the other way around, when you get right down to it. I should have been the one to fear for my mother's safety, for her fragile sanity. At any moment, it was as if she could close here yes and summon, from the murky darkness of her mind, a world only she could see.

I fingered the map of Canada neatly tucked in Bobbie's glove compartment. In the black stretch of land where we sat, with Bobbie's car swallowed like a prey in the belly of the beast, the border in front of us had become an antenna, and the antenna a cursed statue, a monument of war that brimmed under a loose lid I couldn't keep clamped.

"If you close your eyes and let me step on the pedal, you won't know we're crossing a border," Bobbie exhorted, as we sat staring at the invisible line that stretched beyond us.

Rows of bushes along the road, darkened by impending dusk, were clenching inward like fists. The sky was turning violet-dark, and a migration of cars with red taillights flew past us like flocks of cardinals. Somehow it already felt too late to make the crossing. A bullet of sweat slid down my spine's edge. I was no longer capable of making the distinction between what my father called "one wrong move," which was to be avoided at all costs, and the simple human need to act, once it was relatively clear, at least, that no wrong move would be committed.

作品选读（二）

The Lotus and the Storm

(29: The River Flows but the Ocean Stays)
By Lan Cao

When Mai leaves the following morning, James is still asleep. A tapestry of darkness is just beginning to lift. The sun is barely up, a mere speckling of orange. The walls are washed in the pale, gray palette of dawn. She moves about stealthily in the bathroom as she gets ready to leave the room.

Her heart quickens as she takes a long look at him. Mai is fully dressed but she lingers. There is a flicker under his eyelids, a sign of troubled sleep perhaps. The sheets are bunched and knotted against his stomach and she can see his chest moving up and down in quick, ragged breaths. She bends down toward him and kisses his forehead. He does not pull away. Even in his sleep he seems to be leaning toward her. She closes the wooden shutters so he will not be awakened by daylight.

James, she whispers, not out loud but only to herself. The sin his name is drawn out, like an eternal, sibilant whisper. Even his name carries its own after effect; already it is a purple mark foundering deep inside her soul. She knows he is lost to her, and she leaves the room carrying his heart inside her. How surprising, she thinks, that later in life, she is feeling what others feel in their early youth—a sensual jolt and wonder. No matter what happens next, she knows she will be lost to him forever. It is a miracle that she has found him at all. More cannot be asked.

• • •

Later that night she returns to her hotel and checks out. She is told a man had been waiting for her and that he had written her a note. "I will wait for you at Ben Thanh Market," it says. "Or come to the orphanage." At the bottom of the note are the name and address.

She moves into another hotel two streets away. She stays there for more than a week, trying to sort her way through the befuddled grip of her emotions. She ignores his nearby presence in the sprawling market. It is a familiar feeling, nursing yourself back from the precipice of ruined love, the misaligned and scattered selves splintered within. Sometimes these feelings are about James but sometimes they barely attach to a person at all. At those times she is just displaced, weighted down and beset by an intense hunger for life that stirs within, a hunger that can scarcely be met.

When love is experienced and released, where does it go? How does it balance itself on the pinprick of the moment? This much is clear to me. We don't recover from love forged in childhood, in history. We carry it with us. Or more precisely, it just sticks to us. And it is never really forfeited or lost.

• • •

It is early but Mai makes her way to Ben Thanh Market. She will return to the very spot where she first saw James. The note says he will wait at Ben Thanh Market but that was written more than a week ago. And certainly at this early hour he will not be there even if he still plans to wait. Still, she is filled with hope. Vendors are just beginning to set up. She finds her way back to that spot where she first saw James—by the bun bo Hue noodle cart. The vendor she is looking for is there, fanning herself with a conical straw hat. When Mai asks, she is immediately told where the American lives.

That evening, spurred by a freighted sense of urgency, she takes a cyclo to Hai Ba Trung Street and, after crossing several intervening alleys, arrives at a cul-de-sac called Alley Number 9. The sidewalks are wet. The moon looms overhead. Mai walks silently along the reticulated backstreets, in search of the 100 block where she has been told his house can be located. She hurries past a disordered row of crude, boarded-up buildings, some abandoned and vandalized, their scabby timber pulled off and left in a junk heap of tires and other unwanted items. A motorbike spews gravel as it screeches to a sudden stop with a gasp of the brakes before a repair shop festooned with multicolored pennants. The road, grudging and forlorn, is beaten and rutted and bears the deep imprint of wheeled vehicles. The houses here are of weathered clapboard and cement. Small and narrow, they stand haphazardly next to each other. Some are enclosed by a crisscross of chicken—wire fencing, others by concrete knee-high barricades choked by red spikes of dry, thorny stalks and edged by a sludge of brown slime. A small boy eyes her and beams a big grin.

Mai identifies his house by its pale yellow-ocher walls, hot—pink bougainvillea bush, windows with two broken slats temporarily fastened together: slippage fixed by cords and strings. Butterflies float among the flowering bushes. Birds cast a shadow across the sky as they break the horizon and approach the neighborhood. A ragged doll partially covered by leaves and dirt lies face down near the bottom step. It is late but the street is still crowded with cyclos and bicyclists. She finds a spot across from the house, behind a row of motorbikes parked on the sidewalk, and sits there to watch. She fits her body inside shadows big enough to hide her.

Here is James's life, unveiled like a slow heaving confession in the shaded fringe of dusk. She hears the voice of a little girl and the occasional chirps of crickets asserting their nocturnal presence. Through the mosquito—netting curtains, she sees his silhouette, as if etched against the ivory gauze. The little girl is climbing onto his lap, pulling his hair tenderly. Mai sees her face, sweet, adoring. She is a flower. He offers her a spoonful of something and she pushes the offering away to pursue something of greater interest, painting her father's face instead. After a brief struggle in which she bobs and fidgets, he capitulates with a show of resignation, pledging solicitous stillness so she can adorn his face at will. In the background a woman sends her shadows back and forth as she moves across the room. But what Mai focuses on is what she has many times conjured in her mind, James and the little girl. She has fashioned a paper crown and placed it on his head. In exchange for his cooperation, she is making a show of being more tractable, accepting his offer of food with minimal fuss. The bluster of play subsides. A smell of caramelized pork comes from the open window. Mai takes a deep breath, inhaling and holding it as if for a lifetime.

James walks with the girl toward the refrigerator. He opens it and holds her in midair, suspended inside a cold blast. They both laugh. After a few minutes, James closes the door and hoists the child up on his shoulders, father and daughter in sweet complicity. The girl points at the window and James glances out with a dark questioning. Still carrying the child on his shoulders, he walks out the door, to the level patch of grass in front. Mai feels as if someone were holding her and squeezing her tight.

"Over there, Daddy," the girl exclaims, struggling to wriggle free. James submits to her wishes. He eases her down his back but keeps his arm half—clasped around her body. The little girl twists loose and runs to the bottom of the steps. She scoops up her doll and shakes it clean of dirt, rearranging its hair and dress before embracing it. She reassures the doll that they will sleep together tonight. She puts the doll in a sitting position and squats down to talk to it. This is the little girl who will rescue him. She is changing him already, Mai thinks. Things won't fall apart. Light from the house is at his back, emitting a soft glow, absorbing him in its vast repose. Something is marrying him to the night. And in turn, it, the evening, the place itself, is opening up, embracing him in its fold.

James hangs a cigarette between his lips, cupping his hand over it as he strikes a match. After several tries, the sulfur tip flares. A stray cat yowls as it slowly strides along the street with proper melancholy and presumptuous propriety. The little girl takes a few inquisitive steps forward, calling out to the cat, and then running toward it. Meow, meow. James's eyes follow his little girl's every move. He edges closer to the street, confronting, scanning for her movement.

"Khanh, come back," he calls when the little girl ventures too far for his comfort. Only a short flight of steps separates the house from the street. "Khanh."

The name claws at Mai's heart.

James takes a long drag of his cigarette, letting the smoke settle in his lungs. A woman's voice, more harsh than necessary, I think, calls for him. The voice is beckoning him in flat but heavily accented English. James in turn calls for his child. He finds her by the curved walk. He taps her bottom before scooping her up and carrying her against his chest back into the house. Before he enters, he turns briefly toward us as if to impart a final, valedictory glance.

Mai and I stand still together in the purple presence of the evening, watching the little house return to its internal torque. The woman takes the child from James, then returns her to him before their backs turn and they disappear from our line of vision. Slowly the house recedes and dwindles as lights are dimmed, then turned off. Darkness takes over. I think Mai knows what she is witnessing. It won't do to hold on to the form of things. This is a scene she has entered late and from which she will leave early. Still, we both feel something move through us, maybe a realization that we can accept something less than perfection.

•   •   •

Mai stays in Saigon for a few more days and then, before leaving, decides on the spur of the moment to take a drive outside the city. You don't have to go far from Saigon to see the country. The rice fields surprise her. They lie flat, without much ceremony, embracing a piercing, green consciousness.

She has hired a driver to take her around. The road, one among many arterial feeds that surround Saigon, is newly paved but there are long, drawling stretches of rutted asphalt. There are no monuments, no tourist attractions here. Nothing majestic. Only the dramatic compression of green in quadrilaterals. She is not sure why she is doing what she is doing, only that it feels right.

Mai remembers how our mother was pleased when the pale green of her jade bracelet deepened over time into the rich, verdant green of a rice field, which for her augured health and prosperity.

She does not know what to do or where to go. She merely asks to be driven. The engine rumbles and its internal bearings click smoothly each time the driver shifts gears. Everything is peaceful now, though years ago this was the site of ferocious military campaigns. The hard eyes of history can still be felt. The names of towns, some painted, others in grouted signs, appear parabolically through the windshield, but Mai and I remember them through the varnish of war, as battlefield names only. The highway unravels its black asphalt strip flanked by bright emerald green. Mai and I both remember that our father talked often about rice fields, that he once solemnized and imbued them with formidable characteristics—defiant, hard—spirited. Here they are—something immense and simple. Despite the intervening years of triumph and loss, goodness can still be found here.

Although Mai has no conscious memory of the countryside—it was not safe to drive far from the capital city during the war—she feels something so familiar here, as if she were going toward a known place. Toward a still point. That point in the present that carries a scent from the past but is not afraid of it and so welcomes the future without fear.

Suddenly, she (and I too) see why the fields are so familiar. The realization comes as a surprise. Mai asks the driver to stop. She steps out. The air smells of palm thatch and tropical wetness. We are surrounded by green, like the interminable white of a Virginia snowstorm. Despite the elemental difference, this vast green is but an alternate version of the wintry white expanse when harsh lines and edges are muffled and softened. Its beauty too sinks right into your skin. Boundaries are erased here, contours blurred and diffused.

Far away, beyond the sculpted curve of a hill, Mai sees a small thatched house clinging to its shadow, rising foglike from the field as if it were a reflection of life's true, miniaturized reality. Something about it, an injured, ill-fated aura perhaps, touches her to the core. She has been opened up and my sudden window into her is matched by her window into mine. The barricades between us have weakened, perhaps for good.

Mai too wants what I want—for us to be reconciled and integrated in a shared web. When we return to Virginia, she will get the help we need to heal. Right now, we both feel it, a full immersion into the furious center of the other's life.

The countryside opens itself fully to us, as if everything we see before us now has already been seen and felt through the ages. It is something intensely and viscerally familiar, like an inheritance passed down from parent to child. Mai and I marvel at the way a small thatched house soaks in this landscape and this rice field, fully exposed to the battering elements. Stripped to its essentials and fully aware of its impermanence and vulnerability, there is not even a possibility of pretense or posturing. Despite its weary pride, one large monsoon would knock it to the ground.

We linger in this moment, immersing ourselves in its attendant spirit. Mai sees a group of children playing hide-and-seek among concrete markers bearing the names of soldiers from an old war that still haunts today's many battles. The same way rows and rows of gravestones haunt the weed-choked earth, spirits from generation to generation float, wounded and invisible in the air. Now and then there are high-pitched shrieks of laughter and jubilation. Palm tops stir and sway against the sky.

This moment we want to prolong soaks in the shadows of life, then. The future bends backward to mirror the past. We can almost see our sister and mother and father, in a row, all dead but not. Mai thinks of James. She knows I do too. And the name alone makes her smile.

7 (Linh Dinh, 1963—) 丁令

作者简介

丁令 (Linh Dinh, 1963—)，越南名为"Đinh Linh"，美国越南裔诗人、作家、翻译家和摄影师。他出生于越南西贡（Saigon），1975年逃难到美国，在美国费城定居，2018年回到越南。2005年，他在英国东英吉利大学（University of East Anglia）担任研究员。从2002至2003年，他旅居意大利，任国际作家议会客座作家。他曾担任宾夕法尼亚大学（University of Pennsylvania）与德国莱比锡大学（University of Leipzig）的客座教授。

丁令代表作品有，故事集《假屋》（*Fake House*, 2000）与《鲜血与香皂》（*Blood and Soap*, 2004）；诗集《酒鬼拳击》（*Drunkard Boxing*, 1998）、《当一切被清空》（*All Around What Empties Out*, 2003）、《美国塔特》（*American Tatts*, 2005）、《无边的身体》（*Borderless Bodies*, 2006）、《果酱警报》（*Jam Alerts*, 2007）与《一个奶酪狂欢》（*Some Kind of Cheese Orgy*, 2009）以及小说《爱如恨》（*Love Like Hate*, 2010）。《爱如恨》获得了巴尔科内斯小说奖（Balcones Fiction Prize）。他的作品被提名"2000年最佳美国诗歌奖"、"2004年最佳美国诗歌奖"与"2007年最佳美国诗歌奖"等。

选段分别选自小说《爱如恨》的第3章和故事集《假屋》中的标题故事"假屋"。《爱如恨》通过一部家庭传奇描绘了过去半个世纪越南的变迁，是对战后越南社会中浅薄的人际关系、物质主义、机会主义、放荡和不那么浪漫的性互动的讽刺。前一选段中对于美国梦的追求揭露了战后越南社会开始采用"小资本主义"和西方文化价值观的时期出现的误导性期望。后一选段中，作者以隐晦和讽刺的语调道出越南裔离散处境下的困境和挣扎。

作品选读（一）

Love Like Hate

(3. LET'S LEARN ENGLISH!)
By Linh Dinh

Having decided that Hoa would marry a Viet Kieu, that her future would be in America, Kim Lan wanted her daughter to study English immediately. There were dozens of English-language schools in Saigon. Any high-school dropout from San Diego to Sidney could get a teaching job there and be paid well for it, if he was white. The locals simply equated white skin with a mastery of the master language. Salman Rushdie or V. S. Naipaul would not have been hired. The less expensive schools used local teachers. There was the Lego Institute, which advertised: "Build your English skill block by block." There was the Gertrude Stein Academy: "To speak, on an endless shelf, there's English." Kim Lan enrolled Hoa at the most prestigious one: the New York School of English. Everyone on its staff was advertised as being a native of one of the boroughs. There was a mural of Manhattan in the school lobby and, standing on a cardboard box next to the registration desk, a foam Statue of Liberty. The school's bold slogan: "ANSWER ALL YOUR QUESTIONS IN ENGLISH WITHIN A YEAR."

Invigorated by her violent hope of acquiring a new language, Hoa threw herself into her studies. Kim Lan marveled at the sight of Hoa bent over her exercise book. She encouraged Hoa to practice her lessons out loud. Single words, phrases, anything. It was pure music to her ear when Hoa said things like, "I do. You do. He does." Or: "Skiing and skating are my favorite sports." Or: "I'm pregnant and I need to have an abortion." She asked Hoa, "How do you say 'mother' in English?"

"Mama!"

"From now on, I want you to call me mama!"

She bought Hoa a nice dictionary with a colorful illustration next to each word. *My First Dictionary*, it was called, "recommended ages: four to eight." Encouraging Hoa to use this dictionary, Kim Lan would say, "Remember Malcolm X!" Kim Lan had discovered Malcolm X in a magazine called *Today's Knowledge*. Although it had few pages and was no bigger than her palm, *Today's Knowledge* was chock-full of information. In the October 1999 issue, it asked: "Did you know that Malcolm X was a black leader against American capitalism? A pimp who rose to prominence while in prison, Malcolm X taught himself English by memorizing every word of a dictionary." Since *My First Dictionary* only had about two hundred words, Kim Lan figured Hoa could memorize the entire dictionary in about a year or so, and be fluent in English just like Malcolm X. In the same issue of *Today's Knowledge*, Kim Lan learned that Ho Chi Minh had taught himself French by scrawling ten new words on his arms each day. That's 3,650 words a year, she thought incredulously, on such spindly arms? Overlaid with a million words, blue-black with knowledge, Uncle Ho's arms lay dimly lit in a glass coffin. Kim Lan thought of Japanese *yakuzas* tattooed from head to toes. *Horimono*, is it?

Kim Lan also enrolled Hoa in an aerobic dance class so she could listen to American music as she learned how to dance like an American. To round out her daughter's education, Kim Lan took Hoa to Kentucky Fried Chicken. The first American fast-food joint in Saigon was a KFC that opened in 1997 near the airport. It had few customers. For the price of a two-piece meal you could feast on five courses at another restaurant. About the only people who ate there were tourists, expats, Viet Kieus and the nouveau riche. Kim Lan took Hoa to this KFC every weekend. It was a glamorous place where the floor was clean and the uniformed employees courteous. Staring at the brightly lit menu overhead, Kim Lan asked Hoa, "What does it say?"

Mustering up all her mental energy, Hoa slowly translated out loud, "Prepared the Colonel's way using the freshest select ingredients for a tangy, sweet, one-of-a-kind, satisfying taste."

"And what does that say?"

"The Colonel's famous freshly baked biscuits served up hot and flaky just like they've been for generations."

Finding the chicken greasy and the coleslaw inedible, they still pronounced everything delicious. Kim Lan ate the jive mashed potatoes with the little plastic fork/spoon while eyeing the Viet Kieus chowing down at adjacent tables. She loved the way their conversations were interlarded with odd bits of English, words such as "good," "you," and "boring." Annoyed by her stares, a Viet Kieu of Hoa's age glared at Kim Lan, shaking his head. "Good good!" she smiled at him, waving a drumstick. The other two English words she knew were "money" and "mama." She scrutinized the Viet Kieus' clothes for clues on how to dress her daughter. *You must look like them if you want to attract them*, she figured. She also took Hoa to the Baskin-Robbins downtown to sample all forty flavors of American ice cream. When Lotteria opened on Nguyen Dinh Chieu Street, Kim Lan and Hoa were among the first to enter. They quickly became fans of the hot squid, rye shrimp and bulgogi burgers. They never found out that Lotteria wasn't American, but Korean fast food.

Lotteria is actually a Japanese company. Why would a Japanese company peddle Korean versions of American fast food under an Italian name? Lotteria is a subsidiary of Lotte Co. Ltd. Its founder, Takeo Shigemitsu, named his baby after Charlotte in *The Sorrows of Young Werther*. He wanted his company's products to be as endearing as Charlotte, and as enduring as Charlotte. Lotte manufactures gum, chocolate and soft drinks. Besides fast-food joints, it owns hotels, department stores, a theme park and a baseball team, the Chiba Lotte Marines of Japan's Pacific League. Even with Goethe batting cleanup, it hasn't won a pennant in thirty years.

A new Saigon fad appeared in 1993. Street vendors started to sell used clothing known as AIDS clothes, not after the disease, but because they had been given by Western aid organizations. For fifty cents you could have an AIDS T-shirt donated the year before by some churchgoer from Toledo, Ohio. For two bucks you could own a frayed pair of AIDS jeans. AIDS belts, purses, shoes and underwear were also available. Kim Lan wouldn't let Hoa touch AIDS clothes. "Sooner or later you'll die from them. I'll buy you real American clothes."

作品选读（二）

Fake House
(Fake House)

By Linh Dinh

FAKEHOUSE

As I sit at my desk eating a ham sandwich (with mayo, no mustard), head bent over the sports section of the Chronicle (Dodgers 3, Giants 0), the phone rings. It's my wife: "Guess who just showed up?"

We haven't seen my brother Josh in over a year. "I'm really sorry," I say.

"Are you coming home early?"

"I… I will."

The last time he came, Josh stayed with us for over two weeks and didn't leave until I had given him a thousand dollars. "Good luck, Josh," I said as I left him at the Greyhound station.

"Thanks, Boffo."

Josh has called me "Boffo," short for "Boffo Mofo," since we were teenagers. He has always fancied himself to be some kind of a wordsmith. He also likes to draw pictures, blow into a saxophone.

Josh lives on the beach in Santa Monica. About six months ago I received a letter from him: "Dear Boffo, How are you? I was squatting in this warehouse with a bunch of people, very nice folks, mostly artists and musicians. We called it the Fake House (because it looked fake on the outside). It had running water but no shower and no electricity. To take a shower, you stood in a large trash can and scooped water from the sink and poured it on yourself. Everything was fine until three days ago. Mustapha—he's a painter—always left turpentine—soaked rags on the floor, and somebody must have dropped a cigarette on one of these rags because the place went up in flames! Poof! Just like that! No more Fake House! Now I sleep on the beach. I am ashamed to ask you this, but, Boffo, could you please send me two hundred dollars by Western Union? I'll pay you back when I can. Your brother, Josh. P.S. Please send my regards to Sheila." (My wife's name is "Sheilah," but Josh has always deleted the *h* from her name—yet another symptom of his overall slovenliness.) I thought, There's no Fake House, no Mustapha, no fire, but I sent him two hundred dollars anyway.

Aside from these begging letters, he also sends me postcards from places you and I would never visit. One postmarked Salt Lake City said simply, "Ate flapjacks, saw pronghorns." One postmarked Belize City said, "Soggy Chinese food."

Why should I care that he ate flapjacks and saw pronghorns in Utah? That he had soggy Chinese food in Belize? But I suspect that for a man like Josh, who has accomplished nothing in this life, these trivial correspondences serve as confirmations that he exists, that he is doing something.

One year a flyer arrived around Christmas with a meticulously drawn image of Joseph Stalin in an awkward dancing pose, with this caption: "No Party Like a Party Congress! Everybody Dances the Studder Steps!"

"Tracy, I… I … I… I … " I am unable to finish my sentence. My secretary smiles. "You're stepping out, sir?"

I nod.

"You'll be back, sir?" I shake my head.

"You're going home, sir?"

I nod again, smile, and walk out of the office. There was an extra sparkle in Tracy's eyes. Perhaps she finds my stuttering, an absurd yet harmless defect, endearing. I've noticed that she has done something strange to her hair lately and that, since the weather has gotten warmer, she shows up most days for work in a curt, clingy dress and a clingy blouse made from a sheer fabric.

Aside from this small, perhaps endearing defect, I am a man in control of my own faculties and life. I manage two dozen residential units and four commercial buildings. Last year I cleared $135,000 after taxes. My wife does not have to do anything. She sits home and watches Oprah, takes tai chi lessons. A month ago she went to Hawaii alone.

I grip the steering wheel with my left hand and massage my left forearm with my right hand. Muscle tone is important. Time also. I do not like to waste time, even when driving. Then I switch hands, gripping the steering wheel with my right hand and massaging my right forearm with my left hand. Then I massage my right biceps while rotating my neck. "A clear road ahead!" I shout. As I drive, I like to reinforce my constitution with uplifting slogans. I never stutter when alone. "Firm but fair!" "Money is time!" Positive thoughts are an important component of my success. It is what separates me from those of my brother's ilk.

Occasionally, while driving, I'd surprise myself with an exuberant act of violence. Without premeditation my right hand would fly off the steering wheel and land flush on my right cheek. Whack! Afterward I'd feel a strange mixture of pride and humility, not because of the pain but because I had felt no pain.

I am in excellent shape for a man of forty—two. I have very little fat and no beer gut. With dinner I allow myself a single glass of chardonnay. Each morning before work I go to the spa and swim a dozen precise laps. Never thirteen. Never eleven. Then I stand still for about two minutes at the shallow end of the pool, with my eyes closed and my hands bobbing in the water, thinking about nothing. Mr. Chow, who is also at the pool early in the morning, has taught me this exercise. After watching me swim, he said: "You have too much yang. You must learn how to cultivate your ying." Or maybe it was the other way around: "You have too much ying. You must learn how to cultivate your yang." In any case he suggested that I stand still at the shallow end of the pool for a couple of minutes each day, breathe in deeply, exhale slowly, and think about nothing.

It is very relaxing, this exercise, but of course, no one can ever think about nothing. As I stand still at the shallow end of the pool, what I must do for the rest of the day comes sharply into focus: Send eviction notice to 2B, 245 Montgomery. Jack up rent from 600 to 625 on new lease for 2,450 Anna Drive. The idiot on the third floor at 844 Taylor has dumped paper towel into the toilet again, flooding the basement. Call plumber. Send bill to idiot…

Josh is my only sibling. He is a year older than me. He is my older brother. When we were kids, Josh was considered by our parents to be by far the smarter one, someone who would surely leave his mark on the world, a prediction he took quite seriously. But the facts have proven otherwise. I have often thought the reason I tolerate these visits by my loser brother, during which he never behaves graciously but often vulgarly, atrociously, and at the end of which I will have to part with a thousand dollars, or at least five hundred bucks, is because he is tangible proof that I have not failed in this life. I'm not a loser. I am not Josh. We have the same background, grew up in the same idiotic city, San Mateo, raised by the same quarrelsome parents, a garrulous, megalomaniacal father and a childish, know—nothing mother. Josh was considered by all to be the smarter one, even the better-looking one. Although we started out with roughly the same handicaps, I was never afflicted by his hubris, never thought I had to leave a so-called mark on this world. I never wanted to be better than people, although, such is life, I am now doing better than just about anyone I know (and certainly better than everyone I grew up with), whereas Josh, who was so convinced of his superiority, has degenerated into a pathetic loser, taking showers in trash cans and living under the same roof with people with names like Mustapha.

It is true that my brother is better-looking than me. Girls were enthralled by him. He lost his virginity at fifteen. I at twenty-three. But as he grew older, this superficial asset became increasingly worthless. Mature women do not care for good looks and a glib conversation. What they want is a roof over their head, a breadwinner, and a father for their children. They like to be warm and clean. What woman will put up with standing in a trash can and having water poured over herself? Although Sheilah and I do not have children, we will when the time is right. There is no hurry.

It is a shame you cannot see my wife because any man who has will concede that she is a strikingly, almost disturbingly, beautiful woman. She has eyes that beg a little but lips that are determined, fierce, without being vulgar or cruel. They are well drawn and not too fleshy. Her smiles are discreet. She is not one of those women who, out of fear and dishonesty, are constantly showing their teeth. She is tall, two, maybe three inches taller than me.

Sheilah is Tracy's predecessor. She worked for me for two years before we started dating. It was she who asked me out the first time. The pretext was her twenty-fourth birthday. She said, "Me and a bunch of friends are going to this French bistro on Ghirardelli Square for my birthday. Would you like to come as my date?"

I noticed she had said "date," not "friend." She did not say, "Would you like to come as my friend?" but "Would you like to come as my date?" Here's that crack in the line, I thought, run for it.

I must admit that although I was attracted to Sheilah from the moment she walked into my office for the job interview, I did not dare to betray my interest. She was out of my league. Even now, five years into our marriage, I still catch myself in moments of self-congratulation. Once I even laughed out loud, shaking my head and exclaiming, "You didn't do too bad..."

Josh, on the other hand, has never been married, has never even had a relationship with a woman lasting more than a few months. Three times he had to borrow money from me to pay for his girlfriends' abortions. It is a good thing, these abortions, considering the kind of father he would have made.

I haven't told you about the incident that prompted me to get rid of him the last time he came to stay with us.

He had been brooding in front of the TV all week, drunk on my wine. When he wanted to borrow my car one night to go into town, I was more than happy to oblige. I even gave him twenty dollars for beer. He left at eight o'clock and came back at around one in the morning. I could tell immediately that he had a girl with him. My wife was asleep but as usual I was up reading. Each night before bed I try to take in at least twelve pages of a good novel. Although a businessman, I do not neglect to develop the left side of my brain. On that night, if I remember correctly, I was reading *The Joy Luck Club* by Maxine Hong Kingston.

Since the guest room is adjacent to the master bedroom, I could hear their voices fairly distinctly. Josh was talking in a near whisper, but the girl was loud. She was black. I could never recall him dating an African-American girl or showing any interest in black women, and was a little surprised by this fact. Of course playing the saxophone, he was always listening to the great black musicians. They were haggling.

"Please."

"You don't got forty bucks?"

"I only have ten."

"Uh—uh."

"I'll give you my jacket." It was actually a ski jacket I had lent him.

...

"Please."

"Get me out of here!"

She left.

It was over in less than a minute. I was so startled by such an unusual incident occurring in my own home that I had no time to react. Maybe I was a little disappointed that something even more bizarre did not happen. My wife had slept through the entire episode. She could sleep through anything: car alarms, sirens, earthquakes. I looked down at her serene, distant face and felt an overwhelming urge to penetrate.

A week, maximum, I decide, massaging my right thigh as I turn into the driveway.

We live in a split-level three-bedroom house with a two-car garage, in an upscale, multi—ethnic neighborhood. My brother is standing inside the plate glass window of the living room, waiting for me. He has on a dirty-looking baseball cap and a black T-shirt. When he comes out of the house, I notice that he has put on weight just in the past year. He has never taken care of his body, never eaten right, never exercised. He trots down the sloping brick path leading to my car, smiling shamelessly. My brother is always most obsequious during the first few days. Sheilah is nowhere to be seen. I step out of the car. "Good to see you, Boffo!" he practically screams. We hug.

"How…how…how are you?"

"Can't complain!"

"Howsa, howsa…Mustapha?"

Josh looks confused. Then he says, "Mustapha died in the fire."

A professional con man, my brother. I place a hand on the back of his neck and start to massage it without thinking. I lead him into my house.

8

(Andrew Lam, 1964—)
安德鲁·林

作者简介

　　安德鲁·林（Andrew Lam, 1964—），越南名"Lâm Quang Dũng"，美国越南裔作家和记者。他出生于南越一个富足的家庭，年少时接受了贵族教育。1975年越南战争结束后，他们一家顺利逃难到美国。安德鲁·林曾就读加州大学伯克利分校（UC, Berkeley），主修生物化学。然而，为了追逐文学梦，他放弃了从医计划，到旧金山州立大学（San Francisco State University）学习创意写作课程。在校期间，他开始为太平洋新闻社（Pacific News Service）撰稿，并在1993年获得专业记者协会（Society of Professional Journalists）颁发的"杰出青年记者奖"。他目前担任新美国媒体（New America Media）的网络编辑。

　　他的作品有散文集《香水梦：越南离散生活的反思》（*Perfume Dreams: Reflections on the Vietnamese Diaspora*, 2005）、《东噬西：在两个半球之间的写作》（*East Eats West: Writing in Two Hemispheres*, 2010），短篇小说集《失乐园之鸟》（*Birds of Paradise Lost*, 2013）。安德鲁·林荣获2006年笔会/超越边缘奖（PEN/Beyond Margins Award），作品登过畅销书和最佳图书之榜。

　　选段分别出自《香水梦》中的《我的越南，我的美国》（"My Vietnam, My America"）与《东噬西》中的《太强的自尊心可能会伤害您的孩子》（"Too much Self-Esteem Can Be Bad for Your Child"）。前一选段讲述了20世纪90年代美国对越南与越南战争的偏见和扭曲，表达了作者对战争和历史的深刻反思。后一选段讲述了东西文化差异以及当前亚裔学生在美国的生存处境。

作品选读（一）

Perfume Dreams

(My Vietnam, My America)
By Andrew Lam

My Vietnam, My America
December 1990

    Sometimes the following scene emerges from my Vietnamese childhood: I am sitting in a slow-moving jeep watching Christmas lights flashing from an old thatched roof under which a GI bargains with a Saigon bar girl in a green miniskirt. I hear the murmur of wet tires on the flooded road, the GI, slaughter, and the girl's flirting curses. The deal is struck. The soldier's strong foreign cologne wafts in the air. His hand reaches for her. She, cursing still, gears herself for the embrace.

    Uncle Sam's soldiering nephew slept once with Miss Saigon, and in the morning both had changed. One goes home haunted by a turbulent love affair, the other, in the aftermath of her tragic ending, dreams of a new beginning in America. If Vietnam has become, to Americans, a buzzword for ll-fought wars, a metaphor for disaster, America has become, to the Vietnamese, the symbol of freedom and happiness. Yes, Vietnam is independent at last. But the Vietnamese impoverished and oppressed, are far from happiness.

    Last spring when I visited Hong Kong's Whitehead Detention Center, some Vietnamese detainees showed me a statue of Lady Liberty made out of tin. They said she symbolized their aspiration toward freedom. Badly copied and smeared by rain, she stood four feet tall on the rooftop of Barrack 24, Section 8, shaking in the wind like an old banana leaf.

    "America?" said a teenager in Section 8, too young to remember the Vietnam War but old enough to have fought in and escaped from the war in Cambodia, where Vietnam was the invader. "America is paradise." And, he speculated in his Hanoi accent?

    "There are no sufferings in America." It is true—from a fleeing refugee's point of view. America becomes everything Vietnam can't be; it is open to interpretation. In America you can avoid Khmer Rouge mines that blow your legs off and reduce you to begging on

Saigon's sidewalks. In America there are no reeducation camps and malaria-infested New Economic Zones where you are forced to grow yams and corn from the hard, bitter soil.

" In America," a Vietnamese who recently arrived in the United States writes home to his impoverished cousins,"you can cook without fire, get money from machines, send letters over telephone wires, watch the world via satellites, drive for kilometers on well-paved roads. In America your children grow taller, smarter, more handsome. Best of all, the government leaves you alone."

In the dark of night, thousands of Vietnamese climb on board old fishing boats for the perilous journey toward the American GI's wondrous home.

Uncle Sam's soldiering nephew, on the other hand, came home traumatized. Now when Americans speak of foreign ventures we are more prudent. The painful memories of Vietnam come back to haunt us and we instinctively ask, "Is it going to be another haunt Vietnam?" Vietnam, in effect, has become a vault filled with tragic metaphors for every American to use.

Ho Chi Minh, the My Lai Massacre, Kent State, Saigon, Hanoi, the Domino Theory: those, among other names, places, and catch-phrases, are listed in the book *Cultural Literacy:What Every American Needs to Know*, by E.D. Hirsch Jr. But what does every American know? Americans shrug. Vietnam is an unhealed wound, the stuff bad dreams are made of, a legacy of defeat and shame. And so on.

"When Americans say 'Vietnam,' they don't mean Vietnam," my uncle complains. He once served as a pilot in the Vietnamese Air Force, flying C-130 cargo planes. Americans don't take defeat and bad memories very well he says. They try to escape them. Americans make a habit of blaming small countries for the bad things that happen to the United States: cocaine from Colombia, AIDS from Haiti... hurricanes from the Caribbean.

But Vietnam—Vietnam is special. What Henry Kissinger described as a "fourth-rate power" had cracked the ivory tower and plagued the American psyche: that hell in a very small place had devastated the bright and shiny citadel. For the first time in history, Americans were caught in the past, haunted by unanswerable questions, confronted with a tragic ending.

But never fear: Hollywood comes to the rescue. It is free with its various interpretations. *Apocalypse Now* describes an American's mythical adventure in a tropic jungle where he confronts other Americans who have been transformed into insane barbarians. *The Deer Hunter* shows a game of Russian roulette being played out for money between an American and some Vietnamese, suggesting Americans and Vietnamese are equally crazy. Insanity explains away otherwise complicated plots and is what we plead in America when we commit hideous crimes. *Tour of Duty* returns to the metaphor of the brutal embrace: Uncle Sam's nephews raping Miss Saigon and then blowing her brains out. Sylvester Stallone carried the war one step further. As Rambo shooting down faceless Vietnamese and sleeping with the beautiful and mysterious Miss Saigon, Stallone led us to believe that he had single-handedly won the lost war for America and restored its pride. Audiences cheered him on.

I know a Vietnamese who makes money acting in Hollywood. He had survived the war and the perilous journey on the South China Sea to come to America, and now he plays Viet Cong, ARVN (Army of the Republic of Vietnam) soldiers, civilians. He is a great actor, but no one recognizes his face. Time and again he dies, spurting fake blood from his torso and heart. At other time she screams in pain, reinterpreting his own past. "Hollywood loves me," he jokes. "I die well."

Watching such movies, Vietnamese old enough to remember the war giggle uncomfortably. These naïve interpretations of the conflict little resemble their own past. Vietnam was a three-sided war, with North and South at each other's throats, but in the retelling, America has appropriated itself as the central figure in an otherwise complex narrative. Some are enraged, but many are resigned. What they know and won't admit to the American audience is that for them history is a series of personal impressions. Fact and details and analysis and fancy interpretations can't capture the truth about Vietnam any more than wildly fabricated war flicks can. Instead, Vietnamese living in America tell their children ghost stories and share their memories of the monsoon rains and harvest festivals. I too store in my brain a million of those memories and myths, none of which have anything to do with America's involvement in the war, but that, as they say, is another story.

Vietnam-America. Whatever happened to that covetous embrace? America-Vietnam. What became of that illegitimate marriage?

Recently I read that a frail, crowded boat carrying refugees from Vietnam entered Malaysian waters with a peculiar sign hanging on its side. It read "USA remains on my boat." Bones, bags of GI bones. Missing remnants from that vicariously lost war, now found and carefully washed by impoverished Vietnamese hands and carried along as a treasure. They hope to bargain the bones for passage to the promised land.

"A set of GI bones is worth a whole family's tickets to the United States," so goes the gossip in Vietnam. Uncle Sam denies such hand-some rewards, but Miss Saigon and her overabundant children dream on. Normalization with the United States is at hand, Americans will send aid, the trade embargo will be lifted, Hanoi is building an American embassy, American delegations are here to excavate oil fields in the Mekong Delta. There is a faint smell of that seductive dollar bill, the familiar scent of a GI's cologne.

I remember the Americans in Vietnam. While my father was an officer in the ARVN during the war, Americans were his allies, North Vietnamese were his foes. Among the things we burned near the end of the war were self-incriminating photos of our American friends. One photo showed my father and his American advisers looking at a military map. There was a picture of my older brother standing next to the actor Robert Mitchum, who visited Vietnam to support the troops. Another photo showed Joanna, an American social worker, smiling sweetly next to my mother. Those pictures and many more went up in smoke to disclaim our haphazard and estranged friendship (although we later fled to America and became Americans).

"Your country didn't deserve all the shit from us," said the pool man at my parents' suburban home. A Vietnam vet, he wore a baseball cap with the word "Danang" on it. "To love your country, man," he continued. "I had a wonderful time there. If I had enough money I'd take a trip from Hanoi to Saigon." I once gave a dollar bill to another Vietnam vet who was panhandling in Berkeley. It old him I came from Vietnam. He threw the money back at me.

Sometimes I am asked how well Americans understand the Vietnam War. I don't know, I answer, but there is this wall in Washington. And you can sense its truth when you are there. All year long Americans come and leave poems and photos and flowers to those who died in Vietnam. Unlike all the memorials in America that depict past triumphs or happy endings, this dark wall stands alone and sacrosanct. If there are ghosts in America, they could comfortably congregate there, for it is the only American place of tragic consequences, this wall that over time has evolved in a tradition similar to that of a Vietnamese shrine.

My last memory of the Vietnam War: April 28, 1975, two days before Saigon fell to the advancing North Vietnamese Army. My family and I boarded the C-130 with other panicked refugees and fled. My father gave the American pilot a gift he had received from an American adviser years before a silver gun encased in a hollow Bible. Two days later the war ended.

Vicky, a social worker who assists boat people in Hong Kong, traveled to the Mekong Delta to understand her clients' past. She encountered a boy who sat on a water buffalo amid a golden rice field. Instead of playing a traditional bamboo flute he had a boom box playing the songs of the Eurythmics. "What do you make of that?" Vicky asked.

"USA remains on my boat," answers the wooden sign. It tells more than it had intended to. And perhaps Stallone is right: Americans did indeed win the war. Vietnamese are ready to be Americans. Vietnamese want VCRs, democracy, Levi's jeans, freedom, Toyotas, happiness. The Vietnamese government offers the Cam Ranh Naval Base to welcome Uncle Sam again, if he ever wants to come back. Miss Saigon winks.

And me. Sometimes I go to a Vietnamese restaurant in San Francisco's Tenderloin District. I sit and stare at two wooden clocks hanging on the wall. The left one is carved in the shape of a florid S: the map of Vietnam. The one on the right is hewn in the shape of a deformed tooth: the map of America. Tick, tock, tick, tock. They run at different times. Tick, tock, tick, tock. I was born a Vietnamese. Tick, tock, tick, tock. I am reborn an American. Tick,tock, tick, tock. I am of one soul. Tick, tock, tick, tock. Two hearts.

作品选读（二）

East Eats West

（TOO MUCH SELF-ESTEEM CAN BE BAD FOR YOUR CHILD）

By Andrew Lam

In the age of MySpace and YouTube and Google Earth, the space between East and West seems to shrink. But in the area of self-perception, especially, there remains a cultural gap that can often be as wide as the ocean.

Take Jeong-Hyun Lim, a twenty-four-year-old business student in Seoul, popularly known as Funtwo on YouTube. His rock rendition of Pachelbel's Canon has turned him into a global phenomenon. Lim's dizzying sweep-picking—sounding and muting notes at breakneck speed—has had some viewers calling him a second Hendrix. His video has been viewed on YouTube twenty-four million times so far.

But Funtwo himself is self-effacing, a baseball cap covering much of his face. No one knew who he was until Virginia Heffernan wrote about him in the New York Times last August. She called his "anti-showmanship" "distinctly Asian," adding that "sometimes an element of fat-out abjection even enters into this act, as though the chief reason to play guitar is to be excoriated by others."

Anyone in the West with this kind of media spotlight and Internet following would hire an agent and make a CD But Lim told Heffernan, "I am always thinking that I'm not that good a player and must improve more than now." In another interview, he rated his playing around 50 or 60 out of 100.

Lim's modesty is reassuringly Asian, echoing the famous Chinese saying "He who is not satisfied with himself will grow." In a classic 1992 study, psychologists Harold Steve and James Stigler compared academic skills of elementary school students in, China, Japan, and the United States. It showed a yawning gap in self-perception between East and West.

Asian students outperformed their American counterparts, but when they were asked to evaluate their performances, American students evaluated themselves significantly higher than those from Asia. "In other words, they combined a lousy performance with a high sense of self-esteem," notes Nina H. Shokraii Rees, author of *School Choice 200: What's Happening in the States*, in an essay called "The Self Esteem Fraud."

Since the eighties, self-esteem for students has been promoted in many school programs, based on the belief that academic achievements come with higher self-confidence. Rees disputes that self-esteem is necessary for academic success. "For all of its current popularity, however, self-esteem theory threatens to deny children the tools they will need in order to experience true success in school and as adults," she writes.

A quarter-century after Stevenson and Stigler's study, a comprehensive new study released last February from San Diego State University maintains that too much self-regard has resulted in college campuses full of narcissists. In 2006, researchers said, two-thirds of the students had above-average scores on the Narcissistic Personality Inventory evaluation, 30 percent more than when the test was first administered in 1982.

Researchers like San Diego State University professor Jean Twenge worried that narcissists "are more likely to have romantic relationships that are short-lived, at risk for infidelity, lack emotional warmth, and to exhibit game playing, dishonesty, and over-controlling and violent behaviors." The author of *Generation Me: Why Today's Young Americans Are More Confident, Assertive, Entitled—and More Miserable Than Ever Before*, Twenge blames self-esteem movement for the rise of the "MySpace generation."

Has the emphasis on self-confidence gone too far in America? Twenge seems to think so, She points to the French tune "Frere Jacques" sung in preschool, for example. French children may still sing the equivalent of "Brother Jack! You're sleeping! Ring the bells!" But in America the once innocuous song has been converted to: "I am special! I am special! Look at me!" No surprise that the little train that could is exhausted: it's been laden with super-sized American egos.

That Asian-Americans dominate higher education in the last few decades in America is also worth noting. Although they make up less than 5 percent of the country's population, Asian Americans typically make up 10 to 30 percent of the student bodies at the best colleges. In California, Asians form the majority of the University of California system. And at the University of California, Berkeley, Asian freshmen have reached the 46 percent mark. Also worth noting is that, of the Asian population in the

United States, two out of three are immigrants, born on a continent where self-esteem is largely earned through achievements, self-congratulatory behaviors are discouraged, and more importantly, humility is still something of a virtue.

In the East, the self is best defined in its relation to others—person among persons-

and most valued and best expressed only through familial and communal and moral deference. That is far from the self-love concept of the West—where one is encouraged to look out for oneself, and truth seems to always originate in a minority of one. And I fear the far end of that experiment will result in collective apathy.

In much of modernizing Asia, of course, individualism is making inroads. The Confucian culture that once emphasized harmony and unity at the expense of individual liberty is now in retreat.

But if there's a place in Asia that sill vigilantly keeps the ego in check, if not suppressed, it's the classroom, for good and bad. In Asia, corporal punishment is still largely practiced. Self-esteem is barely a concept, let alone encouraged. Critics argue that though not known to foster creativity, an Asian education, with is emphasis on hard work and cooperation, sill largely provides the antidote to the culture of permissiveness and disrespect of authority of the West.

In the West, the words "kung fu" largely represent the martial arts. They have a larger meaning in the East: spiritual discipline and the cultivation of the self. A well-kept bonsai is good kung fu. So is a learned mind, and so, for that matter, is the willingness to perfect one's guitar playing. East and West may be commingling and merging in the age of globalization, but be ware—that ubiquitous baseball cap that Funtwo is wearing on YouTube can mislead. It houses very different mentalities in Asia—for when it comes to the perception of self, East and West remain apart.

9

(Kien Nguyen, 1967—)
阮坚

作者简介

  阮坚（Kien Nguyen, 1967—），越南名"Nguyễn Kiên"，美国越南裔作家。他生于越南芽庄（Nha Trang），母亲出身贵族家庭，嫁给了美国人并生下了混血儿子。越南战争结束后母亲家道中落，美国父亲也回到了自己的国家。阮坚与母亲在当时被视为"叛徒"和"异类"，饱受欺凌和压迫。1985年，阮坚通过联合国"有序离境计划"（Orderly Departure Program）离开了越南，几经波折到达美国，后成为一名牙医。他曾在纽约大学（New York University）担任临床讲师。他目前住在加利福尼亚州。

  迄今为止，他创作了三部小说《多余的人》(*The Unwanted*, 2001)、《挂毯》(*The Tapestries*, 2002) 与《殖民时期》(*Le Colonial*, 2004)。1998年，他荣获格林泽娜·凯夫奖（Grinzane Cavour Prize）。

  选段分别出自《多余的人》的第1章和《挂毯》的第1章。前一选段讲述了主人公对美国父亲的想象和对美国生活的期盼，表达了美越混血儿对身份的迷茫和追寻。后一选段讲述了一场特殊的越南婚姻，表达了作者对越南文化传统的反思。

作品选读（一）

The Unwanted

(CHAPTER ONE)
By Kien Nguyen

Nhatrang, May 12, 1972, 7 P.M.

I remember that night quite well. It is my first memory, and the happiest one from my childhood.

The familiar smell of pig roasting on a spit wafted from the kitchen. My mother made cheery noises as she ran from one hallway to the next, giving orders to the help with a hint of pompous confidence. The moist summer air evaporated into a transparent mist all around me due to the kind of heat found only in Nhatrang and only in May. And what I remember most of all is the sense of festivity all around me as the last rays of sunlight disappeared into the ocean, just a few hundred feet away from my window. It was my fifth birthday.

My childhood home, in order to accommodate my mother's passion for living near beautiful beaches, was situated by the water, with the waves murmuring at the foot of the house. The mansion was comprised of three stories and over twenty-four rooms, including at least eight bedrooms. All were furnished with expensive Western furniture thrown together by my mother's own design. And both to give the house personality and to honor my grandfather's last name, Mother named it Nguyen Mansion. From the numerous stories I was told growing up, mostly by my grandparents, I came to understand that my mother built the house during her pregnancy with me, motivated by the idea of having her first baby in her own home. Mother painted the outside of the house the color of eggshells, and, much to her consternation, I always thought the house was just a simple white color that had aged poorly with time. From the main entrance of the house to the front gate lay a large reddish marble pathway that encircled the garden, which housed a kidney-shaped pool. Our gardener, Mr. Tran, had been hired through an agency, and his job consisted mainly of planting and maintaining the many exotic species of flowers around the front part of the house. My mother, in an effort to shield the inside beauty from the outside world, constructed two enormous iron gates, as well as a high barbed-wire fence covered with thick vines, to obscure all within their boundaries. In the old days, I used to play with my toys in the garden while the children playing on the other side of the gate watched me with fascination. According to my mother, those children were either too dirty, or I was too clean, for my association with them. In Vietnam, rich children like myself wore sandals to protect their feet from the dirt and the heat, while poor children like the ones from the other side of the wall ran around barefoot.

That afternoon, before the celebration, much of the activity was centered in the kitchen. I was flying through the crowded rooms with my arms out like an airplane and making buzzing sounds, bumping into people's legs to simulate a crash. My brother and I had made up this clever plan to get treats from the help. Unfortunately, everyone seemed too busy to notice me. In the middle of the main kitchen a group of chefs stood around an enormous table, decorating a gigantic white cake with bunches of red roses, brown vines, and green leaves made from heavy whipped cream and food coloring. On the other side of the room, barely visible in the dark smoke, live fowls awaited their turn to be slaughtered; their frightened cackles rose over the impatient sizzling of the pork. A few steps away, a group of my mother's maids hovered over the busy stove preparing the main courses. One of the women turned on the ceiling fan as her friend strained cooked noodles over the drain. The fog from the boiling water swept up from the pot, adding to the heat in the room.

Looking for a new victim for my airplane game, I spotted a young caterer's apprentice. He was about ten years old and of diminutive size, with dark circles under his eyes. Running through the kitchen with a big bowl of whipped cream, he crashed into me. I knew how fearful our servants were when it came to my mother's wrath. While the boy was making sure I was not injured, I reached into his bowl for a handful of cream. Before he could recover from his shock, I laughed and ran off, lapping the sweetness from my hand.

Upstairs, I decided to take a peek inside my mother's bedroom. She sat regally at her makeup desk, fully dressed in a pale evening gown that glistened under the orange light like a mermaid's scales. Her attention was focused on brushing her long hair, which rippled down her arching back, jet-black and wavy. My mother was not a typically thin Asian woman. She had heavy breasts and round hips, joined by a thin waist. Her eyes, big and rimmed with dark mascara, concentrated on the image before her. Years spent watching my mother gaze at herself in the mirror had convinced me that she was the rarest, most beautiful creature that ever walked the face of this Earth.

My presence startled her. She took her eyes off her reflection, looked at me, and smiled, showing her white, straight teeth. At times I had sat for hours in my mother's bedroom while she confided her beauty secrets to me. I would listen earnestly, not to what my mother said, but to the mesmerizing sound of her voice, always full of wisdom and intelligence.

Her smile faded into a slight frown as she said, "Look at you. What is that all over your face?"

I touched my cheek and felt the remnants of the whipped cream. Licking my fingers, I answered her, "It's for my cake in the kitchen. Can I come in?"

She nodded. "Sure, come in." And then came the scolding. "What a dirty boy, eating in such a manner. Why don't you wait till dinner?"

I sat on her bed and looked at her curiously. Using a small cotton pad, she was pressing white powder onto the backs of her hands.

"What are you doing, Mommy?" I asked.

"I am putting makeup on my hands, darling."

"How come?"

"You are always asking the same question."

"I never remember what the answer is, Mommy."

She paused and held her hands in front of her face, where they stood at attention like two proud soldiers ready for inspection. "I do this because I want people to notice my hands. Aren't they beautiful?"

Along with her fortune, my mother's hands were the ultimate pride in her life. Before she met my father, she had worked as a hand model for a jewelry company. In contrast to her voluptuous body, her hands were long and graceful. Each finger was a smooth cylinder with invisible knuckles and no wrinkles; each nail was defined, extended, well polished, and glossy. She spent hours smoothing the sharp edges of her nails, trimming the out-of-place cuticles, and changing the color of the paint. Not until she was completely satisfied with her hands did my mother apply makeup to her face, a process that would also require a few hours. She said that since her face was not extraordinary, her success would depend on her hands.

As if to prove her point, my mother made sure that her hands were always displayed. They danced in front of her face during a conversation, rested on her cheeks in photographs, or raised her chin when she exercised her power. Sometimes, they daintily held the stem of a champagne glass. Once my mother considered buying insurance for her hands; however, this idea did not meet with approval from my grandfather. I'm sure my mother wished that she had gotten insurance the day I accidentally bumped into her while running down the hallway. The collision broke two of her nails and scratched her fingers, leaving her boiling mad and me with welts on my cheek.

"Is this party for me, Mommy?" I asked as she continued tending to her hands.

"Yes, darling."

"Does it mean I can stay up late tonight?"

"You can stay up a little while after you blow out your candles."

"Will there be any children coming over tonight from my class?" I asked her hopefully.

"No, darling. No other children, just you and your brother. So you can be the star tonight. After all, it is an adult party; you don't want any children here to spoil it, do you?"

"Right, Mommy," I agreed half-heartedly.

I walked to the bedroom window and looked outside. I could see porters carrying cases of Champagne Guy Larmandier into the house. The garden was lit up by multicolored lights, with every shrub transformed into some sort of animal. Next to the pool, behind a couple of rose bushes, a group of musicians tested their electrical instruments. The noise resolved itself into a lively, cheery tune that carried through the thick air. The cooks, maids, and waiters ran back and forth like ants in an ant farm, all lost in their own assignments. The neighborhood children, clustered next to a few adults, gathered around the front gates, staring curiously inside. Should anyone venture too close to the gates, security men would push them away. Over the sounds of celebration, deep in the darkness, the ocean moaned its constant, breathy rhythm.

"When do I get to blow out the candles?" I asked, turning to look at my mother.

"Right after dinner."

"When do we have dinner?"

"When all the guests arrive," she said.

"When will that be?"

"Around nine-thirty." My mother regarded her nails. A pang of dissatisfaction washed over her face as she reached for her bright orange nail polish.

"Can I stay awake after the cake, Mommy?"

"No, darling. After the cake there will be dancing. You are too young to stay up that late. Maybe next year. Now, be a good boy and go play with your brother."

"But he is sleeping in Grandma's room."

"Then go wake him up. Tell Grandma or Loan to dress both of you." She pushed me out of her room and carefully closed the door without touching her nails.

BY THE TIME Jimmy and I changed into the party clothes that my mother had ordered from the Sears catalog, a luxury that few could afford in Vietnam, the guests had finally arrived. From my grandparents' bedroom, we could hear every noise the people outside made. Gazing at each other nervously, we pressed our ears against the thin wall, listening to the footsteps that ran frantically up and down the hallway. The rich smell of cooked spices mixed with the heavy odor of perfume.

Finally, my mother burst into the room with enough exuberance to burn out a light bulb. Her off-white evening gown embraced her, gushing down her body like a stream of silver water. Her hair was bound above her neck in a complicated knot, revealing a diamond necklace and two small diamond earrings. She looked foreign, formidable, elegant as an Egyptian queen. She smiled through her makeup, as she reached for us with bare arms that sparkled with diamonds. We entered her cloud of perfume, and together, hand in hand, we walked into the noisy brightness outside.

 The rest of the evening is a blur. I vaguely recall the laughter, the kisses, the food, the stark colors, the songs, and the mountain of presents that filled my room. I also remember the foreign guests with sandy hair and blue eyes, as well as the anxious talk on everyone's lips about the revolution. Jimmy and I were sent to bed immediately after I blew out the candles on top of my gigantic cake. And I was to sleep for three years, banished from my mother's warmth and sent away to school, leaving behind the special night that was supposed to be mine.

作品选读（二）

The Tapestries

（Chapter one: The Wedding）
By Kien Nguyen

HUE CITY, JANUARY 1916

 During the winter months, the Perfume River was chilly, especially at dawn. The morning of Dan Nguyen's first wedding was no exception. While the sun was still hidden, its early rays reached from behind the Ngu Binh Mountain, stretching pale-yellow fingers over the sky. Thin clouds wafted by, and the wind whipped up whirlpools of mist. Damp tendrils drifted over the jungle of oak trees that climbed the steep mountainside and were lost against the horizon.

 Along the side of the river, a strip of land still lay in darkness. From afar, it looked like the back of a crocodile floating in the water. A few hundred feet away, a sampan moved slowly upstream. Both sides of the boat were painted with red resin from the lacquer tree and highlighted with gold trim in large rectangular patterns—the design reserved for weddings.

 At the vessel's stern, a white-haired man with stooped shoulders sat on the floor. His gnarled hands clenched an oar, and he leaned heavily into its strokes. The man seemed lost in his own world. His eyes, hidden beneath the rim of a torn conical hat, focused on the water. The faded blue peasant shirt on his back was tattered, exposing his bony ribs. Next to him hung a red lantern that illuminated a short stretch of river ahead. The faint sound of the oar moving the water echoed against the silence.

Behind the old man, in the center of the sampan, was a small cabin with a roof built of red-lacquered bamboo stalks lashed together with palm fronds. Across its entrance hung a pink silk screen on which a canary-yellow dragon entwined with its feminine mate, an equally gracious phoenix. Custom dictated that the bride must be concealed from sight. She sat behind the silk barrier, careful not to make a sound while the boat rocked to the helmsman's gentle rhythm.

Just as the sun appeared from behind the purple mountain, the old man guided his bridal sampan toward land. Sunlight broke through the clouds into thousands of tiny golden pennies. The old man squinted, searching the shoreline for a place to dock. He did not have to look far.

Just ahead, where the ground extended into the water to form a long, narrow wharf, twenty people from the groom's family stood in a single file. Most of them wore the *ao dai*, the ceremonial garb reserved for festivities such as this. The costumes were similar for both men and women: a tunic, made out of silk or satin, with a long skirt separated at the waist into two panels, front and back. The men wore their robes over white pants, while the women wore theirs over black—a more subservient color.

The wedding party had prepared the landing site by hanging strings of firecrackers over the branches of the tamarind trees. Upon the arrival of the sampan, the two oldest men began the ceremony by burning purified joss sticks. Then they ignited the firecrackers. The red, petal-like missiles burst into the morning air, stirring flocks of sparrows from their sleep. They flapped their gray wings among the dark branches, adding their screeches to the din. The deafening sound of the explosives was believed to banish evil spirits as the groom's family prepared to accept their new daughter-in-law.

With the help of two young servants, the old man stepped off his boat. He took off his hat and bowed to the elders. His gesture was mechanical yet courteous. He focused his eyes on the crimson debris of the fireworks on the ground. After the last few scattered booms, silence returned to the riverbank, and even the fog seemed to settle back into its original pattern, draped over the oak trees.

From the greeting party, one man marched forward. He was about forty-five years old, and his deep-set eyes peered from beneath bushy eyebrows. His high cheekbones and the downward curve of his mouth made his features appear grim and darkly authoritative. He wore a headdress of black silk, folded into many layers, which framed the crown of his head like a halo. His ao dai was ocean blue, with a subtle, darker, dotted pattern of embroidery, representing the royal symbol of longevity. The fabric was handwoven from a superlative silk, made by the silkworms of the famous Phu Yen Village. Even a rich man could afford only a few such garments. He returned the old man's salutation with a slow bow, then knitted his hands together and faced his palms upward, placing them against his abdomen.

"Greetings," he said to the visitor. "My name is Tat Nguyen. I am the father of the groom. Welcome to our humble town."

The old man's head bowed lower, so that no one could see his lips moving as he spoke. "Thank you, but I am afraid that I can't accept your warm welcome, Master Nguyen. My job is to deliver my granddaughter to your home. It is now done, and so I must bid my farewell. Take her with you to the groom. From this moment on, she belongs in your household, sir."

He stepped aside, leaving room for the groom's family to approach the sampan. A pair of servants came forward and joined the other two on the boat. One stood at each corner of the bridal cabin. Then, with one synchronized movement, they hoisted the cubicle to their shoulders and carried it to the shore.

Master Nguyen lifted a corner of his robe and strode to the cabin. He parted the silk screen with the back of his hand to reveal its small interior. Looking back at him was a woman in her twenties. Dressed in a red wedding gown, she crouched with visible discomfort in the center of the cabin. The moment she saw his face, she recoiled farther into her cramped sanctuary. Her eyes, slanted and wide-set, darted as though she were searching for a way to flee. From years of working outdoors, her body had absorbed so much sunlight that a glow seemed to radiate from her skin. She had a big, flat nose, large mouth, and oversized teeth, which were stained black with the juice of betel nuts. He drew his eyebrows together disapprovingly.

"Master, do you like what you see, sir?" came a female voice from somewhere behind him.

He turned to see an elderly woman whose back was bent so close to the ground that she appeared to be crawling instead of walking. She was the matchmaker who was responsible for this arranged wedding. Trying to meet his stare, she looped her neck like a duck.

"How old is she?" he asked.

"Four and twenty, sir."

His frown deepened. "She is an old maid, isn't she?"

"She is very healthy," the matchmaker replied quickly. "She is as strong as a bull. And look at her breasts. They are heavy. You will be blessed with many grandchildren."

He relaxed his grimace, looked at the bride, and asked, "What is your name, daughter?"

Upon hearing this, the matchmaker turned happily to the others. "The master has approved. He called her 'daughter.' Bring in the musicians!"

A much louder noise from a turn of the street drowned out the old lady's excited cry—the pulsating sound of a drum. Within seconds, a dragon made of glossy painted wood, cardboard, and papier mâché, held up high on bamboo sticks, appeared at the opening of the wharf. From afar, it seemed to float through the village. Young men in white shirts and red pants danced under it to the beat of the drum. Lanterns, shaped like butterflies and fish, burned brightly under the early-morning sun. A soprano sang the ending verse from the famous opera The King's Wedding. Her voice glided to the highest note before it, too, blended with the sounds of revelry. More firecrackers soared through the air, and no one seemed to notice when the old man slipped away to his boat and turned it back downstream.

When the noisy celebration dimmed, the bride shyly answered her father-in-law's question. "My name is Ven, sir."

"Good." Master Nguyen nodded. It was a lowly name that one would give only to a dog, yet somehow it suited her, he thought.

The matchmaker handed him a red veil, which he hung over the bride's head, concealing her face. From that time on, all she could see were the ruby tips of her slippers, yet she was thankful. The sheer fabric became her protective shield. Alone in a strange town, she would rather be led through the ceremony like a blind woman, unaware of the disparaging looks, like the one she had just received from her husband's father. In the back of her mind, a pang of curiosity stirred up, as faint as smoke. What did he look like? She knew nothing about her bridegroom. What of his personality, his likes, his dislikes, even his name? And yet, these things mattered little at this juncture of her life. Like it or not, she was about to be a married woman.

The servants carried her through the streets. The farther they walked, the more vigorously the cabin rocked on their shoulders. She leaned back, closed her eyes, and let herself sway with its movement. The thought of becoming a fine woman in a rich man's home relaxed her aching muscles. The folds of her satin gown trapped her body heat, and she began perspiring. "An elegant lady never sweats." She dimly remembered an old saying she had heard as a child. She reached under the veil and wiped her forehead with the back of her hand.

At last, the bridal party stopped at what seemed to be the back entrance of a house. Someone swept aside the silk curtain of her cubicle and took her callused palm. She recognized the matchmaker's wrinkled hand as the old lady guided her down a muddy path that led to a wooden door.

At the entrance, a burning pot of red coals sat on the ground waiting for her. It was the custom for the bride to step over a blazing stove before setting foot in her new home. The fire would rid her soul of any evil spirits still clinging to it. The matchmaker explained that, according to the astrologer, Ven's unfortunate time of birth required her to enter through the back door and go straight to her honeymoon suite. The rest of the wedding celebration would continue without her.

Ven had to wait for her husband to come and lift her veil. This was another important tradition she had been told that she must follow if she ever hoped to have a long and happy life with this man. Seeing nothing but the tiles beneath her feet, Ven was led through unseen rooms and seated on her bridal bed, alone in the unfamiliar house.

Ven lost count of how many hours she remained alone. From the fading of a few streaks of light on the floor, she could tell that the day had aged into night. Outside the window, the party seemed to be winding down. She could hear the laughter slowly diminish into the slurring of drunken guests. The ebullient opera had ended, and now there was a single, soporific moan of a lute. In the dark, her back throbbed, and the numbness in her buttocks spread down her legs. She was hungry and tired. The gown tightened around her bosom, making it difficult for her to breathe.

Just when she thought she could not wait any longer, Ven heard the squeaking noise of a door as it opened and shut. A small group of people tiptoed into the room. Their whispering sounded to her like the wind rasping against rice paper. The oil lamp on the nightstand by her side flickered into light. Moments later, she heard the intruders withdraw, carefully closing the door behind them.

But Ven could tell that she was not alone. The subtle movement of the furniture, the faint rustle of clothing, and the quiet footsteps moving back and forth kept her frozen in place. It's him, she thought. It must be my husband. Who else could it be? In seconds, her months of waiting would be over. Like a boiling pot of water, the anxiety rose up, and she could hardly control her composure. She sat tightly, watching her hands tremble. She could feel the heat from her husband's body as he approached her. She kept her eyes downcast. Touching the ruby tips of her slippers were two tiny bare feet, just half the size of hers. A small hand reached out and clumsily tugged the veil from her face.

Standing before her was a little boy wearing a groom's costume. He could not have been older than seven. She could see the wide gap of his missing front teeth as he grinned at her, and it came to her that this child was her husband.

She got up from the edge of the wedding bed and lowered the oil lamp until it emitted only a dot of light the size of a pea. Quietly, she took off her restrictive clothing. The boy sat on the bed and watched her with his large, almond-shaped eyes. He inserted his thumb into the gap in his teeth. Ven left her undergarments on and climbed into the bed, pulling the mosquito net over her. As she lay down, her husband snuggled into her outstretched arms. He buried his face in her armpit, sucking his thumb.

She took the boy's wrist and pulled the finger out of his mouth. With an effort, she made her voice low and reasonable. "Young master, you are too old for this habit." He lay still, looking at her. Then he closed his eyes and went to sleep. Ven struggled with an impulse to wipe the drool off his face.

In the dark, she began to understand what her position would be in this rich man's house. They did not marry her to make her a fine lady. They wanted her for slave labor. Yet, being a daughter-in-law, she was not entitled to the salary a servant would have been paid.

To her surprise, Ven found she could not cry. Soon exhaustion claimed her.

10

(Thanhha Lai, 1965—)
赖清荷

作者简介

赖清荷（Thanhha Lai, 1965— ），美国越南裔儿童文学作家，出生于越南西贡（Saigon）（今胡志明市）。北越攻陷西贡时，她和家人离开越南到美国阿拉巴马州避难。她从纽约大学（New York University）获得艺术硕士学位。毕业后，她在一家报社工作，负责越南移民与社会相关的新闻报道。2005年，她发起了一个非营利性活动——为越南走路上学的孩子买自行车。对家乡的情怀以及对儿童的关爱促使赖清荷创作出优秀的儿童文学作品。

迄今为止，她已出版的作品有散体诗《再见木瓜树》（*Inside Out & Back Again*, 2011）、小说《静静地听》（*Listen, Slowly*, 2015）和《蝴蝶黄》（*Butterfly Yellow*, 2019）。《再见木瓜树》荣获2011年美国国家图书奖最佳青年文学奖（National Book Award for Young People's Literature）与纽伯瑞奖（Newbery Honor）等。

选段分别选自《再见木瓜树》中的《生日愿望》（"Birthday Wishes"）与《静静地听》中的第7章。前一选段从儿童的视角展现了越南难民离散生活的无奈与痛苦。后一选段则穿插讲述了主人公在美国与越南不同的生活经历，表达了作者对文化差异和历史的深刻反思。

作品选读（一）

Inside Out & Back Again

(Birthday Wishes)

By Thanhha Lai

Wishes I keep to myself:
Wish I could do what boys do
and let the sun darken my skin,
and scars grid my knees.
Wish I could let my hair grow,
but Mother says the shorter the better
to beat Saigon's heat and lice.
Wish I could lose my chubby cheeks.
Wish I could stay calm
no matter what
my brothers say.
Wish Mother would stop
chiding me to stay calm,
which makes it worse.
Wish I had a sister
to jump rope with
and sew doll clothes
and hug for warmth
in the middle of the night.
Wish Father would come home
so I can stop daydreaming
that he will appear
in my classroom
in a white navy uniform
and extend his hand toward me
for all my classmates to see.
Mostly I wish
Father would appear in our doorway
and make Mother's lips

curl upward,
lifting them from
a permanent frown
of worries.

April 10th
Night

作品选读（二）

Listen, Slowly

(CHAPTER 7)

By Thanhha Lai

    I hear whistling—the kind humans make when trying to sound like a bird. I crawl out of the net, then jiggle to make it hard for rebellious, day-hunter mosquitoes to stab my exposed skin. Mom packed for me, all capris, as I was too busy seething. I can just hear her reasoning: skirts too impractical, shorts too revealing, pants too hot, so let's do capris. Mosquitoes all over Vietnam cheered.

    Thinking of Mom, I run to my luggage, yank free the velcroed pocket, and unzip it to find a palm-sized something inside bubble wrap. Rip... revealing a cell phone and a charger. I take a deep breath and stare. This must be what it felt like to find gold. I actually kiss the cell. I should have known Mom would find a way to circumvent Dad's ban on anything electronic, as not to show off. But I need this. Why did I not find it immediately after talking to Mom yesterday morning? Because life in Vietnam is one body-crushing, must-do, crowd-throbbing, mind-heavy event after another. It takes all my energy just to react.

    I zoom around trying to find an outlet. Nothing. Can life be this cruel? Control, I tell myself, control. I will find a way to charge the phone, then I'm practically back in Laguna.

    I run outside and stop short. A pouting Út stands in the courtyard in yesterday's crumpled pants and T-shirt. Three teenagers, all clutching sun-blocking umbrellas, surround her as if she might run off. I bet they had to pull her toward me the whole way. They wave, a skinny boy and two long-haired girls, all wearing long pants in this sticky heat. Of course they're not scratching or jiggling. Út is, surprise surprise, cradling her pet. The others each hold a basket.

With his umbrella hand, the boy reaches out for one of the older girls' baskets. She's got to be Út's sister, Lan. The same perfect oval face, same movie-star eyelashes, but Lan seems prettier because, let's face it, a buzz cut takes down even the best of us. The boy looks straight at Lan and smiles, not just smiles, but beams the universal signal for "Interested." She looks down, turns really pink, smiles at the ground. Even I'm not that bad in front of HIM. I catch her smile just in time to see a slight overbite.

Before Lan can give him her basket, the other girl jams her basket into his hand. The universal gesture for "You Better Not Be Interested in Her!" This girl looks right at him and wiggles her hips. She actually does that, bold and mocking—such a Montanaish move. The boy swallows; the knot at his throat runs up and down. He decides to carry the umbrella and one basket on the left, and the other two baskets on the right. Poor guy, I can tell this triangle is nowhere near over. The boy steps forward. "Good aft'noon, miss. My name is Minh. I would be honored to serve as your translator if you can forgive my incompetent English. I am studyin' on scholarship and will return as a junior to a boardin' high school near Houston. As you can witness, I am still in the learnin' stage."

My mouth falls open. I want to hug this knotty, sincere boy who's wearing way cool John Lennon glasses. My personal translator! A Vietnamese who speaks superproper English with a Texas accent. You can't make this up.

"Hey, I'm Mia, oops, I guess I'm Mai here. Thank you, thank you, there's so much I want to say. First, please tell Út I'm so sorry."

Bless him, he doesn't ask about what but just does his job. Út answers by blowing air out her nose in a quick puff. What does that mean? She has yet to open her mouth. Bet you anything she hates her braces. Wearing them is a two-year torment, but I'm not about to walk around for the rest of my life with the top row parasailing over the bottom one. Might as well wear my braces loud and proud.

"Xin lỗi," I add for extra sorriness. Út nose-puffs again. I'm going to take that as forgiveness. Onward

"Could you ask Út if that's a frog or a toad?"

He asks. Then the longest answer in Vietnamese: "Only a know—nothing can't tell a frog from a toad! As misdirected as not knowing a horse from a mule. Tell her frogs belong to the family Ra-ni-dae and live in water; they lay eggs there in clusters, the tadpoles hatch, then turn into frogs with webbed feet. Toads belong to the family Bu-fo-ni-dae and live on land. They're bumpy, cracked, scary. I found mine when he was just an egg that somehow broke from a cluster in Cô Hạnh's pond. I've raised him myself."

Translation: "Út thanks you for your inquiry and would like to inform you that she has a frog."

What a pain that Út is! But I make myself smile and nod as if I didn't understand every word the little snot said. We're even in my eyes. I'm done being sorry. For now, I'll keep my listening skills to myself.

I walk toward them and, with the biggest smile, accept the baskets of food.

I have to say Anh before Minh to show respect that he's older. The Vietnamese are all about respect. Anh Minh, it turns out, matches Mom as a super planner. Is this also a Vietnamese thing? All I did was show him the dead phone and he whipped into must-do mode. He says we can't charge it at a more modern house because it's rude to visit relatives during nap time. His group had meant to leave the baskets on the porch, but I was awake so they stayed. We can't charge at his or the girls' homes because if they go there, they might have to nap. Not to worry, he has other plans for my cell.

"Why aren't you napping?" I ask.

"Between the ages of fifteen and fifty, some of us are too burdened with studyin' or workin' to be nappin'."

I love that Texas accent rolling off his tongue. Come to think of it, all those between fifteen and fifty at mine and Bà's welcoming party were girls and women. Anh Minh is the first boy I've seen.

"Where are all the boys and men?" I ask.

"At our shrimp camp."

I'm imagining a summer sleepaway, where boys become men while hatching shrimps and learning the ecosystem of ocean life and mastering the fine points of canoeing and swimming and bonding.

"Whatever you are thinkin', miss, I am afraid you are mistaken. Walk and I shall explain."

I make my face blank, pretending I've been imagining an empty gray box.

Anh Minh leads, gallantly leaning his umbrella over my head and forsaking shade for himself. I tell him I'm protected by SPF on steroids, but he won't listen. Hatless Út follows, with no one offering to shade her maxed-out bronze complexion. She doesn't seem to care. The two older girls go last, giggling and whispering under their umbrellas.

"Our village has joined together to buy a shrimp hatchin' facility by the sea," Anh Minh says. "The men who do not want or cannot get jobs in the city or in the government live and work there, and boys who do not pass the rigorous test into a city high school train there. That way no male finds idle time."

"What if someone doesn't like shrimp work?"

Anh Minh looks at me like I've asked the most illogical question ever. I could defend myself, but why annoy the one person who can make village life easier? I lean into his umbrella and look up and smile at his serious, sincere face.

We're walking in this maze where one—story rectangular houses are built close together, separated by waist-high cement walls. Once in a while, a many-story rectangular house pops up, separated by head-high walls. People really like cement here, pouring it in front and back to create yards. It does make sense to not coax grass out of the ground, then mow and fertilize and obsess about it. Mom's big thing is no lawns. Each house we have bought has a smaller patch of grass, the current one the size of a crib. An automatic sprinkler is forever drowning the yellowing patch. Maybe soon all of us in desert-dry Southern Cal will be graduating to all-cement yards too.

Finally, we're out on a dusty path where swampy rice paddies line each side. I'm so close I could reach down and pluck a rice stalk. But what if I fall in and go nostril to nostril with a water buffalo? I still love them, but from afar.

The red dust kicks up and sticks between my toes in my sandals. Everyone else is wearing flip-flops, which somehow let the dust fly about and rest back on the path. I'm beginning to think Mom has no clue how to dress here.

At an intersection, Anh Minh points to a gigantic tree where roots hang from thick, muscular branches. The tree obviously has roots underground, but other roots droop down and grow into the soil. The spaces in between the hanging roots create natural hiding spots, where I bet kids spend all their time when not napping.

"This tree has outlived every other livin' thing in the village. We guess it could be three hundred years old." Anh Minh glows while saying that, then he actually puts his palms together and bows at the tree. I might as well do it too. Is bowing to trees a Vietnamese thing?

Village life is centered around the tree. In one corner stands a faded, mossy pagoda, its door wide open in the heat. Inside, on tile, dozens of dogs with lolling tongues lie half asleep. Among the dogs and their spilled water bowls, a duck is waddling, sipping here and there. Somehow, perfectly natural.

We head to the opposite corner of the pagoda and into an open market, closed for nap time. Merchants have put newspapers over their goods and handkerchiefs over their faces and are sleeping and snoring on cots spread out next to their stalls. It's like walking through a Vietnamese-village version of Sleeping Beauty frozen under the witch's spell.

I like the quiet.

We walk deeper into the market and stop in front of what looks like a cement hut with a door and no window. I'm wondering what goods are stored in there when Anh Minh makes that open-palm swing to mean "go in." Seeing my alarmed face, he explains, "It is an internet café."

Okay, let's not say "café." You would imagine coffee and muffins and soft lighting and sleepy music and you would be wrong. Imagine instead a hot shack with a tin roof that makes it even hotter and two old computers on DIAL-UP, that's right, DIAL-UP, but I can charge the cell. Thank you, universe. We have time, so I pay the equivalent of ten cents for the slowest internet connection ever.

I log on. After an eternity, I get twenty-nine messages. Some from Mom. Each with an inspirational message about hanging in there and a new SAT word for the day. DELETE, DELETE, DELETE. Being across the world rocks! Most from Montana. A crisis about tan lines, a crisis about too-glossy lip glosses, a crisis about choosing a French, lobster-tail, or waterfall braid. DELETE, DELETE, DELETE. There's an FB notification from Montana. I log on and wait. Mia Le. Weird to see that name. I haven't been her in a while.

OMG, on my wall is a tagged pic of her and HIM at Anita, a beach where almost-teens go to get away from moms and little kids. I click over to her wall. Wait. And wait. Finally, I'm in. More photos, all bikini shots. Did she Photoshop to make her boobs look extra big? How big do they need to be? I don't want her boobs, but I have to confess I do want the attention they get her. Does that make me pathetic and sophomoric?

There HE is, just as I suspected, standing right behind her butt bow. She's smiling over her shoulder. I know that smirk. HE's not smiling back though, kinda looking up, way up. I scroll down and it says HE and she friended the day I left. That means she asked HIM. Still, HE shouldn't have accepted.

What's wrong with me? HE can do whatever. Beads of sweat, mixed with sunblock, slide into my eyes, letting me cry a little.

But I can't indulge and throw myself down. Anh Minh and the girls are standing behind me, not sweaty, but definitely misty, eyes on the screen, looking at the beach photographs. I would give anything to have an hour alone.

Anh Minh, seeing me see him, pretends like he hasn't been staring at the screen and flips his concentration to the tin roof, like it reveals some unsolved theorem. He's already told me he's going to be a mathematician/professor/poet. Please, universe, never let my mother meet him. I can just hear her comparisons and sighs

Út is twisting her mouth and gearing up for questions about Montana, no doubt. I kick my expression into neutral, but my heart is pumping blood to my face. Stop it, feelings, do not show that I'm flustered having seen evidence of Montana and HIM together. I have no idea if my feelings are listening.

The two older girls keep whispering to each other. I've never actually heard them speak. Anh Minh straightens himself, so grateful to have translation to do.

"Who's she with breasts so full?" So begins the froggy one.

"My friend Montana."

"Why is she older in age?"

"She's twelve, my age."

"Twelve? And a baby she has?" Út won't stop with the questions.

"What baby?"

"Her breasts swell for no reason?"

"Believe me, she has reasons."

"Are you certain she's twelve? Did she fail some grades?"

"She's twelve, I told you."

"Are breasts the size of human heads admired in America?"

How can one person be this nosy? I think, but say, "Not her fault they're that size."

"She has to stuff them into tiny triangles?"

"It's Southern California. People wear bikinis to the beach."

"Must she call attention to her buttocks also? Is she trying to mate? But the males are the ones to court the females."

"She's not a duck or a peacock. She's my best friend. She's smart in her own way. She's very happy, really."

"Best friend? She would think of your happiness before her own?"

I make myself nod slowly. I don't know why I'm defending Montana, but I feel like if I don't, my life will fall apart. Út is a pain, pain, pain. I'm in no mood to be interrogated. What does Út know? She's obsessed with a gargantuan frog.

I always talk really fast when agitated, as if words could drown out anxieties. On and on I blab about how Montana and I are borderline teenagers and that means pressure and change and freedom and bodies. I forget to pause to let Anh Minh translate. There's so much to say about becoming a teenager. The more I talk, the more I can fake calmness. HE was looking away from her butt bow, right? I would be able to tell in two seconds if I were standing right there. Dad could not have picked a worse summer for his must-please-my-momma project. My mind obsesses about HIM while my mouth spews out teen facts. Is this what they mean by "split personality"? When I do pause, Anh Minh seems stumped.

"There's no word for teenager in Vietnamese, miss. Numbers in English go from ten to eleven to twelve, then thirteen, fourteen. So the jump from twelve to thirteen has cultural plus spellin' ramifications. But in Vietnamese, we say ten, then ten one, ten two, ten three, ten four, so there's no change. Literally, a teenager would start at ten and that has no meanin' here or over there. The closest we have here is tuổi dậy-thì, which is the age of puberty at fifteen, sixteen."

"Just tell them it's a big deal to go from twelve to thirteen."

"They won't believe me because there's no such change here."

What is the point of having a personal translator if he's going to argue with me about facts, actual facts. Everybody knows turning thirteen is a gigantic marker, the way old people remember where they were when Kennedy was shot or, for the Vietnamese, where they were the day Saigon fell.

What were my parents thinking, dumping me in a place where teenagers do not exist, where every single person eats some form of rice for every single meal, where napping is a public event, where perfectly well-behaved kids are banished from real conversations?

The worst part? No one here would listen to my many, many, many complaints. No one even complains.

11

(Andrew X. Pham, 1967—)
安德鲁·X. 范

作者简介

  安德鲁·X. 范（Andrew X. Pham, 1967— ），美国越南裔作家，也是美国网络平台"Spoonwiz"的创始人。他出生于越南藩切（Phan Thiet），父亲是一名教师，母亲是一名洗衣工，范家中兄弟姐妹六人。越南战争结束后，范的父亲被北越人关进劳改营。几个月后，他获释并带着全家逃亡美国。在途中，他们经历九死一生的磨难到达马来西亚，在雅加达的难民营中度过了18个月。之后，他们一家得到路易斯安那州一个教堂的赞助到美国，最终在加利福尼亚州的圣何塞定居下来。高中毕业后，范考入加州大学洛杉矶分校（UCLA）学习工程学。

  然而，理工科学习并没有淹没范对文学的热爱。他的两部回忆录是《鲶鱼和曼陀罗：穿越越南风景和记忆的两轮旅行》（*Catfish and Mandala: A Two-Wheeled Voyage Through the Landscape and Memory of Vietnam*, 1999）与《天穹：三个战争中的一生》（*The Eaves of Heaven: A Life in Three Wars*, 2008）。凭借这两部作品，范获得了桐山环太平洋图书奖（Kiriyama Pacific Rim Book Prize）、怀廷奖（Whiting Award）与古根海姆奖（Guggenheim Fellowship）。

  本选集分别选取了《鲶鱼和曼陀罗：穿越越南风景和记忆的两轮旅行》与《天穹：三个战争中的一生》两部作品的选段。前一个选段围绕主人公的回忆展开了越南战争期间他们一家艰难逃难的场景。后一个选段以北越"再教育营"为核心，体现了越南战争结束后北越政府对南越人残酷的对待。

作品选读（一）

Catfish and Mandala

(Catfish—Dawn)
By Andrew X. Pham

  I am a Vietnamese-American man. In my work boots, I am of average height, of medium build, and not too ghastly of face. I like going to the movies and reading novels in cafés. If I had to choose one cuisine to eat for the rest of my life, I'd take Italian without hesitation, though I do harbor secret cravings for hickory-smoked baby-back ribs and New Orleans gumbo. And I like buying cookbooks more than cooking. I enjoy tennis, basketball, baseball, football, and, lately, yes, hockey—from the bleachers or in my La-Z-Boy. My choice daily wear is a pair of five-year-old Levi's and a mock turtleneck (I have a drawer-full, all the same size, same brand, different colors). I don't wear yellow, red, orange, or anything bright: they complicate the laundry process. No G-string underwear. Socks, plain white or black only.

  My family arrived in America on September 17, 1977. I was ten. Of the Vietnam War I knew little, recalling only vignettes and images. Too young to know about its politics until I was about to enter American middle school. Fifth grade, Mr. Jenkin's class, I raised my voice against a teacher for the first time. Eighteen months in America, that much English learned. He was lecturing on the history of the Vietnam War. Something he said must have set me off because I shouted at him, summoning forth adults' drunken words I'd picked up eavesdropping: America left Vietnam. America not finish war. One more day bombing, Viet Cong die. One more day! No. America go home! America chicken! Mr. Jenkin colored, a tomato-flush rising from his buttoned collar to his feathery blond hair. I could tell he wanted to strike me, but I knew they didn't do that in America so I didn't say I was sorry. Chopping the air with his hand, he screamed, No! No! Wrong! And five minutes of English I couldn't understand.

  Much later, I realized with some guilt that perhaps his brother had died in the War, and if it had gone on, he might have lost another. I wish I could tell him now that what I really meant was that my father was in prison because of the War. I was shouting about our imprisonment, about the dark wet cells, the whippings, the shootings, the biting rats, and the fists of dirty rice we ate. These things I remember unfogged by the intervening years. Somehow terribly vivid, irreducible.

I was there. After Saigon fell on April 30, 1975, our family fled deeper south, hoping to find a boat that would take us to Thailand. Outside of Rach Gia, a port city, the Viet Cong had set up a road barricade and caught us along with some three hundred people heading toward the coast to flee the country. Women and children were locked, fifty to a room, in a wing separate from the men. We took turns sleeping on wet concrete, side by side. After a month, the women and children were released with permission to go home. The men were either executed or trucked off to the jungle to work.

My mother and I regularly visited my father at the Minh Luong Prison and Labor Camp. We lodged with peasant families and stayed for weeks near the compound so she could watch him working in the field under guard. Hiding behind bushes, I watched him whenever I could find him. Like her, I felt that if I kept my eyes on him, stayed vigilant enough, bad things wouldn't happen. Some nights, she lay awake until dawn after hearing gunshots snap in the nearby woods, where they executed prisoners.

Two decades have thundered by since his imprisonment. Although we rarely talk beyond the safe grounds of current events, education, investment, and work, he has frequently shared his tales about the Viet Cong reeducation camp with me. The adventure stories he had told me as a boy on his knee were replaced by his death-camp saga. I believe it had something to do with my being his first son, with my having been there at the prison watching over him, witnessing what he thought were his death rites. In the years of telling, they became almost as much my stories as his. And this was strange, since my father and I have never shared much, never done father-and-son things, no camping trips, no fishing excursions; no ball games, no hot dogs in the park; no beers and Super Bowl on the tube. Still, the stories passed back and forth between us even when I had grown and moved away. My father, Pham Van Thong, was bequeathing his rarest pearls of wisdom, imparting a sense of value for life.

Of his last days in the death camp, Thong remembers the silence most. It was a thick creature that sat on his chest and lodged its fists in his throat. In the Viet Cong prison hut, he heard only his heart. Above, an indigo sky spilled light into the room, dyeing the gaunt faces of his fellows squatting on the dirt floor, fifty-four prisoners waiting for the execution call.

It came twice every week over the loudspeakers. Sometimes days passed between the calls, sometimes the calls came back-to-back.

Every evening just after they had scraped the last of the rice and the broth from their tins, silence fell as crickets wooed the coming night. The hut stank with fear and the food in their belly soured. Always, someone vomited.

He waded through his swamp of emotions. As the end neared when the indigo was deepest, two feelings remained. Sorrow for his wife, his children. Regret for a thousand things not done, a thousand things not said, a thousand things taken for granted.

His best friend in prison, Tuan, a helicopter pilot, edged close to him. Sitting on his hams, Tuan leaned over and whispered in his ear, "Thong, promise me."

He squeezed Tuan's shoulder. It was December 17, 1975. If they called his name tonight, Tuan would die and his promise would be worthless. Tuan believed the VC would release Thong in a few years. He would carry Tuan's last words to his wife and son. Thong didn't tell Tuan he believed that death was the only way out of Minh Luong Prison.

"Promise me!"

"Tuan …"

"You'll get out soon. Your wife's uncle is a VC colonel—a war hero."

"The bribes didn't work, Tuan. We're broke. Anh borrowed and sold everything we owned."

"No, she'll find a way. Anh is smart." Tuan had never met her.

The gloom obscured his friend's face, but Thong could pick out the hollow cheeks and the wild vacant eyes. Before Vietnam fell, Tuan was a handsome young officer with all the promise of a good military career. He was only twenty-eight. He was married to his high school sweetheart and they had a son. On nights when it was very cold and the prisoners huddled together for warmth, he would speak of her, the way she moved and intimate things. Things not meant for the ears of others, but in this place it was all he had. All that kept him going.

Tuan's quivering voice was rife with self-reproach. "I shouldn't have confessed that I was a pilot. I was scared. When they said the penalty for lying on the confession essay was execution, I lost my mind. I wrote down everything. I confessed everything. Everything I could remember."

Thong didn't.

"Thanh said I was honest. That's why she loves me. I shouldn't have written about my service in the air force."

He wanted to tell Tuan they wouldn't call tonight, wouldn't come for him, wouldn't punish him. But he didn't. It would have been a lie. He wanted to hear Tuan's voice because it might be the last time they talked. A dying man had the right to talk, Thong said, and they were all dying. If the executioner didn't kill them tonight, jungle diseases would kill them soon enough. Then there were the minefields, the hundreds of land mines they were forced to unearth and defuse with shovels. Death always came round, one way or another.

"You'll be all right," Tuan said, reassuring his friend even through his fear. "You're just a teacher. They don't punish teachers."

Tuan didn't know his secret. No one in the prison did.

"They'll let you go soon. You only violated martial law."

Tuan murmured himself to silence. There were nervous movements in the hut. Someone in the far corner retched. The loudspeakers crackled and screeched to life, whipping a charge of adrenaline through the room.

"Bastards!" someone hissed in the dark. "Why at night? Why do they only call at night?"

Silence answered him.

"If they are going to kill me, I want to die in the sun," the man said, his voice rising on a false note of courage. "Why do they only come at night?"

A voice replied from across the darkness. "They are afraid of what they do. It is easier to kill in the dark."

Someone else said, "No laws, no reasons, no mercy."

"It is the way of the Viet Cong. I know them," an old voice said. It was Khuong, the fisherman. He was in his sixties. He had given fifteen years to the Nationalist Army.

The first man shouted out the window, "Cowards!"

"Shut up!" a new voice trilled.

"Yes, shut up. It'll go hard for us if you don't."

The murmurs of consent angered the first speaker. His voice, tinged with fear, became a shout. "You're all cowards. You wait like chickens—they kill you like chickens. When they kill me, I'm not going to kneel. No shooting in the back of the head. I'll look at the eyes of the man who pulls the trigger."

Khuong replied, "You won't. It is dark. The night hides everything."

The loudspeakers blared. "Stand outside your hut when your name is called." Without preamble it rattled off names like a shopping list. "Nguyen Van Tung, Do Nhan Anh, Tran Truc Dang ..."

A wail pierced the hut. A man across the room convulsed on the ground. The loudspeakers boomed, "Vo Ba Sang." Oh... Not the auto mechanic.

"Le Tin Khuong." The village fisherman. "Dinh Yen Than." The pig farmer. "Vu Tan Khai." The town storekeeper. They were killing

all the locals linked to the Nationalists. People were turning in their own neighbors.

Thong stared at his friend. Tuan's family had lived in this province for generations. They both heard it: "Phuoc Tri Tuan."

Then it was over: thirteen names, six from their hut. Tuan retched on his mat and curled up in it shaking. Thong held him. Sang, the mechanic, took his place at the door, seemingly at peace with his lot.

The guards came in with oil lamps. Thong saw the fear, the ugly fear of the spared, and knew his face mirrored it. He saw the terror of the condemned and the way the tallowy light danced wicked shadows on their twisted features. The VC took the fisherman, the farmer, the storekeeper, and another man.

They dragged Tuan away by his ankles. He did not resist and he did not speak. Tuan gave Thong no final look and no parting words. It was so quick and simple how the VC had taken him and plunged them back into darkness.

Thong sat on his mat in a vile mixture of grief and relief. He had learned to block out the VC's "trials" broadcast over the loudspeakers. They invariably followed the same script: an account of offenses against the country, a conviction, and a death sentence—never a defense or a last rite. Occasionally, a few men were not tried. Tuan was the fourth one tried and his crimes were the same as those before and after him.

A long, long silence followed. Then eleven sharp pistol reports, distance—softened. It was over. They never knew what happened to the remaining two men.

Thong woke three hours before dawn. He heard some other early risers moving in the dark and hurried to be the first out of the hut. The smart ones woke early to use the latrine before the morning rush. Not all could go before the guards came to take them out to work.

The bloat-bellied moon sagged low on the horizon and silhouetted the guard tower just beyond the barbed-wire fence. The night sounds of the jungle hummed and the earth was cold and rough beneath his bare feet. Outside the compound, the sentries shadowed the perimeter on their watch, ignoring him.

The latrine was a wooden structure overhanging the edge of a shallow pond inside the prison fence. He snagged handfuls of grass and climbed up the five-stepped ladder. The latrine reminded him of a hangman's platform, the kind in the American Western movies his wife was so fond of. Only this one did not have a hanging post and in place of the trap door was a circular hole situated over the water. The surface beneath the latrine began to churn, roiling with catfish. He squatted over the opening and proceeded. The catfish fought wildly for their meal, leaping out of the water. He shifted to avoid the splashes. And so it went—the fish leaping and him shifting—until the business was concluded and the soiled grass discarded.

As he made his way back to the hut, others strayed out one by one to the pond. The clouds had swallowed the stars on the horizon. He crawled back to his bed and, before he remembered, he moved to huddle against Tuan for warmth. Tuan's straw mat was still there, reeking of the sourness of vomit and the cloying sweetness of urine.

Thong curled up and wound himself tightly in his blanket and Tuan's. The wind snaked through the thatched wall and ran cold tendrils over his scalp. He rolled onto his other side and bumped against Danh, a prison mate who lay perfectly still. Danh could have been dead. Thong could not tell and he did not wake him. If Danh were dead or dying, there was nothing Thong could do and nothing the VC would do besides tossing Danh into the mass grave in the woods and covering him with a thin layer of dirt.

Thong often daydreamed of the time before his world became undone. His Saigon in April of 1975 was another life. A good life that he didn't think could end even in the final days. He was a teacher, three years retired from the military. His wife, Anh, was a tailor in her own shop with three workers. They had made their fortune before the Americans pulled out in 1972 and they had to shut down their business. Comfortably well-off, they continued to work because it was in their nature. They lived in a three-story house and had five children, one girl, four boys. A shining member of Vietnam's tiny middle class.

It had been very different at the beginning. His family were impoverished refugees, fleeing south in 1946 when the Viet Minh took over North Vietnam. Hers were Southerners scratching out a living amid civil unrest. They married without the blessings of either family. Under a leaky roof, they scraped, worked hard, and saved prodigiously. Somehow, they got by on love and rice. Then came the thing—the thing that catapulted them out of poverty—that which he would forever keep behind doors closed to his children.

When the army drafted him, they gave him an officer's commission because he was a college graduate at a time when South Vietnam's annual crop of college graduates was fifty. His fluency in French and English yielded a translator post. In 1967, his education landed him the office of Assistant Chief of Phan Thiet Province, a coastal city-state of central Vietnam. It was a paramilitary post that dealt in psychological warfare. He was only a lieutenant, but under his proctorship were two thousand men. They wrote literature, broadcast Nationalist ideology, pro-American sentiments, and anti-Viet Cong messages. They accused, ridiculed, blamed, and generally vilified the Viet Cong, their actions, their theories, and everything they stood for. His men patrolled the countryside and played Good Samaritans, lending the peasants a hand to win their favor, their loyalty.

They swayed the peasants who did not care which side won the war because they were so hungry and poor. It was difficult for simple farmers and fisher folk to understand how one regime could be worse than another. They paid the poor to spy on the VC movement in the countryside. They kept many from openly joining the VC. They found men to replenish the South Army.

作品选读（二）

The Eaves of Heaven

(34. REEDUCATION)

By Andrew X. Pham

THE SOUTH 1975
34. REEDUCATION

Tin said, "Surround him. Careful, he's poisonous!"

"The bush!" Tung shouted as the snake slithered toward me.

I slammed my shovel into the ground in front of the snake. It coiled up, hissing.

"Cobra! Cobra!" someone shouted.

Tung and I stepped around to block its retreat into the paddy, our shovels ready. It was more than four feet long and as thick as a man's wrist. Tin had found it under the brambles we were clearing. Within moments, half a dozen other inmates converged to help. There was no way we'd let that much meat escape us.

Tin lured the snake to him with a stick. A machete was poised high over his head. The snake struck at the stick. Tin swung and missed.

I came from behind and pinned the snake with my shovel. It squirmed violently to get loose. Tin brought the machete down and severed its head. The body writhed, flopping and gushing blood.

Tung reached for the snakehead, but Tin batted his hand away. "You don't want to do that. It can still bite and pump you full of poison."

As was the custom, Tin dug a hole, scooped up the snakehead with the shovel, put it in the hole, and filled it with dirt. We all went back to work, grinning. More often than not, we considered ourselves lucky to get mice or frogs. A snake this big meant that there would be a few bites to go around. A year ago, I would never consider tasting the snake meat that was offered as a delicacy in the top Chinese restaurants, but now a cobra looked as tasty as a rope of sausages.

I picked up my shovel and rejoined the crew in the irrigation trench. The sky was blue, the day just beginning to broil. We were outside working in the fresh air, waist-deep in creamy mud. I felt very lucky to be here.

I had thought my life was over when the guards took me from the cell that night in Rach Gia. But instead of putting us on trial as they normally did, they loaded us into a tarp-covered truck bed and drove us out of the city. We had expected to be executed at a mass grave in the woods. The truck bounced over the rutted road for half an hour and delivered us to Minh Luong Reeducation Camp.

Our new home was an old South Vietnam military training site. It was where the Viet Cong kept "low-grade" traitors like South Vietnamese regional soldiers and former low-level officials. Compared to Rach Gia and other prisons where they sent the "high-grade" traitors, Minh Luong was a resort. The doors of our cells were not locked and we were free to move around within the compound. We worked outside daily and had opportunities to scavenge in the fields and streams.

Forgotten diversions of my countryside childhood came back to me. I remembered how to snatch grasshoppers from rice leaves, how to flood crickets from their burrows, how to spear frogs in the ponds. Fellow prisoners taught me how to catch mice, snakes, small fish, and small blue paddy crabs. We picked wild berries, greens, herbs, yams, onions, morning glories, and sour leaves. Some things we pocketed to be cooked later, others we popped in our mouths like candy treats. My favorites were crunchy termites and buttery sparrow eggs.

AT lunch, the guards let us build a little fire. Tin tossed the snake onto the flames. The smell of burnt meat soon drew in the crowd. He gave everyone a small piece. We ate it with our tin of rice.

Tin, Tung, and I sat downwind from a cow grazing the grass on the side of the dirt road. It smelled so sweet and milky that the snake meat tasted just like steak in my mouth. Tung said he could sit here breathing cow-scent all day long. Tin and I laughed at the thought of Tung pining after the cows like a lovesick puppy. Tin and Tung were my two closest friends at Minh Luong. Tung was an army corporal, married with a son. Tin was in his early thirties and single. A recent arrival at Minh Luong, he said he was a government official in Saigon. I suspected he was hiding something because he was very intent on finding a way to escape. He discussed his plans with us, trying to convince us to go with him. Of all his plans only one had any chance of success, but it was such an obvious route that every prisoner already knew about it. I had noticed it my first day inside.

Situated on a rice plain, Minh Luong Camp was enclosed by two layers of barbed-wire fences. The back side of the camp had a creek about three hundred yards from the rear fence. One of our first tasks as inmates was to clear the minefields surrounding the prison, so if a prisoner could get past the fence and stayed unnoticed by the guards, he could reach the creek and float away for miles. It was as clear as an open door. It left me wondering why our jailers hadn't bothered to erect some sort of barrier.

"The ground is very wet and soft. We can dig just enough space to crawl under the fence and then swim down the creek with the current," Tin said quietly. "We would have at least six or seven hours before they mounted a search party."

Tung shook his head. "It's a trap. It's just too easy."

"Do you have someone nearby who can help? You can't go far without money," I said. The new government had issued a new currency.

"I know some people in Rach Gia," Tin said.

Tung was not convinced. "Do you really have to go?"

Tin seemed on the verge of saying something, but thought better of it. I was relieved. I didn't want the responsibility of someone else's secret. We recently heard that the Viet Cong had captured the entire data file of the South Vietnam army, containing hundreds of thousands of personnel service records. Countless men would suffer because the bureaucrats who manned the personnel offices had fled without destroying the files. I had heard two of my team leaders in the RD program had been arrested and executed. I suspected that, like me, Tin had been less than forthright on his confession. It was simply a matter of time before they investigated our service records.

"You know you can't go home. That'll be the first place they look," Tung said.

I nodded. "There's no place to hide. Where can you go?"

The country was practically under martial law. People needed permits to leave their hometowns. Each neighborhood had its own party member representative—and spies who knew every resident.

"Cross the border into Cambodia," said Tung.

I looked at Tin; he had already arrived at this conclusion. He grew up in the countryside and was very resourceful in the wilderness. If anyone had a chance crossing the jungle alive, it was Tin.

He had every reason to flee. If I were Tin, a man without a wife or children, I would have been gone yesterday. He was still healthy and strong, as fresh as I had been six months ago. The longer he waited, the greater the chance he would become one of us sickly inmates.

Life in Minh Luong was harsh. Every day we woke in darkness. They marched us out of the compound to work at the crack of dawn. We cleared minefields, exploded charges, cleared brambles, dug irrigation ditches, and repaired roads. Our first meal of the day came at noon with an hour of rest. We labored until dusk. We had two hours to bathe and eat dinner. Some nights they held trials and sentenced those of us whom they claimed had discrepancies in our confessions. Other nights, they sat us down for three hours of reeducation where a party official lectured us about their battle victories; the struggles of the Vietnamese, first against the French Colonialists and later against the American Imperialists; and the ideals and advances of communism. On special evenings, we watched propaganda movies about VC heroes, battles, Ho Chi Minh, and the success of socialism in

Russia and China.

Occasionally, they summoned us from the field, a dozen at a time in the middle of the day, and put us through investigation sessions. We filled out scores of repetitive questionnaires about our family, friends, colleagues, jobs, social views, and political inclinations. We wrote detailed essays on our lives and thoughts. The more we answered, the more precarious our situations became.

"PHAM Van Thong. Come to the door!" the guard shouted.

I jumped, startled. Other prisoners gestured for me to hurry. I came to the door in my boxer shorts. The guard, a young fanatic with an AK-47 slung over his shoulder, stood next to an old man dressed in the ascetic pajama slacks and black cotton jacket of the revolutionaries. I could tell by the deference the guard showed to the stranger that he was a high-ranking party member. The man was in his mid—sixties with hair streaked with white. He was wiry and straight-backed. He had calm eyes.

He introduced himself as my wife's uncle, and I immediately saw the resemblance. Although we had never met, I was well acquainted with my wife's family history. Uncle Ha was my mother-in-law's cousin. During the Great Famine, Anh's entire extended family fled south. When the French came back to Vietnam, Uncle Ha joined the Resistance to fight the French. After the Geneva Accord, he regrouped to the North with the Resistance forces. Uncle Ha returned home after the Liberation to see his family for the first time in twenty years. His mother had always maintained that her son was first and foremost a patriot. Their reunion was a godsend for me.

"You should try to eat more vegetables," he said.

"Vegetables?" I was confused. Prisoners did not get enough food.

"You have beriberi. I've seen many cases. It was a common condition for our Resistance fighters. Unless you get more vitamins, your face and legs will keep swelling, then your vital organs will break down."

I thanked him for the advice. "How is my wife? Is she well? The children?"

"They are all doing well."

"Did Anh come with you?"

"She's at the inn. Spouses are not allowed visitation. You know that."

"Oh, yes, I'm sorry. I forgot."

I realized he was telling me to be cautious. Even though he was probably one of the highest-ranking party members the locals had met, Uncle Ha was careful not to show any impropriety and had not requested to meet me privately without the proctor. These walls had ears. Perhaps he was afraid that I was foolish enough to blurt out something dangerous.

"Your wife asked me to explain to the local authority that you are a good citizen, and that you fled Saigon because you were afraid. You had no intention of leaving the country."

He was saying that I must stick to my original confession, harp along that line in every interrogation, and never deviate. I nodded and said, "Thank you, Uncle. Please tell my wife that the comrades here are treating me well and teaching me the importance of socialism. I am grateful for the opportunity to learn."

Uncle Ha wished me good luck and good health. Then without another word, he turned and left. I was touched because I knew he had a reputation of integrity and high morals. I wondered what made him decide to help me. My mother-in-law and I believe that Uncle Ha, like many fighters of his generation who joined Viet Minh, was more a patriot than a North Vietnamese Party members. Many high-ranking officials and party members of his age were not hardcore North Vietnamese Party members. They had joined Ho's government to defeat a common enemy. They relinquished their political ideology until it was too late to do anything but become reluctant North Vietnamese Party members.

When Uncle Ha went north, he left his mother and eldest daughter, Nga, behind in the care of my mother-in-law. Nga grew up and married a South Vietnamese lieutenant in the Special Forces. He was a decorated soldier who lost an eye in the war and was sent to a reeducation camp after the fall of Saigon. Upon seeing Nga, who could not remember her long-absent father, Uncle Ha mobilized his considerable power and secured the release of his once-enemy son-in-law.

I thought of Aunt Thao's husband, my cousin Quyen, Uncle Ti, my adopted brother Vi, my best friend Hoi, and schoolmates from my village. Every person I knew had brothers, sons, cousins, or uncles on opposite sides of both wars: first the French, then the American. It was a conflict between brothers. No matter which side won, the family lost.

FOR several nights after Tin made his intention known, I stayed awake, eyes and ears trained on the dark spot where he lay ten feet from me. Night after night, he tossed and turned, but never left his sleeping mat. When I had thought his courage had surely deserted him, he vanished. I rose early one morning to go the latrine. Tin's place was vacant. Climbing up to the latrine set over the pond, I knew he was gone. I was the first one up, the only person at the latrine.

We never heard from Tin again. The guards made no announcements about their single escapee. They neither questioned nor punished us for his disappearance. From time to time, his name would come up in conversation, and someone would quip, "I bet Tin is in Thailand by now, drinking whisky and eating roast pork." It would stir up a round of chuckles and more speculations of marvelous things Tin could be doing at that very moment.

One by one, we fell victim to illness, accidents in the minefields, or the Viet Cong's trials. Some were pulled from our ranks without explanation. We never knew if they were released, sent to crueler camps, or executed. After they took Tung away, I often found myself looking to the creek. I could follow Tin to the Cambodian border, but I couldn't leave my family behind.

DURING one interrogation, I collapsed with a high fever. The inspector splashed water on my face, but couldn't revive me. Two prisoners carried me back to my quarters. Fellow cellmates nursed me with aspirin and penicillin from my stash of medicine. Three days and two nights I lay on the cold ground, wrapped in four layers of borrowed clothes, sweating, freezing, delirious. The body was ready, the spirit nearly there. Colleagues had fallen all around me, worthier men had perished, and I was learning to let go of my fears.

I thought of the Buddhist's third truth of existence: Death is a natural condition. There is no way to escape death.

In the long descent, I arrived finally at a place where what I had lost did not matter as much as what I had had, however briefly, in life. Here, I was free of bitterness and sorrow. Things, the essence of them, came to me, caressed me, entered and passed through me like familiar spirits.

Riding the border of sleep and wakefulness, I dreamt of the green fields of March, the yellow wind of summer harvests, the eternal gray of October rain, the blush of Hanoi winters, the gold foil on a champagne bottle buried in Tong Xuyen.

12

(Monique Truong, 1968—)
莫妮卡·张

作者简介

莫妮卡·张（Monique Truong, 1968— ），美国越南裔作家，出生于越南西贡（Saigon）。1975 年，她随同母亲逃难到美国。1990 年，她从耶鲁大学（Yale University）获得文学学士学位，1995 年从哥伦比亚法学院（Columbia Law School）获得法学博士学位。

她创作的作品有，三部长篇小说《盐之书》（*The Book of Salt*, 2003）、《难言之隐》（*Bitter in the Mouth*, 2010）和《最甜的水果》（*The Sweetest Fruits*, 2019），合著《分水岭：美国越南裔诗歌和散文》（*Watermark: Vietnamese American Poetry & Prose*）。她荣获过纽约公立图书馆幼狮文学奖（New York Public Library Young Lions Fiction Award）、古根海姆奖（Guggenheim Fellowship）与纽约公共图书馆青年狮子小说奖（New York Public Library Young Lions Fiction Award）等重要的文学奖项。

选段出自《盐之书》的第 14 章和《难言之隐》的第 22 章。前一选段以"意识流"的叙事手法讲述了主人公在过去与现在的结合中试图找回自我的历程，表达了主人公对身份、历史与文化之间复杂关系的探索。后一选段讲述了主人公在越南战争前后在越南与法国的生活经历，表达了主人公对殖民历史和文化身份的思考。

作品选读（一）

The Book of Salt

(Chapter 14)
By Monique Truong

FAME, you tell me, appears in the irides as a circle of flames.

"Bee, those two are going to bask in it."

"Why?"

Your eyes race toward the door, responding to a knock that is not there. A spasm of shame, I think. You, Sweet Sunday Man, are ashamed of yourself, not me. Ashamed that you chose me, a man who may as well be blind, you think. This October will mark my fifth year with my Mesdames. How could Bee not know? you must think. Sweet Sunday Man, I know. I know when my Madame and Madame wake up in the morning. I know the sounds that come from behind their bedroom door when they think that I am not around. I know the cigars that they smoke. I know the postcards that they collect and the women who recline naked on them. I know the old-woman gases that escape from them, and the foods that aggravate them. Brussels sprouts, if you must know. I know the faces of those who are invited often to dinner. I know the backs of those who are asked never to return. I know the devotion that my Mesdames have for each other. I know the faith that they both have in GertrudeStein.

"Why?" I ask again.

"Stein's books."

"Books?"

"Stein writes books, but they are ... unusual, almost not books at all," you try to explain.

I am impressed anyway. Miss Toklas has a scholar-prince, I think.

"Here," you say, crossing the front room of your garret. You point to a row of books sitting by themselves on a shelf, and you say "Here" again.

I see a spine covered in flowers, one in the yellow of banana peels before they are freckled by the sun, one in the gray of my mother's best áo dài, I pick up a book wrapped in the blue of a Bilignin summer sky, and I leaf through its pages. Like rice paper, I think.

"It's vellum," you say, as you try to take the book from my hands.

"Vellum?" I repeat.

Paper resembling the skin of a calf, you explain with hand gestures and playful caresses against my own. I gladly give the book back to you. "Only five," you tell me with the outstretched fingers of your right hand, "deluxe copies were printed." Words printed on skin, I am still thinking. You carefully place the book back on the shelf and exchange it for another: "Here, this one, this is Stein's latest." I take the book from your hands, balancing its top and bottom edges between the tips of my fingers, mimicking how you held it in your own. Last year, you tell me, was a very good one for GertrudeStein. Not only was GertrudeStein published in 1933, but in 1933 GertrudeStein was also read. This is a minor miracle that you hope, by fixing your eyes on mine, that I can understand. "The Autobiography of Alice B, Toklas," you read to me from the book's cover. Hearing the title only in English, I am still able to understand. My Madame wrote a book about my other Madame. How convenient, I think. GertrudeStein would never have to travel far for her stories. They, I suspect, chase her down and beg to be told. You have stayed in Paris to wait for the French translation of The Autobiography, you tell me. A collector, I think. "I've also stayed here," you whisper, "waiting for you."

And am I but one within a long line of others? Are there wounded trophies who have preceded me? But why ask questions, I tell myself, when you are here with me now. Some men take off their eyeglasses, some lower their eyelids. You lower your voice. Desire humbles us in different ways. Your body comes close, and the scent of lime and bay is all around us. You tilt your head. You kiss my lips, lopsided by a smile. Your breath is warmth spreading across the closed lids of my eyes. Your tongue finds the tips of my lashes, flicking them aside. My Madame's books are set down for the night.

So that we are clear, Sweet Sunday Man, I have known from the very beginning that GertrudeStein is a writer. I just did not know that it was her vocation, her métier, as the French would say. From my first day at 27 rue de Fleurus, I have seen my Madame writing, but then again I have seen other Mesdames busying themselves with the task as well. I assumed it was all the same: letters, lists, invitations extended and withdrawn, thank—yous and no-thank-yous. Every afternoon, Sweet Sunday Man, I see GertrudeStein sit down at her writing table, also known as the dining table at other times of the day. After about a quarter of an hour, as if on cue, she rises, searches for her walking stick, and heads out with Basket for their daily neighborhood chat and stroll. When the studio door clicks shut, Miss Toklas appears, not like an apparition but like a floor lamp or a footstool suddenly coming to life. Sudden, yes, but there all along. Miss Toklas may be practical in nature, even staid in appearance, but she is a sorceress all the same.

First, my Madame pushes in GertrudeStein's chair and gathers the papers and notebooks knocked off the table by her Lovey's hands. When I first saw them I thought of overgrown knobs of ginger or sage sausages pushing against their casings. Either way, assertive and unmistakable, I thought. Next, Miss

Toklas wipes away the ink from the fountain pen, replaces the tip that GertrudeStein has flattened like the top of a volcano, and returns the instrument to its red lacquer box. Opening up a nearby cupboard, Miss Toklas places the box inside and takes out a typewriting machine. She sits herself down at the dining table, not in GertrudeStein's chair but in the one to the right of it, and begins to type. The piece of paper, strapped to the machine, flails up and down as each key comes in for a slap or a kick and always looks to me as if it is resisting.

Before meeting you, Sweet Sunday Man, I never thought twice about Miss Toklas's typing. I thought of it as a typical act of overindulgence, like the careful cutting of meat into bite-sized pieces for a child who is no longer one in age, or a singular act of pampering, like the donning of a new pair of shoes in order to soften their leather for the tender feet of a lover. Miss Toklas is capable of doing both. After hearing your predictions about my Mesdames' purported fame, Sweet Sunday Man, I must admit that I am more curious about the cupboard with the heavy black typewriting machine and the red lacquer box lying inside, like the skeletal remains of a once heftier machine and its elongated heart. Who knows what else this cupboard may hold? I think. My curiosity, which is the term that we in the servant trade prefer, tends to peak on Mondays, and, conveniently, Mondays are also when my Mesdames are absent from the rue de Fleurus for the good part of the day.

At the beginning of everyone else's workweek, my Madame and Madame take a leisurely drive around the city, often followed by a chorus of horns, to attend to their errands and occasionally to their friends. Today is no different. I watch from the kitchen window as GertrudeStein lugs a large satchel of books to their automobile. Miss Toklas follows with two *pâtés en croûte*, one perched in each hand. The "meat loaf," as Miss Toklas calls these pastry-wrapped beauties, are going to the homes of two of their friends. "One who is in poor health and another who is just poor," Miss Toklas said. "Skip the truffles in both," she told me. "It is the meat that they need, not the fuss." Miss Toklas has a judicious approach toward extravagances, culinary and otherwise. Waiting inside the kitchen for tonight's supper is a third pâté en croûte with three times the usual amount of "fuss." After all, Miss Toklasisa sorceress: an act of charity and self—indulgence combined into one. Lucky GertrudeStein is always the intended recipient of truffles and other reserved luxuries. Outside, GertrudeStein is sounding like a race car driver and she knows it. Miss Toklas knows it too and places her hands over her ears. The repeated revolutions of the motor, the sounds of petrol pushed into an unwilling machine, wake the concierge, and he leans out of his window and shakes his fist. "Crazy Americans!" he grumbles. GertrudeStein waves back and smiles, assuming that the concierge must have said something to the jovial tune of "Bon voyage!"

My Mesdames are too trusting. They never assume the worst about those around them. Though, sometimes, I think they are just careless about what they care about. Either way, it is an unusual trait in an employer of domestic servants. I once worked for a Monsieur and Madame who placed a chain around the icebox before they went to bed at night. You can keep the damn cold, I thought. I had another Madame who padlocked the door to the toilets before she left the house. The nearby café, as I was forced to discover, required the price of a drink with every flush. Madame, your kitchen sink will have to do when my bladder is too full and my pocket is too dry, she should have heard me thinking. The worst, though, was a Monsieur who locked up the kitchen knives at night and wore the key around his waist. They are the instruments of my trade, for goodness sake! You, Monsieur, do not trust me with your life, but you trust me with your meals? Absurd, *n'est—ce pas*?All of this is to say that I was anticipating a security measure or two with my Madame and Madame as well, but their cupboard opens quietly, easily.I see table linens, bundles of tea-stained cloth tied with mustardy strings, a sort of graveyard for ruined tablecloths, napkins, and runners. I am not surprised that Miss Toklas would save such things. Odd, though, that she would store them in this cupboard, I think. But what was at first glance undeniably cloth turns into reams and reams of paper, as my eyes adjust to the sight, to the ivoried remains of what must be decades' worth of GertrudeStein's one-quarter of an hour. What you would have given to see this, I think. Opportunity presents itself to me so rarely. I am amazed that I still recognized it. Yes, I think, what would you give? Endless Sundays drenched in cathedral bells, the left side of your bed, a good-night kiss instead of a good-bye one, a drawer for my razor and comb, your eyes warm on my face when I am serving you tea in my Mesdames' studio, your desire for me worn there like a red bloom in your lapel.

*   *   *

Every Saturday, I wait. My presence, just inside the entrance to my Mesdames' kitchen, ensures that all the cups are steaming and that the tea table stays covered with marzipan and butter-cream-frosted cakes. Always discreet, almost invisible, I imagine that when the guests look my way they see, well, they see a floor lamp or a footstool. I have become just that.

"Hardly! You're not nearly as bright or useful."

Thank you, Old Man, for showing me the error of my ways.

At the edge of a crowded room, held in place by the weight of my shoes, thick-soled and cracked by the cold, I wait. The heat of so many bodies crowded together but not touching keeps the studio at a comfortable temperature, but the feeling of cold is, for me, a relative thing. Every Saturday, I search this gathering for Sweet Sunday Man's face and catch only glimpses of his back. But today, I tell myself not to be afraid. I will not be cast adrift. It is not only a matter of time. I do not need a reflection in a mirror, red on the blade of a knife, proofs that this body of mine harbors a life. I have my Madame and Madame. As long as I am with them, I have shelter. I am in the center of a hive, and it is Sweet Sunday Man who is the persistent bee. The honey that he craves is the story that he knows only I can tell. Last Sunday when I told him about the cupboard and what my Mesdames have stored inside, his breath left him. Sweet Sunday Man wanted to know the exact number of notebooks. He wanted to know the order of the type-written pages. He wanted to know the exact words that GertrudeStein had written and that Miss Toklas had dutifully typed. I shook my head and shrugged my shoulders. In his excited state, Sweet Sunday Man forgot that the English language is to me a locked door. His breath left him again. He sat down at his desk, and I took that as a sign to begin preparing our evening meal. For the rest of the day, the usual rhythm of our routine prevailed. I cooked and he read. I caught him stealing glances, though. Admiringly, I thought. A sea change, I hoped.

But today's tea is like all the others. At 27 rue de Fleurus, even the furniture attracts more attention than I do. That cupboard is getting glances from all directions. Light from some unseen source is licking at its dark wood, sticking to it like wet varnish. Being at the center of attention can make anything glow, I think. Ah, I should have known. Sweet Sunday Man liked my story about the cupboard. He liked it so much that he repeated it. To everyone in the studio, from what I can see. Sweet Sunday Man, there is a fire at 27 rue de Fleurus. When you and the other guests show up for Saturday tea and see the flames, do you rush in to save my Mesdames, the contents of their cupboard, or their cook? The correct answer is Basket and Pépé. My Madame and Madame, as everyone knows, can take care of themselves. The cupboard also needs no assistance because Miss Toklas would run back into the burning apartment until every sheet of paper touched by GertrudeStein was safe in her arms. As for the cook, the assembled guests would scratch their heads and ask, "The Steins have a cook?"

Sweet Sunday Man, I did not consider my stories about my Mesdames then or now in terms of a barter and trade but as an added allure, a bit of assurance. With my continued "curiosity," I knew that I could offer you something no other man could. With my eyes opened, sensitive to these Mesdames of mine, my value to you I thought would surely increase, double and sustain itself. Value, I have heard, is how it all begins. From there, it can deepen into worth, flow into affection, and artery its way toward the muscles of the heart. My mistake, always my mistake, is believing that someone like you will, for me, open up red, the color of a revelation, of a steady flame. I long for the red of your lips, the red of your life laid bare in my mouth. But I forget that you, Sweet Sunday Man, are flawed like me. You are a dubious construction, delicate but not in a fine-boned way. Delicate in the way that poor craftsmanship and the uncertainty resulting from it can render a house or a body uninhabitable. Dubious, indeed. I hide my body in the back rooms of every house that I have ever been in. You hide away inside your own. Yours is a near replica of your father's, and you are grateful for what it allows you to do, unmolested, for where it allows you to go, undetected. This you tell yourself is the definition of freedom. As for your mother's blood, you are careful not to let it show. You live a life in which you have severed the links between blood and body, scraped away at what binds the two together. As a doctor, you should know, blood keeps a body alive.

Sweet Sunday Man, I marvel at the way that you can change from room to room. I envy the way that you carry yourself when you are in the studio, surrounded by the men who think of you as one of their own. The looseness of your limbs speaks of physical exertion for sport and not for labor. Your movements, large and deliberate, signal a life that has never known inhibition. You, Sweet Sunday Man, take full advantage of the blank sheet of paper that is your skin. You introduce yourself as a writer. You tell stories about a family that you do not have, a city in which you have never lived, a life that you have never fully led. You think yourself clever, resourceful, for always using the swift lines of a pencil and never the considered stroke of the pen. You shy from the permanence of ink, a darkness that would linger on the surface of the page and the skin. You are in the end a gray sketch of a life. When you are in the studio, I see your stance, its mimicked ease and its adopted entitlements. When we are together in your garret, I recognize it as an assumption that you try to rid yourself of, shaking it free from where it clings to your body. In there, in the only rooms in this city that we in truth can share, your body becomes more like mine. And as you know, mine marks me, announces my weakness, displays it as yellow skin. It flagrantly tells my story, or a compacted, distorted version of it, to passersby curious enough to cast their eyes my way. It stunts their creativity, dictates to them the limited list of who I could be. Foreigner, asiatique, and, this being Mother France, I must be Indochinese. They do not care to discern any further, ignoring the question of whether I hail from Vietnam, Cambodia, or Laos. Indochina, indeed. We all belong to the same owner, the same Monsieur and Madame. That must explain the failure to distinguish, the lapse in curiosity. To them, my body offers an exacting, predetermined life story. It cripples their imagination as it does mine. It tells them, they believe, all that they need to know about my past and, of lesser import, about the life that I now live within their present. My eyes, the passersby are quick to notice, do not shine with the brilliance of a foreign student. I have all of my limbs so I am not one of the soldiers imported from their colonies to fight in their Grande Guerre. No gamblers and whores joined to me at the hip so I am not the young Emperor or Prince of an old and mortified land. Within the few seconds that they have left to consider me before they stroll on by, they conclude that I am a laborer, the only real option left. Every day when I walk the streets of this city, I am just that. I am an Indochinese laborer, generalized and indiscriminate, easily spotted and readily identifiable all the same. It is this curious mixture of careless disregard and notoriety that makes me long to take my body into a busy Saigon marketplace and lose it in the crush. There, I tell myself, I was just a man, anonymous, and, at a passing glance, a student, a gardener, a poet, a chef, a prince, a porter, a doctor, a scholar. But in Vietnam, I tell myself, I was above all just a man.

作品选读（二）

Bitter in the Mouth

(Chapter 22)

By Monique Truong

The story of my life, according to DeAnne Whatley Hammerick, began in the fall of 1955, thirteen years before I was born. Young Thomas, twenty-three years old, was in his third and last year of Columbia Law when he met a young woman named Mai-Dao. She was twenty years old and a senior at Barnard. She was a rare bird in his eyes. Young Thomas told her that he was from the South. She told him that she was from the South too. He, unlike many Americans at the time, knew that her country had been partitioned into North and South just the year before. Well, I would have never known; you don't have even a trace of a southern accent, he replied in his leisurely drawl. Then, he fell in love right there on the steps of Low Memorial Library, while the corridor of trees, which led from the street into the wide plaza before them, turned colors. He fell in love, even though Mai-Dao had told him that she was engaged to a young man back home. The school year ended, and she returned to her hometown and young Thomas to his. Before she left New York City, she gave him the photographs of their time together. What she couldn't say to him was that she couldn't keep the photographs. These things, if kept, were always found. They traded their mailing addresses, and he, like a teenage girl, promised to write. He did. He wrote to her many times after he returned home to Charlotte, once after he moved to Shelby, and one more time in 1960, on the day that he moved into the blue and gray ranch house in Boiling Springs with his new bride. Mai-Dao, like a teenage boy, didn't reply.

Over the years, as the name of Mai-Dao's country became a household word even in Boiling Springs, Thomas couldn't see the news of her country's civil war, the deployment of U.S. troops there, and the body bags that returned without thinking of her. In 1968, the year that she gave birth to me, though he didn't know that back then, he thought of her as he watched her hometown—it was the southern capitol, so he thought that it would keep her safe- exploding on his television set. He hoped that she was far away from there. He imagined her back in New York City. He tried to imagine how her world had changed. He tried not to think about her, a married woman, as he was a married man.

On April 30, 1975, Thomas and DeAnne sat riveted in front of their television set as Dan Rather announced that Saigon was "now under North Vietnamese Party control." DeAnne remembered her husband closing his eyes and keeping them shut as he listened to the reporter announcing that Saigon had been renamed Ho Chi Minh City.

The letters addressed to Thomas began arriving at the blue and gray ranch house soon after. They were postmarked Chapel Hill, so DeAnne wouldn't have paid much attention to them, except for the foreign name in the return address.

Then came the telephone call on the night of July 5. It was 11:30 P.M, and DeAnne and Thomas were already side by side in bed. Thomas hung up the receiver and ran out of the house, still in his pajamas. DeAnne heard her husband's car door slam shut. When she heard his car door open, it was 4 P.M. the following day. She went to the front door of the blue and gray ranch house, and I was asleep in his arms.

Thomas had to tell DeAnne the story of my birth mother's life, or what he knew of it. That was DeAnne's precondition for agreeing to my adoption. DWH, the truth teller now, told me that she, in fact, didn't feel like she had a choice. Thomas had already made up his mind. She might as well get the whole story in the process, DeAnne thought. She also thought that it would be better (for her) if she made the decision then and there to believe that what her husband, Thomas, was telling her was true.

DeAnne asked to see the photographs. Then she asked to see the letters. She told Thomas that he had to throw everything away. He promised her that he would. He didn't. After he passed away, she found the photographs in his office. The letters she didn't find there. DWH said that when Thomas showed the letters to her she couldn't bring herself to read them. The handwriting was all curves and delicate loops, and all she could imagine was the body of the woman who wrote the words. DeAnne made Thomas read the letters aloud to her. So as I slept in the guest bedroom of their house,

Thomas and DeAnne sat at the kitchen table and talked for the remainder of the day.

Mai-Dao wrote her first letter to Thomas on May 1, 1975, one day after the fall of Saigon. Mai-Dao had been in Chapel Hill for almost a year already. Her husband, Khanh, an assistant professor of economics at the University of Saigon, was a postdoctoral fellow at UNC, and after much bribing and string pulling back in Saigon,

she and their six-year-old daughter had been able to join Khanh in September of '74.

Mai-Dao took with her to Chapel Hill the last letter that Thomas had sent to her in Saigon. Since the first day of her arrival in his home state, she had been taking mental notes of what she liked about his South, so that she could share them with him. Then she reread his letter, dated December 10, 1960—he*'d written to her on our wedding day, Linda*—and the letter reminded Mai-Dao that she knew nothing about his life in the fourteen years since then. Thomas must be a very different man now, Mai-Dao thought. So she set aside the idea of writing to him and tried as best as she could to settle into her new temporary home, a trailer that Khanh had rented for them in order to make the most of his small monthly stipend. She thought it was a storage shed when they first drove up to it. The interior was the size and width of a corridor in the three-story villa that her father had given to them as a wedding present back in Saigon. Khanh reminded her of how lucky they were to be here and not there.

That became her mantra in the months to come: lucky to be here and not there. She enrolled her daughter in the first grade and was amazed at how quickly a young child could pick up a new language, like it was just a shiny new toy. Mai-Dao audited classes in the art history department of UNC and thought often about traveling up to New York City and seeing the Metropolitan Museum of Art again and, of course, her beloved Central Park. Khanh told her that there was no money for such a pleasure trip. She looked at her husband, amazed at how the young man who had shown up for their dates in a chauffeured car had changed. She couldn't have imagined that he would become so serious and practical, with worry lines cut deep into his forehead. Lucky to be here and not there, she reminded herself. She went to the library and checked out a cook-book—the first one she had ever read—and fed her husband and daughter American-style meals, which the cookbook author, Betty Crocker, assured her were both economical and nutritious. Mai-Dao wasn't a very good cook, so every once in a while she and her daughter would go to the supermarket and indulge in the American snack foods and sodas that she had missed so dearly when she was in Saigon. "Thomas, did you know that there is a soda in Vietnam that tastes exactly like Dr Pepper?" Mai-Dao asked, in the first of her eight letters to him. *I don't know why, Linda, but that always stuck in my head. Maybe because of your grandma. You know how she drank that stuff like water.*

On April 30, 1975, Mai-Dao and Khanh and their young daughter had sat in their rented trailer home in front of a small TV set, one of the few things they owned outright here, and had watched in disbelief as "there" disappeared. Mai-Dao started to cry when she saw the word YESTERDAY appear at the bottom of the tiny screen, the white text superimposed over the footage of the evacuation of Saigon. Khanh whispered in her ear that she shouldn't cry in front of their daughter. Mai Dao stopped, though she knew that it wouldn't change a thing. Her father was a general in the army. Khanh's father was one as well. When Dan Rather reported that South Vietnamese servicemen and their families were among the seventy thousand South Vietnamese who had made it safely to Thailand, Khanh turned to his wife and said that they would hear something from their families soon.

How? she wondered. Who would have had the forethought in the chaos of an evacuation to write down the address of a son and daughter who were lucky enough to be in a city called Chapel Hill? Even its name sounded distant and safe, Mai Dao thought.

Over the next day or two, while her husband went to his office at the university to make the necessary telephone calls, listing their names with the International Red Cross, and trying to reach his distant relatives in Paris, Mai-Dao tried to keep herself from thinking about her mother being shoved and pushed into a helicopter or into a boat—*if my mother was lucky*, Mai-Dao reminded herself—by cleaning the trailer home, washing every item of clothing that the three of them owned at the Laundromat, and writing a long, belated letter to Thomas. "I'm here with my husband and my daughter" was how Mai-Dao began her letter. *Thomas choked up when he read those words to me, Linda. I could have told him to stop reading, but I didn't.*

DWH had been speaking very slowly, pausing in between words, stopping in midsentence. The incomings, given such a cadence, were acute and more assertive than usual, as if the tastes triggered by the words literally had more time to sink in. I had to excuse myself from the kitchen table. I went into the living room and telephoned Kelly at the Greek Revival. I asked her to bring over a bottle of whatever she had. It wasn't even noon, but Kelly, in true form, didn't ask why, didn't sound a bit surprised, and came by the blue and gray ranch house in less than fifteen minutes with a bottle of bourbon, two-thirds full. Kelly came to the back door of the house, said good morning to DWH through the screen door, handed me the bottle thoughtfully hidden inside of a fancy shopping bag underneath a layer of tissue paper, and was on her way again after she had squeezed my hands so hard that my fingers almost went white.

I poured for myself a juice glass full of bourbon and asked DWH if she wanted one as well. I couldn't remember at that moment whether I had explained to DWH about the ameliorative effects of alcohol. We had discussed cigarettes and their effects on my condition during our morning talks, but I wasn't sure whether the topic of alcohol or sex had reached the breakfast table yet. It didn't matter, because DWH answered yes. *You know, your grandma loved to mix that stuff with her Dr Pepper.*

Iris's truth serum of choice, I thought.

13

(Viet Thanh Nguyen, 1971—)
阮清越

作者简介

阮清越（Viet Thanh Nguyen, 1971— ），越南名"Nguyễn Thanh Việt"，美国越南裔作家和批评家，出生于越南邦美蜀（Ban Me Thuot）。1975 年，他随父母逃难到美国并定居下来。1992 年，他从加州大学伯克利分校（UC, Berkeley）获得英语与族裔研究学士学位，1997 年从同一所大学获得英语专业博士学位。毕业后阮清越到南加州大学（University of Southern California）任职。

迄今为止，阮清越创作了颇多优秀的作品，主要有专著《种族与抗争：美国亚裔文学与政治》(*Race and Resistance: Literature and Politics in Asian America*, 2002)、非小说类书籍《永不消逝：越南与战争记忆》(*Nothing Ever Dies: Vietnam and The Memory of War*, 2016)、长篇小说《同情者》(*The Sympathizer*, 2015)和《践诺者》(*The Committed*, 2021)，以及短篇小说集《难民》(*The Refugees*, 2017)等。《同情者》斩获 2016 年的普利策小说奖（Pulitzer Prize）、代顿文学和平奖（Dayton Literary Peace Prize）、卡耐基优秀小说奖（Carnegie Medal for Excellence in Fiction）、埃德加最佳处女作奖（Edgar Award for Best First Novel）与美国亚太文学奖（Asian/Pacific American Award for Literature）等诸多奖项。

选段分别选自《永不消逝：越南与战争记忆》与《难民》。前一选段主要讲述了作者对"公正的记忆"（just memory）的理解、感悟和探索，体现了他作为越南裔对历史与文化独特的理解。后一选段《黑眼女人》（"Black Eyed Woman"）从一个越南裔年轻女性的视角讲述了"鬼魂回家"的离奇故事，描绘了战争给越南裔留下的创伤阴影。

作品选读（一）

Nothing Ever Dies: Vietnam and The Memory of War

(Just memory)
By Viet Thanh Nguyen

THIS IS A BOOK on war, memory, and identity. It proceeds from the idea that all wars are fought twice, the first time on the battlefield, the second time in memory. Any war could prove this claim, but the one that serves personally as a metonym for the problem of war and memory is what some call the Vietnam War and others call the American War. These conflicting names indicate how this war suffers from an identity crisis, by the question of how it shall be known and remembered. The pairing of war and memory is commonplace after the disasters of the twentieth century, with tens of millions of dead who seem to cry out for commemoration, for consecration, and even, if one believes in ghosts, for consolation. The problem of war and memory is therefore first and foremost about how to remember the dead, who cannot speak for themselves. Their unnerving silence compels the living—tainted, perhaps, by a touch or more of survivor's guilt—to speak for them.

Inseparable from this grim and mournful history are more complicated questions. How do we remember the living and what they did during times of war? How do we remember the nation and the people for whom the dead supposedly died? And how do we remember war itself, both war in general and the particular war that has shaped us? These questions gesture at how new wars cannot be fought unless a nation has dealt with its old wars, however imperfectly or incompletely. The problem of how to remember war is central to the identity of the nation, itself almost always founded on the violent conquest of territory and the subjugation of people. For citizens, garlands of euphemism and a fog of glorious myth shroud this bloody past. The battles that shaped the nation are most often remembered by the citizenry as defending the country, usually in the service of peace, justice, freedom, or other noble ideas. Dressed in this way, the wars of the past justify the wars of the present for which the citizen is willing to fight or at least pay taxes, wave flags, cast votes, and carry forth all the duties and rituals that affirm her or his identity as being one with the nation's.

There is another identity involved as well, the identity of war, "the genesis of a nation's soul," as novelist Bob Shacochis puts it. Each war has a distinct identity, a face with carefully drawn features, familiar at a glance to the nation's people. The tendency is to remember any given war, to the extent it is remembered at all, for a detail or two. Hence, World War II is the "Good War" for many Americans, while the tragedy in Vietnam is the bad war, a syndrome, a quagmire, a stinging loss in need of healing and recuperation. The inclination is to remember wars like individuals, separate and distinct. Wars become discrete events, clearly demarcated in time and space by declarations of war and ceasefires, by the inscription of dates in history books, news articles, and memorial placards. And yet all wars have murky beginnings and inconclusive endings, oftentimes continuing a preceding war and foreshadowing a later one. These wars often do not take place only in the territories for which they are named, but spill over into neighboring countries; they are also shaped in war rooms and boardrooms distant from the battlefields. Wars are as complex as individuals, but are remembered by names that tell us as little as the names of individuals do. The Philippine—American War implies symmetry between two nations, yet it was Americans who seized the Philippines and instigated the carnage. The Korean War implies a conflict between Koreans, when China and the United States did more than their fair share of the fighting. In the case of the Vietnam War, Americans invented the name, an odd handcuffing of two nouns that has become normal through constant repetition. So normal, in fact, that even if the name is abbreviated to Vietnam, as it so often is, many people still understand it to mean the war. In response, many have protested that Vietnam is a country, not a war. But long before this cry, some of the Vietnamese (the ones who eventually won) had already begun calling it the American War. Still, if the Vietnam War is an inadequate name in the sense that it misleads us about the war's identity, is the American War any better?

This name excuses the various ways in which Vietnamese of all sides also own the war, from its triumphs and its disasters to its glories and its crimes. Not least the name encourages Vietnamese people to think of themselves as victims of foreign aggression. As victims, they are conveniently stricken with amnesia about what they did to one another and how they extended their war westwards into Cambodia and Laos, countries that a unified Vietnam would strive to influence, dominate, and even invade in the postwar era. These ambivalent meanings of the American War are matched by those found in the Vietnam War. While that name has come to represent American defeat and humiliation, there are also elements of American victory and denial, for the name limits the war's scale in space and time. When it comes to space, either name effaces how more than just Vietnamese or Americans fought this war, and how it was fought both inside and outside of Vietnam. When it comes to time, other American wars preceded it (in the Philippines, the Pacific Islands, and Korea), occurred at the same time (in Cambodia, Laos, and the Dominican Republic), and followed it (in Grenada, Panama, Kuwait, Iraq, and Afghanistan). These wars were part of a century-long effort by the United States to exert its dominion over the Pacific, Asia, and eventually the Middle East—the Orient, broadly defined. Two landmark years bracketed this century. In 1898, America seized Cuba, the Philippines, Puerto Rico, and Hawaii, inaugurating an overseas expansion of American interests that ran into unexpected resistance in 2001, with 9/11 and the ensuing conflicts in the Middle East. The real American War was this entire American Century, a long and uneven expansion marked by a few periodic high-intensity conflicts, many low-intensity skirmishes, and the steady drone of a war machine's ever-on going preparations. The result is that "wartime has become normal time in America."

To argue over the Vietnam War or the American War is thus to argue over false choices. Each name obscures human losses, financial costs, and capital gains, as well as how the war also blazed through Cambodia and Laos, something both the Vietnamese and the Americans wish neither to acknowledge nor remember. The North Vietnamese sent troops and materiel through Cambodia and Laos, and the U.S. bombing of these efforts, as well as the civil wars that flared up in both countries, killed approximately four hundred thousand in Laos and also seven hundred thousand in Cambodia during what the journalist William Shawcross sarcastically called the "sideshow" to the war. If we count what happened in a bomb-wrecked, politically destabilized Cambodia during the Khmer Rouge regime of 1975–1979 as the postscript to the war, the number of dead would be an additional two million, or close to one-third of the population, although some estimates say the count was only 1.7 million, or about a quarter of the population. The body count in Vietnam for all sides was closer to one-tenth of the population, while the American dead amounted to about 0.035 percent of the population.

In tabulating a war's costs and consequences, postscripts should count as well as sideshows, both of which are erased in the names of the Vietnam War or the American War. They contain the damage to the years 1965–1975, to the country of Vietnam, to a death toll of about three million. Counting the sideshows in Cambodia and Laos would raise that number to around four million, while adding the postscripts would make the total approximately six million. Refusing the war's given names acknowledges that this war, like most wars, was a messy business not easily or neatly contained by dates and borders. To deny it a name, as I will do by sometimes simply calling it the war, clears a space for reimagining and remembering this war differently. Denying this war its name also acknowledges what everyone who has lived through a war already knows: their war needs no name, for it is always simply the war. Referring to another war, her own, the writer Natalia Ginzburg says, "We will never be cured of this war. It is useless. We are people who will never feel at ease, never think and plan and order our lives in peace. Look what has been done to our houses. Look what has been done to us. We can never rest easy again."

This war—admittedly, my war—was not even fought only between the two sides in the two names, American and Vietnamese. In reality, these nations were fractured, the United States into its pro—and antiwar factions and the Vietnamese into north and south as well as... ideological positions which did not divide neatly with the geography. The war also had other national participants, Cambodians and Laotians bearing the brunt, but also many South Koreans. To see how they remembered their war and have themselves been remembered, as I will do, is not an attempt at total inclusion and total recall, since I pass over other participants in silence (Australians, New Zealanders, Filipinos, Thai, Russians, North Koreans, Chinese …). But expanding the story to include people outside of Vietnam and the United States is my gesture at both the need to remember and the impossibility of total memory, since forgetting is inevitable and every book needs its margins. Still, my desire to remember as many as I can is a reaction to the lack of inclusiveness found in many, and perhaps most, memories of the war, or at least the ones circulating before the public. What these public memories show is that nations and peoples operate, for the most part, through what I call an ethics of remembering one's own. This ethics has national variations, with the Vietnamese more willing to remember women and civilians than the Americans are, the Americans more willing than the Vietnamese to remember the enemy, and neither side showing any inclination for remembering the southern Vietnamese, who stink of loss, melancholy, bitterness, and rage. At least the United States gave the southern Vietnamese who fled as refugees to American shores the limited opportunity of telling their immigrant story and, by so doing, inserting themselves into the American Dream. The Vietnamese government only offered them reeducation camps, new economic zones, and erasure from memory. Little surprise, then, that the exiled southern Vietnamese also insist, for the most part, on remembering their own. For both nations and their diverse constituents, including the defeated and exiled Vietnamese, an alternative ethics of remembering others is the exception, not the rule. This ethics of remembering others transforms the more conventional ethics of remembering one's own. It expands the definition of who is on one's own side to include ever more others, thereby erasing the distinction between the near and the dear and the far and the feared. Working from both ends of the ethical spectrum, from remembering one's own to remembering others, I thread together the memories of my war's dramatis personae, men and women, young and old, soldiers and civilians, majorities and minorities, and winners and losers, as well as many of those who would fall in between the binaries, the oppositions, and the categories. War involves so many because war is inseparable from the diverse domestic life of the nation. To think of war solely as combat, and its main protagonist as the soldier, who is primarily imagined as male, stunts the understanding of war's identity and works to the advantage of the war machine.

A more inclusive memory of war is also an outcome of the struggle to build what the sociologist Maurice Halbwachs called collective memory, where individual memories are made possible by memories already inherited from the communities to which we belong, which is to say that we remember through others. The critic James Young revises this through his model of collected memories, where the memories of different groups can be brought together in the reassuring style of American pluralism. Any potential dissent between these groups and their memories is tamed by a "ritual of consensus" that is the mythical American Way, says scholar Sacvan Bercovitch. Whether we speak of collective memory or collected memories, these models are only credible if they are inclusive of the group by which they are defined, however great or small. So it is that a call for war is usually accompanied by a demand that the citizenry remember a limited sense of identity and a narrow sense of the collective that extends only to family, tribe, and nation. Thus, the inclusiveness of the American Way is, by definition, exclusive of anything not American, which is why, even today, American memories of the war usually forget or obscure the Vietnamese, not to mention the Cambodians and Laotians. Those who are against war call for a broader human identity that would include those we had previously forgotten, hoping that such expansiveness will reduce the chances of conflict.

This desire to include more of one's own or even others runs into problems both personal and political, for neither individual nor collective memory can be completely inclusive. Total memory is neither possible nor practical, for something is always forgotten. We forget despite our best efforts, and we also forget because powerful interests often actively suppress memory, creating what Milan Kundera calls "the desert of organized forgetting." In this desert, memory is as important as water, for memory is a strategic resource in the struggle for power. Wars cannot be fought without control over memory and its inherent opposite, forgetting (which, despite seeming to be an absence, is an actual resource). Nations cultivate and would monopolize, if they could, both memory and forgetting. They urge their citizens to remember their own and to forget others in order to forge the nationalist spirit crucial for war, a self—centered logic that also circulates through communities of race, ethnicity, and religion. This dominant logic of remembering one's own and forgetting others is so strong that even those who have been forgotten will, when given the chance, forget others. The stories of those that lost in this war show that in the conflict over remembrance, no one is innocent of forgetting.

作品选读（二）

The Refugees

(The Black Eyed Woman)

By Viet Thanh Nguyen

Fame would strike someone, usually the kind that healthy-minded people would not wish upon themselves, such as being kidnapped and kept prisoner for years, suffering humiliation in a sex scandal, or surviving something typically fatal. These survivors needed someone to help write their memoirs, and their agents might eventually come across me. "At least your name's not on anything," my mother once said. When I mentioned that I would not mind being thanked in the acknowledgments, she said, "Let me tell you a story." It would be the first time I heard this story, but not the last. "In our homeland," she went on, "there was a reporter who said the government tortured the people in prison. So the government does to him exactly what he said they did to others. They send him away and no one ever sees him again. That's what happens to writers who put their names on things."

By the time Victor Devoto chose me, I had resigned myself to being one of those writers whose names did not appear on book covers. His agent had given him a book that I had ghostwritten, its ostensible author the father of a boy who had shot and killed several people at his school. "I identify with the father's guilt," Victor said to me. He was the sole survivor of an airplane crash, one hundred and seventy-three others having perished, including his wife and children. What was left of him appeared on all the talk shows, his body there but not much else. The voice was a soft monotone, and the eyes, on the occasions when they looked up, seemed to hold within them the silhouettes of mournful people. His publisher said that it was urgent that he finish his story while audiences still remembered the tragedy, and this was my preoccupation on the day my dead brother returned to me.

My mother woke me while it was still dark outside and said, "Don't be afraid."

Through my open door, the light from the hallway stung. "Why would I be afraid?"

When she said my brother's name, I did not think of my brother. He had died long ago. I closed my eyes and said I did not know anyone by that name, but she persisted. "He's here to see us," she said, stripping off my covers and tugging at me until I rose, eyes half-shut. She was sixty-three, moderately forgetful, and when she led me to the living room and cried out, I was not surprised. "He was right here," she said, kneeling by her floral armchair as she felt the carpet. "It's wet." She crawled to the front door in her cotton pajamas, following the trail. When I touched the carpet, it was damp. For a moment I twitched in belief, and the silence of the house at four in the morning felt ominous. Then I noticed the sound of rainwater in the gutters, and the fear that had gripped my neck relaxed its hold. My mother must have opened the door, gotten drenched, then come back inside. I knelt by her as she crouched next to the door, her hand on the knob, and said, "You're imagining things."

"I know what I saw." Brushing my hand off her shoulder, she stood up, anger illuminating her dark eyes. "He walked. He talked. He wanted to see you."

"Then where is he, Ma? I don't see anyone."

"Of course you don't." She sighed, as if I were the one unable to grasp the obvious. "He's a ghost, isn't he?"

Ever since my father died a few years ago, my mother and I lived together politely. We shared a passion for words, but I preferred the silence of writing while she loved to talk. She constantly fed me gossip and stories, the only kind I enjoyed concerning my father back when he was a man I did not know, young and happy. Then came stories of terror like the one about the reporter, the moral being that life, like the police, enjoys beating people now and again. Finally there was her favorite kind, the ghost story, of which she knew many, some firsthand.

"Aunt Six died of a heart attack at seventy-six," she told me once, twice, or perhaps three times, repetition being her habit. I never took her stories seriously. "She lived in Vung Tau and we were in Nha Trang. I was bringing dinner to the table when I saw Aunt Six sitting there in her nightgown. Her long gray hair, which she usually wore in a chignon, was loose and fell over her shoulders and in her face. I almost dropped the dishes. When I asked her what she was doing here, she just smiled. She stood up, kissed me, and turned me toward the kitchen. When I turned around again to see her, she was gone. It was her ghost. Uncle confirmed it when I called. She had passed away that morning, in her own bed."

Aunt Six died a good death, according to my mother, at home and with family, her ghost simply making the rounds to say farewell. My mother repeated her aunt's story while we sat at the kitchen table the morning she claimed to have seen my brother, her son. I had brewed her a pot of green tea and taken her temperature despite her protests, the result being, as she had predicted, normal. Waving the thermometer at me, she said he must have disappeared because he was tired. After all, he had just completed a journey of thousands of miles across the Pacific.

"So how did he get here?"

"He swam." She gave me a pitying look. "That's why he was wet."

"He was an excellent swimmer," I said, humoring her. "What did he look like?"

"Exactly the same."

"It's been twenty-five years. He hasn't changed at all?"

"They always look exactly the same as when you last saw them."

I remembered how he looked the last time, and any humor that I felt vanished. The stunned look on his face, the open eyes that did not flinch even with the splintered board of the boat's deck pressing against his cheek—I did not want to see him again, assuming there was something or someone to see. After my mother left for her shift at the salon, I tried to go back to sleep but could not. His eyes stared at me whenever I closed my own. Only now was I conscious of not having remembered him for months. I had long struggled to forget him, but just by turning a corner in the world or in my mind I could run into him, my best friend. From as far back as I can recall, I could hear his voice outside our house, calling my name. That was my signal to follow him down our village's lanes and pathways, through jackfruit and mango groves to the dikes and fields, dodging shattered palm trees and bomb craters. At the time, this was a normal childhood.

Looking back, however, I could see that we had passed our youth in a haunted country. Our father had been drafted, and we feared that he would never return. Before he left, he had dug a bomb shelter next to our home, a sandbagged bunker whose roof was braced by timber. Even though it was hot and airless, dank with the odor of the earth and alive with the movement of worms, we often went there to play as little children. When we were older, we went to study and tell stories. I was the best student in my school, excellent enough for my teacher to teach me English after hours, lessons I shared with my brother. He, in turn, told me tall tales, folklore, and rumors. When airplanes shrieked overhead and we huddled with my mother in the bunker, he whispered ghost stories into my ear to distract me. Except, he insisted, they were not ghost stories. They were historical accounts from reliable sources, the ancient crones who chewed betel nut and spat its red juice while squatting on their haunches in the market, tending coal stoves or overseeing baskets of wares. Our land's confirmed residents, they said, included the upper half of a Korean lieutenant, launched by a mine into the branches of a rubber tree; a scalped black American floating in the creek not far from his downed helicopter, his eyes and the exposed half-moon of his brain glistening above the water; and a decapitated Japanese private groping through cassava shrubbery for his head. These invaders came to conquer our land and now would never go home, the old ladies said, cackling and exposing lacquered teeth, or so my brother told me. I shivered with delight in the gloom, hearing those black-eyed women with my own ears, and it seemed to me that I would never tell stories like those.

Was it ironic, then, that I made a living from being a ghostwriter? I posed the question to myself as I lay in bed in the middle of the day, but the women with their black eyes and black teeth heard me. You call what you have a life? Their teeth clacked as they laughed at me. I pulled the covers up to my nose, the way I used to do in my early years in America, when creatures not only lurked in the hallway but also roamed outside. My mother and father always peeked through the living room curtains before answering any knock, afraid of our young countrymen, boys who had learned about violence from growing up in wartime. "Don't open the door for someone you don't know," my mother warned me, once, twice, three times. "We don't want to end up like that family tied down at gunpoint. They burned the baby with cigarettes until the mother showed them where she hid her money." My American adolescence was filled with tales of woe like this, all of them proof of what my mother said, that we did not belong here. In a country where possessions counted for everything, we had no belongings except our stories.

14
(Le Thi Diem Thuy, 1972—)
黎氏艳翠

作者简介

黎氏艳翠（Le Thi Diem Thuy, 1972— ），越南名"Lê Thị Diễm Thúy"，美国越南裔诗人、小说家和表演艺术家。她生于越南藩切（Phan Thiết）的一个小村庄。1978年，她随父亲离开越南，辗转到了新加坡的一个难民营。几个月后，她与父亲到达美国，与来自越南、柬埔寨和老挝的难民一同住在废弃的美国海军营。两年后，黎的母亲和姐姐经过马来西亚的难民营到达美国，一家得以团聚。1998年，黎氏艳翠与母亲回到越南。2001年，黎母病逝，安葬于越南老家。父亲在2003年搬回越南定居下来。童年的不幸、"船民"逃难和离散的生活经历对黎氏艳翠造成了无法磨灭的创伤烙印，同时也为她的艺术创作提供了鲜活的素材。

1990年，她就读于马萨诸塞州的汉普郡学院（Hampshire College），研究文化与后殖民文学。在1993年，她到巴黎研修和学习文化。

她的戏剧作品有《火红的夏天》（*Red Fiery Summer, 1995*）与《我们之间的身躯》（*The Bodies Between Us, 1996*）。她的小说有《我们都在寻找的匪徒》（*The Gangsters We Are All Looking For, 2003*）。黎氏艳翠荣获了古根海姆奖学金（Guggenheim Fellowship）与美国奖学金（USA Fellowship）。

选段出自《我们都在寻找的匪徒》中的《棕榈》（"Palm"）这一章节，讲述了黎氏艳翠一家初到美国时的场景，从一个孩童纯真的视角展现了越南难民在美国生存的血泪历史与心酸经历。

作品选读

The Gangsters We Are All Looking For

(Palm)

By Le Thi Diem Thuy

The swimming pool was in the courtyard, beyond the rusted iron gates of the small red apartment building my father had found when Mel asked us to leave his place. One of the gates had hung lower than the other after my mother backed into it that summer, trying to park our family's new used Cadillac.

The night this happened, we had dragged our mattresses out of the bedroom and were lying on the living room floor, with the front door open to help break the summer heat. Other families in our building had done the same. I could hear voices all around. After a while, Ba fell asleep, but Ma and I lay awake, restless. She rolled out of bed and walked into the kitchen. I thought she was going to pour herself a glass of water. Instead, she took Ba's keys, which were hanging from a nail on the wall, and fishing her pocketbook out from under the mattress signaled for me to come with her.

Ma didn't know how to drive. We got into the car, and she threw her pocketbook on the dashboard. She put both hands on the steering wheel and rocked it back and forth.

"Let's see if this works," she said, slipping the key into the ignition. When the engine started, she smiled and patted the steering wheel. She practiced a couple of times, backing out and pulling into the parking space, and when she felt confident about those maneuvers, she backed the Cadillac into the middle of the street and turned on the lights. We sat there for a minute, giggling. She said, "This is easy. It's easier than riding a bicycle. We can't fall off!" She drove down the very middle of the street, gunning toward stop signs, taking wide left turns, bumping the windshield wipers on by accident so they swayed back and forth, making small squeaking sounds all the way around the block.

Like everyone else in the building, my father heard the crash. As he came running down the stairs, others came walking out of their apartments. Reassured to know that no one in their family was responsible for the present commotion, people leaned over the second-floor railing or ambled across the courtyard, gathering to see what had happened, and to whom.

My father fixed my mother with a look, but before he could say anything, she argued that it wasn't her fault. The car was as big as a boat, she said. Thank... the gates were there, or else the Cadillac would have shot straight into the pool. "And where," she asked, waving her hand toward the passenger seat, "would that have left the child and me?"

My father opened the driver's side door so my mother could step out of the car. I opened the passenger door myself and stepped out. Ma leaned back into the car and grabbed her pocketbook from the dashboard. She didn't have much money in it—she never would—but she liked carrying it everywhere she went. In one motion, she swung the pocketbook under her left arm, fixed it in place by pressing her left elbow tight against her side and reached for my hand. She calmly walked me up the sixteen steps back into our apartment.

Ba climbed into the Cadillac, gently backed it away from the mangled gates, turned the car off and remained sitting in the driver's seat, with the doors closed, the windows up and the lights off, thinking. He then drove the car to the house of a family friend; one of the four uncles Ba and I had come with to America and had lived with for two years, before Ma arrived. The uncle worked as a mechanic at a local garage and he was the one who convinced Ba to get Ma the used Cadillac, a "Welcome to America" present. Ba woke the uncle and, without any kind of explanation, told him that the car was too big. It was too much. He needed something else. The uncle sat up and reached for the pack of cigarettes he kept beside the bed. He thought it was a shame about the Cadillac, but said he understood. Ba gave the uncle the keys to the Cadillac and, a week later, the uncle brought by an orange Mercury Cougar. He said he knew it wasn't much smaller, but it was the best he could do. He threw the keys to Ba, and Ba hid them from Ma.

The morning after Ma crashed into the front gates, the landlord came by to check on the busted washing machine in the laundry room. As he approached, he saw the gates wide open, one of them dented and hanging by a hinge. Between them, the pool lay like a bright blue sheet. It rippled slightly but otherwise it was calm. When he reached the gates, he tried to close them. One gate swung forward easily but the broken one had to be picked up and walked into position. He felt uncomfortable doing this. It was like walking a drunk. But he did it anyway.

As the landlord half carried, half dragged the gate closed—inadvertently shutting himself out of his own courtyard—he silently cursed his tenants. He suspected each and every one of those living in the building's sixteen units. They were all capable of having done this. They were people who broke things: the washing machine, screen doors, kitchen sinks, windows, the back gate and now the front. And they let their children run wild.

Out of the corner of his eye, the landlord saw something flutter. It was an empty rice bag, hanging in an open window of the house next door. Years ago, that house, like many on the block, had begun as something pretty, with yellow curtains in the windows and flowering bushes out front. Had they been roses? It was so long ago. Now the house was nothing more than a shell. When a fire gutted the place, the owners never came to fix it or even to tear it down. The landlord noticed that the neighborhood children had taken over the house; tattered bits of cloth, like the empty rice bag, hung in the windows; the front yard, burnt dry by the sun, was littered with branches of eucalyptus and their cones, as if they'd been blown there by a summer storm.

On the other side of his apartment building was a Church of Jehovah's Witnesses. It was covered in beige stucco and, with its two small watchtowers, looked like a miniature castle on a cake. All it lacked, thought the landlord, were a couple of sentinels, one in each tower to keep guard over the neighborhood.

A baby cried. A woman's voice tried to console it, murmuring in a language the landlord didn't understand. These sounds came from somewhere up on his second floor.

The landlord looked at the gates to his apartment building. They were crookedly yet firmly in place, one leaning heavily against the other. He struggled with the gates for a moment before managing to push his way through.

On his way past the swimming pool, he bent down and picked up some leaves that had gathered in a corner. He cupped the leaves in his hand and felt the water drip between his fingers. Holding his hand away from his body so as not to drip water on himself, the landlord went to see about the washing machine.

I lived upstairs, in a one-bedroom apartment with my mother and my father. She worked as a seamstress, doing piecework at our kitchen table. He worked as a welder at a factory that made space heaters. Neither of them wanted to be doing it; Ma wanted to have a restaurant, and Ba wanted to have a garden. On weekends, my mother liked to watch kung fu movies at the Chinese movie theater on El Cajon Boulevard and my father liked to drink with his friends.

The three of us slept in one room. My parents' double bed was separated from my single bed by a side table with a lamp on it. The base of the lamp was a figurine of an old Chinese man crouching on a rock, his wide pant legs pushed up past his knees. In his hands he held a fishing pole, and his eyes were forever fixed on one spot in the pool of light that was cast back down on the table.

That was the summer when the older boys in the neighborhood started diving off the second-floor railing into the swimming pool in the courtyard below. From our front windows, we would see one boy after another stand poised on the railing for a minute, bend his knees, push off and disappear as the other boys, each waiting his turn, hooted their approval.

From where she sat working at the kitchen table, my mother had a clear view of the divers. "Someone is going to die trying to fly like that," she'd say, carefully feeding small pieces of fabric through her sewing machine. Her words were drowned out by the sewing machine's noise and the boys' cries of "Jump! Jump! Jump!" "Hurry up!" "C'mon!"

I didn't know how to swim then, so my mother told me never to go near the pool. That summer, as I sat with her while she worked, she would issue her warnings. About the pool she told me, "Look at you; you're as small as a mouse. The water is much deeper than you think." About cars she said, "They can hit you and keep going." About the needle on her sewing machine she said, "Watch your fingers; it can move much faster than you can run!" And about boys she warned, "They will try to press you into it."

I wasn't scared. I was curious. I wondered about the swimming pool. How deep was it at its deepest point? How many people would that be, if they stood stacked, each on the shoulders of the one before, with all those beneath holding their breath for how long? What did it feel like to jump as I'd watched the older boys do, leaping off the railing with a sudden push of their feet? Some of them made funny faces on their way down. Some ran in place, their arms and legs racing in the air. One boy, imitating Road Runner, bugged out his eyes and yelled, "Meep, meep!" Others closed their eyes and looked like they were sleeping. They pressed their arms fast against their sides, pointed their toes and plunged into the water like knives. As fast as they fell, the boys popped up again, laughing. Each boy's hair would be plastered against his forehead, every strand shining and neatly in place, as if he was headed for the first day of school or a church Communion or a meeting with a girl.

That summer, with my parents asleep in the bed next to mine, my father lying on his back, his breathing like a whistle, my mother lying on her side, one arm thrown across his chest and her long hair fanning out behind her, I'd lie awake and think about things.

With the sheet pushed down to my waist and one arm cushioning my head, I'd gaze at the rectangular shape of the window above my parents' bed and picture fish in the sea, their gills fluttering like eyelashes; clouds of sand roaming the desert for thousands and thousands of miles; the bright green streak of a gecko darting across a wall; how it felt to ride a horse and whether it made any difference whether it was a black or a spotted one.

15

(Dao Strom, 1973—)
姚·斯托洛姆

作者简介

姚·斯托洛姆（Dao Strom, 1973— ），美国越南裔艺术家，出生于越南西贡（Saigon），越南战争结束前，她随同家人到加利福尼亚州生活。她毕业于爱荷华作家研修班（Iowa Writers' Workshop），目前居住在俄勒冈州的波特兰。

她擅长将文字、声音和视频混合起来创作别具心裁的艺术作品。迄今为止，她创作了诸多颇有影响力的作品，有诗集《乐器》（*Instrument*, 2020）以及它的音乐伴奏《旅行者颂》（*Traveler's Ode*, 2020）、诗歌《你总是'异类'》（*You Will Always Be Someone From Somewhere Else*, 2018）、回忆录《我们本来就是温柔的人》（*We Were Meant To Be a Gentle People*, 2015）、小说《女孩和男孩的温柔秩序》（*The Gentle Order of Girls and Boys*, 2006）与《草屋顶，锡屋顶》（*Grass Roof, Tin Roof*, 2003）。凭借作品，她入围鞭炮诗歌奖（Firecracker Award in Poetry），荣获了创意资本艺术家奖（Creative Capital Artist Award）与俄勒冈州文学艺术职业奖（Oregon Literary Arts Career Fellowship）。

选段出自小说《草屋顶，锡屋顶》的《关岛，1975》（"Guam, 1975"）和《女孩和男孩的温柔秩序》中的《邻居》（"Neighbors"）。前一选段主要讲述了主人公在越南战争结束后逃难到关岛并生存的辛酸经历，表达了作者对战争和难民历史的反思。后一选段讲述了主人公一家作为难民在美国的生活经历，表达了作者对离散、文化与历史之间关系的探索。

作品选读（一）

Grass Roof, Tin Roof

(Guam, 1975)

By Dao Strom

My brother has told me about clinging to the legs and riding on the boots of American GIs in the refugee camp in Guam where we waited a month for passage to the States in May 1975. They were impressively large, these men, and utterly fascinating to my brother, who was nine. The soldiers assisted the Red Cross workers, hauling supplies, setting up tents, handing out blankets, food rations, medicines. With rifles on their shoulders, they patrolled the fenced perimeters of the camp, and my brother and the other boys he played with would watch them. Sometimes they would dare each other to run up behind and touch the soldiers—on the leg, the hand—or say one of the few English phrases they'd recently learned: "Hello, how you do?" or "You number one!" or "Goddamnit." The soldiers would say words in return and make friendly gestures, but my brother could not understand English well. The first few times this happened he froze in shyness, then took off running again the second the soldier's conversation paused. Steadily he grew bolder, though, and lingered longer, as the other boys did.

The GIs gave them small items—packs of gum, a cigarette or two, a candy bar, magazines or comic books, a pencil, a dog tag, wallet pictures of themselves in uniform, and, occasionally, swigs of soda or beer. Some soldiers played with the boys, swinging them around, turning them upside down, hoisting them high onto their shoulders. One time, a boy, as he was being let down, wrapped himself around his soldier's leg, and the soldier proceeded to walk with him sitting on his boot. The other boys thought this was hilarious. Soon it became a ritual game between the boys and the soldiers. Each time the boys saw a soldier walking by, they would run after him, and whoever reached him first would throw himself at the soldier's khaki-covered leg and clamp on. The soldiers mostly humored them, plodding on without pause, or feigning confusion and effort at walking. The boys would hold on for as long as they could, usually just ten or twenty yards, from one end of a row of barracks to the other, then would fall away, rolling across the ground and dramatically acting out a death. There were one or two boys who were clingers to a more severe degree, however, and inadvertently Thien became one of these. Something in a particular soldier's presence caught him one afternoon. He could not let go. For more than half an hour, he clung to this soldier's leg, and the soldier took him on all his errands, to the laundry room, to the post office, to the area behind the mess hall where GIs and kitchen staff stood to smoke, to a building full of other soldiers to get some papers signed. The soldier never glanced down to acknowledge Thien, but his silence was powerful—it exuded a manner of benevolence that was extremely mellow, personal, and unusual. Thien hung on despite the discomfort of sitting so long in this position (his hands were leaving sweat marks on the soldier's pants) and the soldier let him. When others passed and made comments or pointed, the soldier responded only in brief, semiserious tones; that he did not laugh or joke with his peers told Thien something. There was an agreement between them, he and this soldier.

The ride ended when an older American, not in uniform, passed them crossing the commons and barked some commands at Thien's soldier who, now, at last, turned his face toward Thien. His eyes were small in his wide, smooth face, giving the impression that they looked out from somewhere hidden. His look was apologetic but conspiratorial. Thien grinned in understanding, let go, went on his way. For days afterward, though, this soldier's expressions and mannerisms stayed with Thien. He tried to copy them, to smile with a small upturn of his lips and exude the same mysterious, accepting silence. Remembering the soldier was slightly pigeon-toed, Thien began to turn his toes in when he walked. He looked for the soldier to pass their area of the camp every day. Finally, he spotted the soldier one evening outside the mess hall, standing beside another boy, one of those whom Thien played with regularly. The soldier had his hand on the other boy's shoulder. When Thien saw this, a bottled fury rose inside him. He rushed at the other boy, knocking them both to the ground. The two wrestled and rolled in the dirt, pulling hair and clawing at faces.

The soldier broke them apart. His expression was startled but amused. He held them apart with a hand on each boy's chest, his arms stretched out wide.

作品选读（二）

The Gentle Order of Girls and Boys

(Neighbors)

By Dao Strom

Trevor was not the first foreign boyfriend Leena had had, and she initially treated him as she had all the others, with equal parts remove and submission and occasional fits of passion. She had been doing this act for so long, in fact, that she believed in it each time just as whole-heartedly as she relied on its passing and on her resilience: she would always be ready to fall anew.

What she did back then was not an official form of prostitution, more like seduction, or role-playing, as she thought of it. She showed interest, she feigned ignorance; she received gifts and special allowances; in short, she got to enjoy herself. For a period of time, she had ensured her exemption from government harassment by sleeping with certain policemen and municipal leaders under the pretext that she was to find out things about them for certain other men in leadership positions—some of whom she also slept with. Then there were the businessmen from Korea and Japan, and then came the travelers from Europe and eventually the States. She counted on the transience and loneliness of these men and found the ones from the West especially receptive to her and often quite kind in a way that was new to her. She met her first Western foreigner in 1990; Trevor came along in 1995. By that time she had changed her name and had mastered just the right combination of Orient (she had gleaned this to be a romantic but inaccurate, and somewhat generalized, vision of Asian cultures) and sophistication. The name Leena she had taken from one of her earlier Western boyfriends, a Swede, who had told her she looked like a Vietnamese Paulina Porizkova. That was in 1991, before she had ever seen a fashion magazine from the West. He was the one who had left her a British Vogue, and she had found it—for many months—to be very instructive.

The truth was Leena loved men. She always felt sympathy for them. She saw their lust and even their violence in a vulnerable light, for she had seen how they would forsake much in the pursuit of a little bit of pleasure; how even the strongest could be swayed by characteristics that to her were just a given: an appearance of softness, simple prettiness, the willingness to surrender. Men liked to be surrendered to. That was, she believed, another unignorable fact of nature. This need (she could spot it in most men who had it) could prompt them to give her things and to give things up to her. And no matter what they did in the rest of their lives, no matter what significant positions they held in the outside world, no matter what they claimed, she went away with the knowledge that she had known them in their starkness, in the beauty or ugliness or pitifulness of their surrender to a moment totally sensual and senseless. Her surrender was not a big deal: she did it every day, and never, truly, lost anything by it. She did not think about all this explicitly but felt it, in a way, to be a justification of her particular talents in the world. But she was sincere, too, and she made a point of treating all she received and witnessed with care. She had an emotional conscience. It required her to be present for whomever she was with.

After she and Trevor met, she traveled several times with him to other parts of Vietnam, and every now and then they would pick up other travelers, inviting them back to their hotel. Always, before getting married, they took separate rooms at hotels, with Leena claiming to be his interpreter or travel guide. They picked up men and women, usually foreigners, young adventure-seeking types. The first time it occurred, Leena had not been fully aware of what was happening. They had been talking with a young Chinese-American woman at a café, and Trevor was showing her a lot of interest, but not in any manner that seemed licentious to Leena. He was insisting she come see the view from the rooftop of their hotel (a hotel in Hue, overlooking the Perfume River), and Leena had thought nothing of it, because it seemed to her that Trevor was kind and polite to everyone, had in him this streak of helpfulness and genuine concern—not about rescuing people from tragedy so much as wishing to ensure they have a good time. Like a bartender, Leena thought. They walked back to their hotel, the three of them, and it was only by the way the hotel clerks glared at them across the lobby that Leena became aware of there being another kind of energy in the air. She saw then what they saw: two Asian women going up the stairs with one well-dressed, slightly older American man—the type of man who could afford to pay for two rooms. That was new to her.

Trevor monitored pleasure like someone dealing cards, as if there was an unspoken etiquette to it that he wanted to be sure to respect. He was clearly the one in charge but was not forceful, not overexcited or even passionate; he asked if certain actions would be okay before he performed them. Leena relinquished herself to him totally, as if it were a competition between her and the other woman as to who could abandon herself more completely. She felt it to be a dark and tender act, whereas with other men tenderness was not something she had associated with submission. At moments Trevor sat back and just watched, everything in him seeming to be already sated. She understood then that he understood the nature of his own lust and inherent power, as a man and as a man with money, looks, and poise, and from this knowledge he had derived an attitude of seeming benevolence, of luxury even: he was confident that whatever he desired he could acquire.

Another time, on a boat in Ha Long Bay, with a group of other foreign businessmen and a few hired girls like herself, after much drinking and imbibing of other substances, Leena found herself at one point in a narrow passageway in the boat's hold, being fondled and pressed upon by two men. Trevor came down the ladder and looked at them. He said, "Not you," to one, and, with some prying, got him away from Leena. To the other one he said, as the man's hands went groping up her legs, "You let her touch you first." Leena felt strangely endeared to him at moments like these—for his being older than her, for his peculiar way of caring: how he would send her out into the thick of things yet still keep a firm hold on her, still give direction. She felt he protected her. And that loving him meant she must follow, looking only at the trail he made for them as they went, and not at anything else.

They married in Vietnam and then had to wait a year for Leena's paperwork to be processed. Trevor traveled frequently between Southeast Asia and the States during that time, and that impressed everyone Leena knew—family and friends. A man who could move so freely about the world was surely a prize. Leena believed it, too.

16

(Bich Minh Nguyen, 1974—)
阮碧铭

作者简介

阮碧铭（Bich Minh Nguyen, 1974— ），美国越南裔小说家，1974年出生于越南西贡（Saigon）。1975年4月越南战争结束后，她被家人带着逃难到美国，定居密歇根州的格兰德拉匹兹市。她毕业于密歇根大学（University of Michigan），获得艺术硕士学位。她曾在普渡大学（Purdue University）和旧金山大学（University of San Francisco）任教，目前是威斯康星大学麦迪逊分校（Wisconsin-Madison）的创意写作教授。

迄今为止，她创作的作品有回忆录《偷食佛龛供品》（*Stealing Buddha's Dinner*, 2007）、小说《矮女》（*Short Girls*, 2009）和《先锋女孩》（*Pioneer Girl*, 2014）。她的作品斩获了"美国国家图书奖"（National Book Award）、"国际笔会杰拉德与基金奖"（PEN/Jerard Fund），且登上了《芝加哥论坛报》（*The Chicago Tribune*）"年度最佳图书"榜。

选段分别选自《偷食佛龛供品》中的《亚洲快餐》（"Fast Food Asian"）和《矮女》中的第16章。前一选段讲述了主人公与家人在亚洲餐厅吃饭的故事，表达了美越文化之间的差异以及主人公对美国饮食文化的迷恋。后一选段讲述了主人公在经历磨难之后的醒悟和反思，表达了作者对创伤历史和现实生存的考量。

作品选读（一）

Stealing Buddha's Dinner

(Fast Food Asian)
By Bich Minh Nguyen

At home, I kept opening the refrigerator and cupboards, wishing for American foods to magically appear. I wanted what the other kids had: Bundt cakes and casseroles, Chee‧tes and Doritos. My secret dream was to bite off just the tip of every slice of pizza in the two-for-one deal we got at Little Caesar's. The more American foods I ate, the more my desires multiplied, outpacing any interest in Vietnamese food. I had memorized the menu at Dairy Cone, the sugary options in the cereal aisle at Meijer's, and every inch of the candy display at Gas City: the rows of gum, the rows with chocolate, the rows without chocolate. I knew the spartan packs of Juicy Fruit as well as the fat pillows of Bubble Yum, Bubbalicious, Hubba Bubba, Chewels, Tidal Wave, the shreds of Big League Chew, and the gum shaped into hot dogs and hamburgers. I knew Reese's peanut butter cups, Twix, Heath Crunch, Nestlé Crunch, Baby Ruth, Bar None, Oh Henry, Mounds and Almond Joy, Snickers, Mr. Goodbar, Watchamacallit, Kit Kat, Chunky, Charleston Chew, Alpine White, Ice Cubes, Whoppers, PayDay, Bonkers, Sugar Babies, Milk Duds, Junior Mints. Bottle caps, candy cigarettes, candy necklaces, and wax lips. Starburst, Skittles, Sprees, Pixy Stix, Pop Rocks, Ring Pops, SweeTarts, Lemonheads, Laffy Taffy, Fun Dip, Lik-m-Aid, Now and Later, Gobstoppers, gummy worms, Nerds, and Jolly Ranchers. I dreamed of taking it all, plus the freezer full of popsicles and nutty, chocolate-coated ice cream drumsticks. I dreamed of Little Debbie, Dolly Madison, Swiss Miss, all the bakeries presided over by prim and proper girls.

When Rosa cooked on some weekend nights she kept to a repertoire of sloppy joes made with ketchup, tacos with ground beef flavored with spices from the cupboard, meat loaf tinged with cumin, Mexican rice, goulash, pot roast cooked in a pressure cooker until the meat was soft and stringy, and her specialty dish of sopa-ground beef, stewed tomatoes, and egg noodles cooked in a skillet until the noodles burned. These were sensible, no-waste foods. But she wasn't immune to convenience, sometimes buying boxes of instant mashed potatoes or scalloped potatoes, whose hard slices looked just like plastic before they got baked in seasoning mix and milk. Rosa would also consent to a few cans of Beefaroni, frozen Banquet pot pies, and boxes of brandless macaroni and cheese. I was always begging her to buy the boxed lasagna kit from Chef Boyardee. I loved to assemble the lasagna, careful to spread the sauce and cheese so each layer contained equal allocations. If no one was looking I would eat a cold half spoonful of the sweet, beef-tinted sauce. I loved to sniff the grated cheese and let a pinch of it dissolve on my tongue. It was a sharper, smellier smell than the Colby and generic singles Rosa occasionally bought; usually, though, we just wore down the brick of government cheese she got a few times a year from the surplus pile at the Hispanic Institute. She drew the line at Hamburger Helper. Despite my private opinion, she believed she didn't need such a helper and certainly not at those prices.

As with clothes shopping, sales trumped all. I believed she would have fed us Cracker Jacks and Ding Dongs every day if they had been on permanent markdown. She also had clear preferences, like olive loaf instead of bologna, orange Faygo instead of Crush, raisin cookies instead of chocolate chip. She sprinkled wheat germ on grapefruit and bought maple sugar oatmeal over peaches and cream. These small differences accumulated within my growing stockpile of shame and resentment, as if Rosa herself were preventing me from fitting in and being like everyone else. I wrinkled my face at her sopa and the mound of rice she served with shards of dry chicken. I scowled at almost everything we ate, even Noi's pho, shrimp stews, and curries. I wanted to savor new food, different food, white food. I was convinced I was falling far behind on becoming American, and then what would happen to me? I would be an outcast the rest of my days.

But Rosa did not want to be like the Vander Wals next door. She called their midwestern dinners bland, sticking out her tongue for emphasis. She might cook a pot roast, but it was different— richer, she insisted, with real flavor. White American food was as repugnant to her as tulips and the Dutchness and conservatism they represented. Not that I understood this then. I didn't know that Rosa might have felt oppressed in this cold climate, suffocated and isolated. I hadn't arrived at that point yet. I was still in the stage of longing: all I wanted was to sit at the dinner table and eat pork chops the way my friends did. Because I could not, because our household did not, I invested such foods with power and allure.

Rosa had put an end to my father's bringing home candy and gum and Pringles, but when he got a craving he pursued it. He loved Jell-O parfait from the deli aisle, sweet gherkins, braunschweiger, Chicken in a Biskit, two—liter bottles of pop, and cream-filled wafer cookies dyed pink and orange. (I tried to pit him against Rosa's shopping, encouraging him to consider French onion dip to accompany the bargain bag of Jays, or better yet Tato Skins for their "baked potato appeal," as the commercials promised.) He was fond of gadgets and purchased the first microwave oven on our street. I bragged about it to all of my friends. The microwave was so American in its efficiency and sleekness, with its green digital display and buttons that beeped whenever I touched them. In a flash I could make my favorite snack of instant cocoa and baked potatoes.

One thing the whole family could agree on was fast food. Like the Chicken Coop, which offered up tubs of fried chicken with delicate, super-crispy coatings that smelled of butter, herbs, and fat. Happy were the evenings my father brought home an extra-large bucket, with sides of coleslaw, biscuits and honey, and mashed potatoes and gravy. Anh and I liked the drumsticks for their portability and ease, and because kids on Shake 'n Bake commercials always looked so happy crunching on them. Crissy only ate the white meat of the breast. My father, uncles, Noi, and Rosa reached for the thighs where the meat was darkest and juiciest. When at last only bones remained, cleaned by my father and Noi, Anh and I picked up the little fried bits left at the bottom of the bucket. We tipped it back into our wide-open mouths to catch every last crumb.

The Chicken Coop napkins were printed with laughing roosters and somber psalms. Upon the wicked He shall rain snares, fire and brimstone, and a horrible tempest: this shall be the portion of their cup. The words turned translucent from the grease on our hands. When I asked Rosa what such sayings meant she snapped, "They mean nothing," and threw the napkins away.

In the fall of 1982 Burger King launched a campaign to make the Whopper America's number one hamburger. My father happened to love the char-grilled taste of Whoppers—the tomato and onion, creamy with mayonnaise and ketchup; the thin slices of pickle. Burger King was a family treat, and any car ride toward it meant blissful calmness; no one dared to fight and ruin the experience. One day my father heard that Burger King was running a fantastic promotion: to celebrate winning a national taste test they were giving away free Whoppers for one day only. All you had to do was step up to the counter, say, "Whopper beat the Big Mac," and you'd get a free Whopper Junior, one per person. To the Burger King my family urgently repaired, wondering if we would get there in time, and if the place would run out of burgers. There was quite a line at the restaurant, which created an audience for each person's statement. My father spoke the words proudly, having rehearsed them in the car. Rosa went next, then Crissy and Anh, then me. I froze. Suddenly it felt like everyone was staring at me, and I lost the ability to speak. For one terrible minute I was the stupid, funny-looking girl to mock and deride.

My father nudged me, then made at skiing clicking sound. It was the noise he made when he was getting angry. I knew how swiftly that noise could escalate into a shout, his red-faced temper taking over. He would hurl keys, plates, shoes—anything nearby—against a wall. Out of the corner of my eye I could see my sisters looking intently away, as if already separating themselves from me, freeing themselves from tangential blame. I leaned forward and whispered, "Whopper beat the Big Mac."

My father clapped, and I got my burger. He ordered fries and pop for everyone, and as we claimed a table I saw how happy he was. He was practically cackling, as though being here with our free Whoppers signified some true victory.

Noi was the holdout. She might go along with us to Burger King, and would even accept a few fries, but her disdain for the place was as visible as the paper crowns Anh and I wore while we ate. Noi had little use for American food. She would have preferred to avoid it completely, but she couldn't ignore the way I started pushing her beef and onion sautés around my plate. I hadn't stopped liking her food—*cha gio* and pickled vegetables still held an iron grip on my heart—but now I knew what real people ate. And in my mind I used that term:real people. Real people did not eat*cha gio*. Real people ate hamburgers and casseroles and brownies. And I wanted to be a real person, or at least make others believe that I was one.

The closest Noi came to cooking American food was making french fries her way, wedge-cut, served with vinegar and lettuce, and thin steaks pan-fried with onion and garlic. These, along with a bowl of my favorite misoup-shrimp-flavor Kung-Fu ramen-made lunches and dinners to dream about. Still, I knew that no one at school had homemade french fries, or ramen. No one at school knew how I really ate. They didn't know how much time I spent thinking of dinner, of stolen popsicles, of ways for a Whopper to rise up and beat, once and for all, the Big Mac.

For I realized that the other kids scorned Burger King. McDonald's was the cool thing, and at recess girls clapped hands with each other and sang,Hamburger, filet-o-fish, cheeseburger, french fries, icy Coke, thick shakes, sundaes, and apple pies.They even had birthday parties in the McDonald's playroom, where each girl got her own Happy Meal with a Strawberry Shortcake figurine. The Whopper had a long way to go to beat the Big Mac. In the gaze of my classmates I understood the satisfaction of symmetrical yellow arches. Even the hamburgers were tidier, more self-contained; no one at McDonald's spilled onion and ketchup with each bite. The very word McDonald's rolled more easily off the tongue—a sturdy lilting name, nothing there to make fun of, against the guttural, back-of-the-throat emphasis of Burger. Once in a while Chu Cuong and Chu Dai alleviated my fast food sorrow by taking my siblings and me to McDonald's. Despite my father and Burger King's campaign, Chu Cuong had developed a fondness for the Big Mac, and he always ordered dessert: apple or cherry pies, deep-fried, gorgeously oblong and brown and burning hot as they slid out of their thin cardboard sleeves.

Chu Cuong and Chu Dai were also the ones who drank extravagant amounts of Sprite, shunning the two-liters of RC and Squirt we usually had in the house. They let us kids keep the cans for the deposits—ten cents in Michigan, which added up fast for candy purchases. Chu Cuong would toss his empty pop cans into the backseat of his blue Thunderbird and wait until they piled up, a shimmering mosaic of silver and green. Then after we collected them in trash bags he'd ferry us to Meijer's bottle return center. Carrying the sacks across the parking lot, he was like a vision of a Vietnamese Santa.

Next door, the Vander Wals' oldest daughter, Jennifer, was almost my age. She was blond with matching socks and unscuffed shoes. When summer emerged we found ourselves face to face across the strip of grass that separated our driveways, just bored enough with our siblings to become friends with each other.

Jennifer introduced me to the concept of homemade, which I only associated with American food, when she gave me half of a cookie her mother had baked. Nestlé's Toll House, she called it, and I thought, You name your cookies? But it was like no cookie I had ever had. It was crumbly and rich, the chocolate chips bearing no resemblance to the pinpoints found in Chips Ahoy. In our house, cookies came from Keebler, Nabisco, or, more frequently, the generic company whose label shouted "COOKIES" in stark black letters. Once in a while, at my father's request, Rosa brought home Voortman windmill cookies, or the cream-filled pink and yellow wafers that were as dull to me as graham crackers.

The concept of homemade cookies struck me as suspect and impossible. "What do you mean, your mom made them?" I demanded.

Jennifer tried to explain the flour and sugar and Crisco, her mother's big mixing bowl and cookie sheets. I had thought all American food came from a package and some mystical factory process. The idea that a person could create such a thing at home was a revelation. And then, a desire.

I wondered how many more layers of discovery stood between me and true Americanness. I decided that even if Rosa wouldn't let me change my name, I could change myself anyway. I could keep secrets: from my white friends at school and from my family at home. At school I was good, as neat with my homework as any other girl and just as well behaved. At home I stole food, sulked in my grandmother's closet, and in fits of unexplained rage threw Rosa's clean clothes down the laundry chute.

It was exhausting, this secrecy, this effort to be normal, and I took to wandering the house at night when everyone else was asleep. I liked being invisibly in-between, a shadow dissolving into itself. My father and stepmother believed in silence and fear; they made strict rules to contain their possible unraveling. In truth, I had a thousand questions about my face and my race, but it was so much easier to deny them than to speak out loud and court the embarrassment and shame that always lay in wait for me. As I stood at the living room window, the street lamps seemed to cast an eerie glow over the neighborhood. I wrapped myself in the yellowed nylon curtains my stepmother had hung and wondered what it would be like to live in any other house.

作品选读（二）

Short Girls

(Chapter 16)

By Bich Minh Nguyen

At sunset they ate Van's birthday cake on the back patio, using the furniture that was being sold to a professor at the university. Then a cleaning service would come in to shine the floors downstairs and shampoo the carpets upstairs. "It'll be all new again," Van said with a hint of melancholy. Linny was impressed by what she could only call Van's fortitude. So far she'd never even seen her shed a tear for Miles, though Linny attributed that, more likely, to Van's inborn sense of privacy.

"I bought you some clothes for your birthday," Linny told her. "And you can't return them."

"I'm not talking about clothes again. Not if you want to hear about Dad and Nancy Bao."

Linny was surprised. "What about them?"

"I saw her when I went home to see Dad. She came over to the house, and she didn't know I was going to be there."

Linny exchanged a look with Tom. "I told you!" she exclaimed. "Why didn't you tell me this before? They really are still together."

"That's the thing I was trying to figure out, because I don't think they are. Nancy came over to take care of the house."

She explained how Nancy, surprised to see Van there, had told her that she sometimes stopped by to check on Mr. Luong, bringing him a few sweet bean pastries or a magazine he might like. She had been the one to tell him about the reality TV show audition, after reading about it in a newspaper. She had also been helping him tidy up the house a little, get things organized. She had kept the living room credenza dusted, the sticks of incense replenished.

When Van asked Nancy why she did all this, she simply said that people in the community cared about Dinh Luong.

"That's all I got out of her," Van finished. "She probably thinks we're bad daughters for not being there all the time to take care of Dad. And I think she must blame me for Na, which I guess is deserved."

"That wasn't your fault," Linny said quickly at the pained look crossing her sister's face.

"Anyway, this still doesn't answer the question about them. There may be nothing more than an old friendship. Maybe there was more once, but I don't think there is now. It just didn't seem like it."

"I did notice sometimes," Linny said, realizing it as she spoke, "that when I would visit Dad the house wouldn't be as dirty as I thought it would be. I thought it was you, or that he cleaned and shopped only when he remembered to or when he felt like it. But that doesn't mean there isn't something else going on with Nancy." She turned to Tom. "What do you think? You live in that town—you hear the gossip."

"I don't know any more than you do," he admitted. "I never saw your dad and Nancy in the car and I've never heard anyone gossip about them. Lots of people have said that Rich and Nancy hardly ever talk to each other but who knows what that means. Who does talk to Rich Bao?"

Linny couldn't help thinking the mystery extended beyond her father and Nancy, out to their friends, their community and generation, the stories they told and wove about Saigon. Maybe it was their own way of making sense of how they'd gotten from Vietnam to America. That whole generation had its own language, its own clinging to tradition. What are your children going to understand? Her mother had said, meaning they were going to be thoroughly American. The idea had scared her. It was one of the reasons she wanted Linny and Van to go to Vietnam with her.

Maybe Van was thinking about their mother too, because she said, "Look at the sky."

The stars had started to pop out even before the sun fully set. Linny wondered if her sister was trying to keep that last moment in Ann Arbor, trying to take it all in. "You know what? Mom will never know that all this stuff has happened. I feel like we should tell her that you're moving."

Sitting next to her, Tom took her hand.

"I used to think that all the time," Van said. "Maybe that's why Dad stays where he is."

"Maybe."

But it seemed a revelation to Linny, a possible answer to his identity. All her life Linny had thought of him whenever she stood on her tiptoes, straining to reach a package of pasta or a box of tea on a high shelf. She thought of him when in a crowd, craning to look around people's heads, careful to keep track of elbows so as not to get slammed in the face. She thought of him too when entering a room with tiled floors. She had tried to see, or maybe couldn't help but see, the world from his point of view.

She remembered being a tiny girl, staring at people's legs while waiting for some parade—maybe a Fourth of July festival or the Tulip Time celebration in the lakeside town of Holland. All Linny recalled was seeing other people's thighs. Pant legs and skirts all around her, close enough for Linny to see the weave of cotton and the sparkle of poly. Her mother had kept her close, her father standing nearby with Van. On that one day they had seemed like sentries. And then Linny had grown up—though not as up as she had hoped and assumed. She remained, and Van too, the short girls their father had told them they would always be.

In the early shadows of dusk, Linny accepted this. Words hovered in front of her *The Short Girl Café*. Bright reds and yellows. Oncidium orchids. And Linny, years from now, sitting down at a table with her father, her sister, Tom. And more. No menus, just rounds and rounds of plates brought out to them on the longest day of the year. Then they would go outside or up to a roof, just in time to get as much of the sky as they could bear. It's what Linny will have learned to wait for. All that blue. She will see it again and again, crossing the world to follow it home. Each time she will hold out her hand, wishing to save just a little of it, to try to catch the falling hour.

17
(Thi Bui, 1975—)
裴施

作者简介

　　裴施（Thi Bui, 1975— ），美国越南裔插画小说家（graphic novelist）和画家。1975年1月，她出生于越南西贡（Saigon）。越南战争结束后，父母带着襁褓中的裴施与其他子女坐船逃难，到了马来西亚的一个难民营。三年后，裴施一家得到美国人的资助，离开了难民营，移居美国。裴施目前在加州艺术学院（California College of the Arts）任教。

　　2017年，裴施出版了她的第一部插画小说《尽力而为》（*The Best We Could Do*, 2017），记录了她们一家作为难民的生活经历，深入探讨了移民、战争和代际创伤的主题。这本书被提名2017年美国国家书评协会奖（National Book Critics Circle finalist）与2018年艾斯纳奖（Eisner Award finalist），2018年获得美国图书奖（American Book Award）。2019年，她与越南裔作家阮清越合作创作了儿童绘本《海盗鸡》（*Chicken of the Sea*, 2019）。阮清越和他的儿子艾里森负责故事的构想和写作，裴施与自己的儿子负责插画的部分。这本书倾注了阮清越与裴施对孩子的爱，记录了父母与子女之间美好的交流经历。

　　选段出自《尽力而为》中的第9章《火与灰》（"Fire and Ash"），讲述了主人公一家在美国的成长经历和心酸历史，表达了作者对战争历史、难民身份和文化冲突的反思。

作品选读

The Best We Could Do
(Excerpt)

BY Thi Bui

CHAPTER 9
FIRE AND ASH

Má found us our own apartment as quickly as possible.
We received food stamps and assistance for families with children at first...
U.S. DEPARTMENT
FOOD C
VALUE
...but we got off welfare as soon as Má could support us with her job.
On $3.35 an hour and countless sacrifices,
little by little
my parents built their bubble around us-
our home in America.

They taught us to be respectful,
to take care of one another,
and to do well in school.
Those were the intended lessons.
The unintentional ones came from their unexorcised demons...
...and from the habits they formed over so many years of trying to survive.

152　美国越南裔文学作品选
An Anthology of Vietnamese American Literature

Our most important possession was this unassuming brown file folder—

—in which my parents placed the most essential pieces of our identity.

Our birth certificates, translated and notarized,

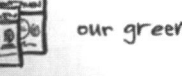

our green cards,

and our Social Security cards.

When we began school, we were each given a brown folder of our own.

Into this folder went our report cards,

certificates and awards,

and the annual class picture.

No individual school pictures. Those were too expensive.

When I was nine, my parents passed the test to become American citizens, and our naturalization papers went straight into the Important Documents folder.
Eventually, Lan's and Bich's folders reached capacity,
and the awards became wooden plaques and shiny trophies that adorned their bedroom.
SCIENCE
Má's friend from work often drove them to School functions.
I don't understand why your husband won't go to your kids' awards nights!
Such bright kids- why wouldn't he be proud of them?
Sigh. It's just not our way to show it so much.
By the time Lan and Bich graduated high school and went to college,
CLASS OF '84 VALEDICTORIAN
CLASS OF '86 SALUTATORIAN
Má had acquired her own certificates,
piecing together lunchtime workshops and night courses to build up the career she had begun on the assembly line at three dollars an hour.

Hằng, you're such a good student.
Would you stay on as a teaching assistant next term?
What do you think?
It means I'll have to keep driving you at night.
I have my license.
I can drive.
It's different here! You won't be able to do it.
You know, you could use the course credits I earn...
...and study something you like.
Bố tried his hand at graphic design,
PLATT COLLEGE
while Má continued courses in mechanical drafting.
I loved looking at the drawings they each made.

But what I loved more were the nights when they were at school, because Lan and Bich would come home from college to watch us.
I remember two kinds of spaghetti...
Wow, meat sauce AND squash and mushrooms?
...and bedtime stories from "The Iliad."
After Paris steals Helen and runs away with her...
...Agamemnon leads the Greek fleet to attack the city of Troy.
I'd lie there, savoring the luxury of spending time together...
...the marvel of being told STORIES in BED, and the curious FREEDOM of being home without our parents.

One night when I was fourteen...
Thi.
Do you want to watch a movie? Bố rented "Die Hard."
Okay!
It was Tết.
DIE HAR
That's why my parents happened to be at home.
CRASH POW
Lan and Bích came home a lot less
We're studying tonight, Má.
and Tâm and I were left alone more.
Move your head.
CRASH

158　美国越南裔文学作品选
An Anthology of Vietnamese American Literature

Thi Bui 159

160　美国越南裔文学作品选
An Anthology of Vietnamese American Literature

The fire had started downstairs.

The old couple- smokers with emphysema-

-fell asleep with a lit cigarette.

Their oxygen tanks exploded.

This is the night I learned what my parents had been preparing me for my whole life.

304

Thi Bui 161

162　美国越南裔文学作品选
An Anthology of Vietnamese American Literature

18

(Vu Hoang Tran, 1975—)
陈禹申

作者简介

陈禹申（Vu Hoang Tran, 1975— ），美国越南裔作家，出生于越南西贡（Saigon）（今胡志明市）。他从塔尔萨大学（University of Tulsa）获得学士学位，从爱荷华作家工作室（Iowa Writers' Workshop）获得硕士学位，从内华达大学拉斯维加斯分校（University of Nevada, Las Vegas）获得博士学位。他目前在芝加哥大学（University of Chicago）教授创意写作课程。他荣获过怀丁奖（Whiting Award）和劳伦斯基金奖（Lawrence Foundation Prize）等重要奖项。他的作品在《南方评论》（*Southern Review*）、《哈佛评论》（*Harvard Review*）、《密歇根季评》（*Michigan Quarterly Review*）与《安提俄克评论》（*Antioch Review*）等重要期刊上发表。

《龙鱼》（*Dragonfish*, 2015）是陈禹申的代表作，也是目前为止唯一一部已出版的作品。这部小说讲述了一名奥克兰警察在拉斯维加斯苦寻越南裔妻子的故事，引发了种族、身份、创伤记忆与文化冲突等问题的思考。

选段出自《龙鱼》的第二章和最后一章。前一选段围绕搜集"失联"妻子的信息展开。在最后一章中，主人公揭开了所有有关妻子的谜团，更进一步了解了妻子的过去。罗伯特发现，他与妻子之间存在的不仅仅是感情问题，而是更加深层的种族问题、殖民历史和战争经历方面的问题。

作品选读

Dragonfish

(Chapter 2)
By Vu Hoang Tran

WHEN SUZY LEFT-ME, it was easy at first. No children. No possessions to split up. No one really to care. I was an only child, my parents both years in their graves, and her entire family was either also dead or still in Vietnam. After eight years together, I'd gotten to know maybe two or three of her friends, and the only things my police buddies knew about her was her name and her temper.

She gave me the news after Sunday dinner. I was sitting at he dining table, and she approached me from the kitchen, her mouth still swollen, and said, "I'm leaving tomorrow and I'm taking my clothes: You can have everything else." She carried away my half-empty plate and I heard it shatter in the sink.

The first time I met her, I knew she was fearless. I was responding to a robbery at the flower shop where she worked. She'd been in America almost a decade, but her English was still pretty bad. When I arrived, she stood at the door with a baseball bat in one hand and bloody pruning shears in the other. Before I could step out of the patrol car, she flew into a tirade about what had happened, as though I'd been the one who robbed her. I understood about a quarter of what she said—something about a gun and ruined roses—but I knew I liked her. That petite sprightly body. Her lips, her cheekbones: full and bold. Firecracker eyes that glared at people with the urgency of a lit fuse. We found the perp two miles away, limping and bleeding from a stab wound to his thigh. The pruning shears had done it. Suzy and I married four months later.

I was thirty-five then, an age when I once thought I should already have two or three kids, though I suspected she, at thirty-thee, had given little thought to her own biology, let alone he passage of time. When I proposed, she agreed on the spot, but only if I was okay with not having children. She was not good with kids, she said, and having them would hurt too much, two reasons she repeated when I brought it up again a year later and third time the year after that. I always figured she'd eventually change her mind.

Her real name was Hong, which meant "pink" or "rose" in Vietnamese. But it sounded a bit piggish the way Americans pronounced it, so I suggested the name of my first girlfriend in high school, and this she did give me, though her Vietnamese acquain-tances still called her Hong.

When we married, neither of us seemed to have any worldly possessions beyond our clothes and the car we drove. It was like we had both, up until the time we met, lived our adulthoods at some cheap motel, so that we knew nothing about domesticated life beyond paying bills and doing laundry. We combined all our savings and bought an old townhouse near Chinatown that I repainted and she furnished—a luxury she'd apparently never had and one she indulged in with care and sincerity, down to the crucifixes that adorned every room and the two brass hooks on the wall of the entryway, the one for my coat a little higher than hers.

In our first year, we bonded over this novelty of owning a home, of living with another human being and building a brand-new life together with chairs and tables and dishes and bath towels. We were happy, I realize now, not because of what we actually had in common, but because we were fashioning this new life out of things that had never existed for either of us.

I'd stop by the flower shop every afternoon during my patrol to visit her. We had two days of the week together, and we spent it fixing up the townhouse, exploring local consignment shops, trying out every cheap restaurant in Chinatown, then going to the movies (Westerns and old black- and-white detective films were her favorite) or walking the waterfront, where the smell of the ocean reminded her of Vietnam. For a long time I didn't mind losing myself in her world: the Vietnamese church, the food, the sappy ballads on the tape player, her handful of "friends" who with the exception of Happy hardly spoke a lick of English, even the morbid altar in the corner of the living room with the grue-some crucifix and the candles and pictures of dead people she never talked about. That was all fine, even wonderful, because being with her was like discovering a new, unexpected person in myself.

But after two years, I realized she had no interest in discovering me: my job, my friends, my love for baseball or cars or a nice steak and potato dinner. She hardly ever asked me about my family or my upbringing. She must have assumed, because of her silence about herself, that I was equally indifferent to my own past. She didn't know that until her I had not thought of Vietnam since 1973, when I was eighteen and the draft ended and saved me from the war, and that all of a sudden, decades later, this distant country—this vague alien idea from my youth—meant everything again, until she gradually embodied the place itself, the central mystery in my life. The least she could do was share her stories, like how happy her childhood had been and how the war upended everything, or what cruel assholes the North Vietnamese Party were, or how her uncle or father or neighbor had died in battle or survived a reeducation camp, or *something*. But she'd only say her life back home was "lonely" and "uninteresting," her voice muted with hesitation, like she was teaching me her language and I'd never get it anyway.

Gradually, an easy distance settled between us. I found I loved her most when she was sick and had no choice but to let me take care of her. Feed her. Give her medicine. Keep her housebound, which she rarely was for more than a day. And since I'd apparently reached the limit of what she was willing to give me, I grew fond of any situation where she'd talk about herself, even if it was her waking in the night from a bad dream and then, in the grip of her fright, waking me too, so I could lie there in the darkness and listen to her recount it.

She had bad dreams constantly. Recurring ones where I had cheated on her and hurt her in some profound way and she's beating me with her fists as violently as she can and yet all I'm doing is laughing and laughing as she throttles me in the face. Sometimes it's another man in this dream, though she'd never say who that might be—perhaps a lover from her past whose sins she was now mistaking for mine. Then there were the dreams where she's murdered someone. Not just one person but a lot of people. She doesn't murder them in the dream, she's only conscious of having done it and must now figure out how to cover it up. In one version, she has buried them under piles of clothes in the closet. In another, she has shoved them into the washer, the' dryer, that large cabinet in our laundry room where she kept all the strange pickled foods I could never force myself to like. And the entire time, all she can think about it is that she has killed people and that her life is now over.

I remember her describing one dream where she's walking for hours through an empty furniture store and someone is following her as she makes her way across beautiful model bedrooms and kitchens and living rooms. Even as she climbs the stairwells from one floor of the store to the other, the person keeps following her, their footsteps loud and steady. I asked if she ever saw what the person looked like, and she said she couldn't make herself stop or turn around in the dream, and that all she wanted was for the person to catch up to her, take her by the shoulder, and show their face.

To church every Sunday, she brought along a red leather-bound journal, worn and darkened with age, and held it in her lap throughout Mass like a private Bible, except she never opened it. She said it was a keepsake from the refugee camp and that it made her feel more right with God at church, whatever that meant. At home, it lay on the altar beneath the crucifix. I opened it once. The first few pages, brittle and yellowed, were written in someone else's handwriting, the rest in Suzy's tiny Vietnamese cursive, which was already hard to read. I tried translating the first page with a bilingual dictionary but could get no further than the opening sentence. Something about rain in the morning and someone's mother yelling at them. Suzy once forgot the book at church and didn't realize it until bedtime. She wanted to go right then and there to retrieve it, insisting, "Someone is always there!" But I refused to let her go. At dawn the next morning, after a long, sleepless night, she drove to church and came home with the journal clutched to her chest like a talisman, her eyes red from crying. She did not speak to me the rest of the day.

She could go an entire week without speaking. A way at first to punish me for whatever I had done to anger her, though gradually, almost every time, her silence outlasted her anger and became a retreat from me and into herself, an absence actually, as though she had gotten lost in whatever world she had escaped into. Her temper—that flailing beast inside her that she herself hated—would retreat as well, and the only thing left between us until she spoke again was what we had said and done to each other when we fought: about money we didn't have and the children we weren't having, about what to eat for dinner, about my poor driving and my poor taste in clothes and a million other things I can't remember anymore. I always played my part, stubborn and mouthy as I am, my own temper always burning brightest before hers exploded. She'd go from yelling at me to lunging at me, those eyes erupting out of her face as she slapped and punched my chest or seized my neck with both hands. Both of us knew she was not strong enough to hurt me, and on a certain level I think she went out of her way to avoid it, never throwing or breaking anything in the house, never once using anything but her hands and her words. Even as I held her wrists and let her scream at me, let her kick me in the stomach or the legs, it sometimes felt as though she were asking me—with her hateful, pleading eyes—to hold her back and tie her to the mast until the storm passed. Because inevitably she'd crumple to the floor and cry herself into a numb silence and eventually into bed, where she would begin withdrawing from me and the world.

Sometimes we didn't need an argument. She'd be talkative and affectionate in the morning, and then I'd come home in the evening and she'd seem afflicted with some flu-like melancholy that only silence and aloneness could treat. So I learned to let her be. I turned on the TV in the kitchen during dinner. I turned up the music in the car as she sat staring out the window. I spent more and more time with friends at the bar or at our weekly poker game. I slept in our spare bedroom, which was otherwise never used.

Once or twice a year, I'd startle awake in the middle of the night and find myself alone in bed, the house empty, her car still parked in the driveway. An hour later the front door would open and she'd be barefoot in her nightgown and a jacket, having taken one of her nocturnal walks through the neighborhood... knows what for or where to. She'd crawl back into bed with-out explaining anything, despite my stares and my questions, and in the morning I'd notice the dirty bottoms of her feet, the stench of cigarettes on her clothes, the whiff of alcohol on her breath. One evening I came home from work and every single light in the house was on, and she was out back beneath the apple tree, curled up and asleep on the grass, empty beer bottles lying beside her with crushed cigarettes inside.

Then, after a few days, sometimes as long as two weeks, without any hint whatsoever of reconciliation, she'd crawl into my arms while I lay on the couch watching TV, roll over in bed and bury her face in my chest, join me in the shower and lather me with soap from my head to my feet. I never knew how to feel in these moments, whether to love her back or commence my own week of silence. Not until she started talking again, recounting some funny incident at the flower shop two weeks before, or describing some movie she'd seen on TV at three in the morning, would I then feel her voice burrow into me, unravel all the knots, and bring us back to wherever we were before the silence began. Then we'd make love and she would whimper, a childlike. thing a lot of Asian women do, except hers sounded more like a wounded animal's, and that would remind me once again of all the other ways I felt myself a stranger in her presence, an intruder, right back to where we were.

And yet we still kept at it, year after year of living out our separate lives in the same home, of needing each other and not knowing why, of her looking at me as though I was some longtime lodger at the house, until I came to believe that she was both naive and practical about love, that she'd only ever loved me because I was a cop, because that was supposed to mean I'd never hurt her.

The night I hit her was a rainy night. I had come home from the scene of a shooting in Ghost Town in West Oakland, where a guy had tried robbing someone's seventy-year-old grandmother and, when she fought back, shot her in the head. I was too spent to care about tracking mud across Suzy's spotless kitchen floor, or to listen to her yell at me when she saw the mess. Couldn't she understand that blood on a sidewalk is a world worse than mud on a tile floor? Shouldn't she, coming from where she came, appreciate something like that? I told her to just fuck off. She glared at me, and then started with something she'd been doing the last few years whenever we argued: she spoke in Vietnamese. Not loudly or irrationally like she was venting her anger at me—but calmly and deliberately, as if I actually understood her, like she was daring me to understand her, flaunting all the nasty things she could be saying to me and knowing full well that it. could have been gibberish for all I knew and that I could do nothing of the sort to her. I usually ignored her or walked away. But this time, after a minute of staring her down as she delivered whatever the hell she was saying, I slapped her across the face.

She yelped and clutched her cheek, her eyes aghast. But then her hand fell away and she was flinging indecipherable words at me again, more and more vicious the closer she got to my face, her voice rising each time I told her to shut up. So I slapped her a second time, harder, sent her bumping into the dining chair behind her.

I felt queasy even as something inside me untangled itself. There'd been pushing in the past, me seizing her by the arms, the cheeks. But I had never gone this far. The tips of my fingers stung.

Everything happened fast, but I still remember her turning back to me with her flushed cheeks and her wet outraged eyes, her chin raised defiantly, and how it reminded me of men I'd arrested who'd just hit their wives or girlfriends and that preternatural calm on their faces when I confronted them, the posturing ease of a liar, a control freak, a bully wearing his guilt like armor. It made me see myself in Suzy's pathetic show of boldness. She'd never been as tough as I thought, and now I was the bad guy.

She spit out three words. She knew I understood... She said it again, then again and again, a bitter recitation. I barked at her to shut her mouth, shoving my face at hers, and That's when she swung at me as if to slap me with her fist, two swift blows on my ear that felt like an explosion in my head. I put up an arm to shield myself and she flailed at it, still cursing me, until finally I backhanded her as hard as I could, felt the thud of my knuckles against her teeth.

She stumbled back a few steps, covering her mouth with one hand and steadying herself on the dining table with the other until she finally went down on a knee, her head bowed like she was about to vomit. Briefly, she peered up at me. Red milky eyes, childish all of a sudden, disbelieving. I watched her rise to her feet, still cradling her mouth, and shamble to the sink and spit into it several times. I watched her linger there, stooped over like she was staring down a well. I didn't move—I couldn't—until I heard her sniffling and saw her raise herself gingerly and reach for a towel and turn on the faucet.

As I walked upstairs, I listened to the water running in the kitchen and the murmuring TV in the living room and the rain pummeling the gutters outside, and everything had the sound of finality to it.

In the divorce, she was true to her word and I was left with a home full of eggshell paintings and crucifixes and rattan furniture. It was a testament to the weird isolating vacuum of our marriage that she was able to immediately and completely disappear from my life. Her flower shop had closed down a year before and she had been working odd jobs around town: cutting hair, selling furniture, I rarely kept up. I had known so little about her comings and goings or the people she knew that once she was gone I had no way of even finding out where she was living, Even Happy had quietly disappeared.

Months later, after the divorce was finalized, with a little help from within the department I found out she had moved to Las

Vegas. I sold the townhouse and everything in it and tried my best to forget I had ever married anyone. I went on a strict diet of hamburgers and steaks.

But two years later, a few months before my trip to Vegas, I bumped into Happy at the supermarket. Instead of ignoring me or telling me off, she treated me like an old friend, which didn't surprise me too much. She had always lived up to her name in that way, and actually looked a lot like Suzy without her glasses: a taller, more carefree version. She said she, too, had moved to; Vegas for work and was in town for the summer to visit family.

I asked her out to dinner that night. Afterward she came home with me. We shared two bottles of wine and I let her lead me to the bedroom, and it wasn't until we finished that I realized—or admitted to myself—my true reason for doing all this. With her blissfully drunk and more talkative than ever, I asked about Suzy. She told me everything: how Suzy had become a card dealer in Vegas and met up with this cocky Vietnamese poker player who owned a fancy restaurant and a big house and apparently had some shady dealings in town, and how she quit her job and married him after knowing him a month, and how everything had been good for about a year.

"Until he start losing," Happy declared casually, sitting back against the headboard. She fell silent and I had to tell her several times to get on with it. She looked at me impatiently as though I should already know, as though anyone could've told the rest of the story.

"He hit her," she said. "She hit him too, but he too strong and he drink so much. Last month, he throw her down the stair, break her arm. I see her two week before, her arm in a sling, her cheek purple. But he too rich for her to leave. And always he say he need her, he need her."

"Did she call the cops? Why didn't she go to the cops?"

I stood from the bed, my head throbbing from the wine and all that I was imagining. I knocked the lamp off the nightstand.

Happy flinched. She had put her glasses back on, as if to see me better. After a moment, she said, "Why you still love her?" There was no envy or bitterness in her voice. She was simply curious.

"Who said I did?"

She checked me with her eyes as though I didn't understand my own emotions.

I tried to soften my voice, but it still came out in a growl: "Is it just the money? What—is he handsome?"

"Not really. But you not either." She patted my arm and laughed.

"You know what? I'm gonna go to Vegas and I'm gonna find this fucker. And then I'm gonna hit him a little before I break his arm."

This time she laughed hard, covering her mouth and regarding me with drunken pity. "You a silly, stupid man," she said.

Chapter 18

As I DROVE OUT of the city, the sun shone as intensely as it had the previous morning. The sky was the color of the Pacific in July. The farther south I drove on the 15, the less snow I could see. Only a few unmelted patches on the shoulders of the highway, the broken lumps on the tops of passing cars, spitting flurries onto my windshield. It was strange to see green palm trees swaying in the breeze and beyond them the vague warm mountains, because in the bright sunlight, if you squint, it all seems like a vision from some tropical island.

I held on to that thought to lessen the pain in my head. To bury as much as I could of the last two days.

It was my second and my last time leaving Las Vegas. The farther away I got, the more I felt I was shedding some pitch dark side of myself that the place had awoken. Maybe it was my most genuine side. It doesn't matter ultimately—who you think you are. Sonny and Happy had died, and mourning one and cursing the other made me no more wiser about the things that people do to each other. In the end, good and bad people perish all the same.

I felt inside my duffel bag for the videotape. It was still there, though its value was lost on me now. It would never tell me where Suzy went or what new life she would find for herself. It would never tell me what she had actually written me or what else had happened in that hotel room. All it contained were darkened glimpses of two people whose love for each other somehow lasted for over twenty years.

Two hours out, I stopped at a gas station to fill up my car and change out of my bloody clothes. I threw away the food and painkillers Junior had given me and bought a bottle of ibuprofen, some cold sandwiches and hot coffee, and a pair of cheap sunglasses to cover up my bruised eye and shade myself from the harsh sunlight.

It was still desert all around me, gray mountains behind brown mountains, miles of hoary creosote bushes blanketing the flat land like a bed of thorns. I ate all the sandwiches sitting on the frigid hood of my car and drank my coffee slowly and decided I was never coming back to this or any desert.

Only then did I call Tommy.

As soon as he heard my voice, he said, "What the hell did you do, man?"

"I can explain the girl," I said.

"What girl? There's no girl. All I see is a suitcase at my front door with fifty... inside and a note with your name on it. And oh yeah, your badge."

He grilled me with a string of questions, but I wasn't listening. I hung up without saying another word.

I sat in the car for a while, sifting through my surprise, my disappointment, and eventually the realization that I shouldn't have been surprised at all.

I considered tossing the videotape then. Run over it with my Car first. Burn it and let it melt into the desert dust. If Mai was gone now, why hold on to anything else, especially this?

But I kept it. I would never watch it again, but somehow it felt right to save this one reminder. At least it wasn't some heartfelt memento of something we once had. On the tape was everything I knew about her and everything I would never know. That wasn't enough, but at least it was real.

19

(GB Tran, 1976—)
陈家宝

作者简介

陈家宝（GB Tran, 1976— ），美国越南裔作家和漫画家。1975年4月，他的父母逃难到美国并定居美国卡罗来纳州。1976年，陈家宝出生于美国南加州。年少时，陈家宝对他父母的家族历史和战争经历并无过多了解，他的父母也未曾向他谈及过多。直到越南的祖母去世，陈家宝随父母回越南奔丧，开始了解了他的家族历史。

这一"探亲"经历为他的写作提供了丰富的素材，创作了回忆录《越美：一趟家族旅行》(*Vietnamerica*, 2011)。这本书以漫画形式讲述了殖民时期祖父母的心酸家史以及在越南战争前后父母的逃难与难民经历。该书获得了插画家协会的金奖（Society of Illustrators Gold Medal），并被列入《时代周刊》的十大插画回忆录。

这部回忆录以红、黑、黄三种颜色为主色调，描摹出其艰辛的家族历史，以精湛的艺术技巧和叙事策略创造出综合视觉、听觉和触觉的"创伤联觉"（the synesthesia of trauma）效应，给读者展示了一部有关越南家庭四代人的"记实录"。

选段出自《越美：一趟家族旅行》，讲述了主人公随同父母亲回越南奔丧，并开启寻根之旅的故事，展现了出生在美国的越南后代对"根与路"的反思与探索。

174　美国越南裔文学作品选
An Anthology of Vietnamese American Literature

作品选读

Vietnamerica

(Excerpt)

By GB Tran

Three months ago, in the fall of 2006, my mom's mom died.

It was hard to think of Thi Mot as "Grandma." I'd only been to Vietnam to meet her once before this trip.

It was so late in her twilight years that physically and mentally she was already pretty far gone.

176 美国越南裔文学作品选
An Anthology of Vietnamese American Literature

It was a bizarre coincidence: Mom's mom and Dad's dad, my last two surviving grandparents, dying within a few months of each other.
Why didn't you tell me the Vietnamese mourn in white instead of black?
I wouldn't have worn this freakin' oven.
YOUR BEING HERE IS ALREADY MORE THAN HE DESERVES.
YOUR MOTHER DIDN'T COME.
YOU DIDN'T HAVE TO EITHER.

178　美国越南裔文学作品选
An Anthology of Vietnamese American Literature

GB Tran 179

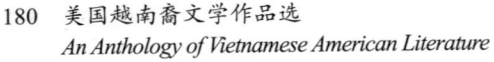

An Anthology of Vietnamese American Literature

To him, she's a remnant of a life without his own father. Just another fixture in Grandpa's posh and sterile home.

The building itself a reward from the Communist party after their victory over the Americans in 1975.

Plaques and medals chronicle Huu Nghiep's lifetime of loyalty and service.

First against the Japanese, then French, and finally American invaders.

Did he kill a foreign legionnaire for this one? Maybe a marine?

Probably neither. A doctor, his purpose was to SAVE lives. After the war ended in '75, Huu Nghiep started writing.

CARING FOR AND RAISING CHILDREN BY HUU NGHIEP

Irony's a bitch.

182 美国越南裔文学作品选
An Anthology of Vietnamese American Literature

IT WAS WEIRD. AWKWARD. CREEPY.
I MEAN, WAS SHE REACHING FOR ME OR HER DEAD HUSBAND?
C'est étrange!
She's right, though. You two look exactly alike.
HONK
BEEP
BEEP
Same posture, same hair, same nose!
Act the same, too: whenever I visited Huu Nghiep after you escaped to America, he barely said a word.
It was just like NOT talking to you!
Toward the end, he even turned away visiting the bigwigs because he said he was too tired.
PAT PAT PAT
CHEW CHEW
HMPH.
SO THE REVERED HERO OF THE REVOLUTION PREFERRED SELF-EXILE TO FACING THE CORRUPT NEW GOVERNMENT HE GAVE HIS LIFE FOR.
How'd he die?
DON'T KNOW.
You didn't ask?
NO.
Why not? Aren't you curious?
NOPE.
NOT REALLY.
...
CHK CHK
But he's your Dad!
THE IDEALS HUU NGHIEP DEVOTED HIS LIFE FIGHTING FOR WENT UP IN SMOKE.
GIVEN HOW EVERYTHING TURNED OUT, I THINK HE DIED MORE OF A BROKEN HEART THAN ANYTHING ELSE.

184　美国越南裔文学作品选
An Anthology of Vietnamese American Literature

Vinh wants to rent a car and drive us back to Saigon for our flight home.
HE DOESN'T NEED TO GO TO ALL THAT TROUBLE.
They want to.
They really want to see us off at the airport.
What about Huu Nghiep's widow?
WHAT ABOUT HER?
Don't you think you should see her one more time?
It might be your last.
Dinner's ready!
Gia-Bao, eat this!
It's the most delicious part of the pig!
Translation: "Most artery clogging, heart-stopping part."
After dinner we'll all go for a joyride!
Except you, Gia-Bao!
You need to jog off all that pork!
VVVRRRM

Thank you for visiting me again before returning to America.
YOU'RE WELCOME.
?!
Hey, Dad...
You and Mom left in '75 with nothing but the clothes on your backs, right?
YES.
And before that, Huu Nghiep disappeared when you were just a baby?
WE LEFT EVERYTHING BEHIND.
...
CORRECT.
And you didn't contact him for over 50 years—
YOUR POINT?
How in the hell did that get here?!
TRAN HUU TRI '72

WE'RE LEAVING.
But—
NOW.
I forgot to mention Dad was a painter. He doesn't talk about it.
He never went to school for art, just devoted every second of his free time to it.
After trying for more than a decade, he finally got his big break in 1975.

188 美国越南裔文学作品选
An Anthology of Vietnamese American Literature

IVAL
ARTURE
GATE 2
GATE 3
Neither Mom or Dad had a chance to do that for their parents.
Whether they actually wanted to or not...
BLAM
Or whether their parents deserved it...
Is another story.

20

(Aimee Phan, 1977—)
艾米·潘

作者简介

艾米·潘（Aimee Phan, 1977— ），美国越南裔作家，1977年出生于加利福尼亚州的橘子郡。她在加州大学洛杉矶分校（UCLA）获得英语学士学位，在爱荷华作家研究中心（Iowa Writers' Workshop）获得硕士学位。2005年至2007年间，她在华盛顿州立大学（Washington State University）担任英语助理教授，目前在加利福尼亚艺术学院（California College of the Arts）任教，并与家人居住在加利福尼亚州伯克利市。

迄今为止，她创作了两部小说《我们不应该见面》（*We Should Never Meet*, 2005）与《查瑞张的再教育》（*The Reeducation of Cherry Truong*, 2013）。她还写了很多散文，包括《城市家庭的代价》（*The Price of Urban Family Living*）与《他们来自何方》（*Where They Came From*），这些文章发表在纽约时报（*The New York Times*）、《弗吉尼亚季刊》（*Virginia Quarterly Review*）、《今日美国》（*USA Today*）与《俄勒冈人》（*The Oregonian*）等美国重要期刊报纸上，广受学界和读者好评。她的小说《我们不应该见面》入围桐山小说奖（Kiriyama Prize）和2005年美国亚裔文学奖（Asian American Literary Awards）。

选段分别选自《我们不应该见面》中的故事《莲小姐》（"Miss Lien"）和《查瑞张的再教育》中的《家族树》（"Family Tree"）。前一选段讲述了悲惨的越南女性生活，表达了殖民历史对无辜越南百姓带来的创伤阴影。后一选段讲述了主人公在越南"再教育营"的磨难历史，表达了作者对战争历史和创伤经历的探索。

作品选读（一）

We Should Never Meet

(Miss Lien)
By Aimee Phan

The war is far away, their father assured them, far up in the north. We are safe here.

Because he was their father, because they never remembered him ever being wrong, they tried to believe him.

This time, Lien remembered where she was. She didn't have to open her eyes. Though the river breeze drifting in from the window was cool, biting even, the thin blanket clung to her back, already soaked with sweat. Long strands of hair pasted to her cheeks. The pungent aroma of peppermint oil tingled her nose. Lying on the sleeping mat these past two days, she recognized every sound the midwife and her servants made. Shuffling feet kicking up dust from the dirty floor. The steady drip of sheets and rags wrung clean. Jugs of water splashing into shallow clay bowls. The persistent, steady chorus of moaning and whimpering from the other girls. Lien vainly remained silent, hoping the others would recognize the dignity in swallowing back the pain. Hoping they would follow her example. But they didn't care. Their bodies, so recently torn open, were still in shock and ached, bled, and throbbed, resentful of what they'd been put through.

The midwife was making her rounds, checking temperatures and bandages while chewing on betel nuts. Lien sat up when she came near. Sparks of colors swirled around her eyes. She tightened her grip on the blanket to steady herself.

When can I leave?

The midwife placed her palm on Lien's forehead. What about the child?

Lien blinked several times and inhaled stale air. When can we leave?

The midwife spread her lips, revealing black-lacquered teeth. Lien realized she must have come from a family of wealth. Lien wondered how the woman had fallen from her upper status. The war, probably. It explained her bitterness. She disdained this place as well, thought she didn't belong here either.

You haven't paid me yet, the woman said.

Lien had been in and out of consciousness for the past two days. She knew the little money she did have, stuffed deep in the stitching of her clothes, was gone by now.

I will pay you back.

You had a difficult labor. We had to send for a boy to help hold you down.

I have nothing to offer you now, unless you want me to work the payment off. Around them, girls shuffled about the house, changing bedsheets, sweeping the dirt floor, tending to others either recovering or approaching labor. The midwife had enough people working off debts.

The midwife's eyes were distracted by something. Lien followed the woman's gaze to her wrist. A thin jade bracelet, her last possession of value. Without hesitating, Lien wrapped her fingers and wrenched it off, ignoring the dull pain it left behind.

I will be back for it when I have your money.

You can stay one more day, the midwife said, taking the bracelet from her and slipping it inside her blouse pocket. The bleeding should stop by tomorrow.

It is only a safety precaution. It is nothing to worry about. We can always use more room in this house with the new baby.

These were the things Lien's father kept saying while he, her mother, and grandparents began digging for a bunker behind their house. Almost every family in the village was building one. A ditch dug up for every house. Children started standing closer to their parents, holding on to their legs. The shelling, once barely audible in their village, was increasing in volume and frequency. The earth shook from these mounting explosions, unstable, uncertain, rattling the people who depended on its rich soil for their livelihood.

At first their father insisted the children concentrate on rice planting while the adults tended to the bunker. He said the rice was more important, the foundation of their family and the entire country. They depended on the crop for survival. Nothing should ever come before it or compromise its growth.

It promised to be an abundant crop. The monsoon season had provided plenty of water, and the mud's consistency was especially soupy this year. If successful, they would have enough rice left over to sell to the market for extra food and supplies to stock up for the dry season.

Though Lien sternly instructed her brothers and sisters to watch the paddy, she couldn't help also feeling curious about the adults' new project. She found herself walking along the edge of the paddy close to where they were digging and setting up plates of cement for the bunker walls. She prodded the buffalo absentmindedly with her bamboo stick as it plowed the field, all the while watching her father and grandfather fit the poles along the walls. She could only see the tops of their heads, light with dust and bent close together, like they were deep in conversation.

Perhaps we should send the women and children away, Lien's grandfather said. In the bunker's trench, they couldn't even see Lien.

Where would we send them? her father said. We don't know anyone in Can Tho.

They should go to the city. It's better protected. They will be safer there.

We have no money. We can't afford to. And we can't leave the land unguarded.

What good is this land going to do you if your family is dead?

Crazy old man. Has the village been attacked yet? I only agreed to build this bunker because you wouldn't stop nagging. No one is going to die. You heard Dat, it will never get this far south.

I am crazy? All my life this country has been at war, on my very land. How did I raise a son so blind?

The buffalo snorted loudly, restless from standing still for so long. Lien's father and grandfather looked up, squinting at the sun.

What are you doing, Miss Lien? her father asked. What do you need?

Nothing. The buffalo is just tired. She slapped the ox on the back with her stick, and they walked on.

The common room in the midwife's house was divided into five sections with bamboo screens for every two sleeping mats. The girl sharing Lien's partition, who'd given birth yesterday and slept most of the afternoon away, awoke just when the sun was setting, soft yellow light drifting over as her eyes fluttered open. A slow smile appeared on her face, her arms lazily stretching over her head. She was beautiful, with shiny waist-long black hair and delicate slender hands.

I'm starving. She sat up a little and looked over at Lien. When is supper?

Soon.

Ay—yah. The girl lay back suddenly, but her smile only grew wider. You think it would get easier after a few times, but it never does. Her eyes scanned Lien head to toe. Your first?

Lien nodded.

Oh, look at this one. One of the midwife's servants was walking toward them holding a small bundle wrapped in cloth. The girl held her arms out for it, quickly cradling and cooing at it softly. This will be a handsome one. Daddy's an American GI. Beautiful green eyes. But it's too soon to tell if it will get those.

Do you want to see your baby?

It took Lien several moments to realize the midwife's servant was talking to her. Even then Lien couldn't speak, only staring back at the servant's expectant eyes, then the girl's. Both were waiting for Lien's response, ready to judge her. Finally, reluctantly, Lien nodded.

The girl had pulled her blouse down to breast-feed the infant. Lien turned on her back so she could stare at the ceiling.

It's all right, the girl said after the servant left. I wasn't sure about looking at my first either, knowing I had to give it up.

Lien rolled her head to the side and looked at her. Where did you take it?

There's this orphanage run by some Catholic nuns. The girl shifted the infant so she could sit up more easily. They take every child in, no questions.

How far is that from here?

Just outside of Vinh Long. About fifteen kilometers north. The girl smiled sympathetically. You know, this baby could help you, if the father's an American. That's why I'm keeping this one.

Lien didn't say anything.

Unless you don't want to see the father. Once again the girl's eyes traveled the length of Lien's face and body, as if she could tell just by looking at her. Unless it was bad. Then no one could blame you for getting rid of it.

Lien twisted in her sheets until she found a comfortable position facing the wall. I can't keep it.

They were silent then, the only sound in the room the persistent, greedy suckling of the infant. Lien resisted the urge to cover her ears, though the nursing only grew louder and more desperate.

They had to be quiet. The roof of the bunker was made up of thin layers of straw and sand. Lien held her brother An in her lap, urging him to stop wiggling and hushing his crying. No one spoke. The family spent most of the time listening to the fighting and burning above, trying not to envision the worst.

When it had been silent for nearly five hours, and her father deemed it safe, they emerged from the bunker with tentative steps, squinting, like it had been years since they'd seen the sun and breathed fresh air, instead of only two days.

We're alive, Lien's mother reminded them. We need to be thankful we are alive.

But as the family wandered around their property to assess the damage, they could not remember that. It didn't matter that the house was spared.

Most of the livestock had been stolen from their cages. The vegetable garden was covered in shrapnel. They found their water buffalo near the main road slaughtered, rotting, covered with flies. But the worst of it was the rice paddy. The crop was ruined. The smell of fire drifted through the air. They'd have no rice for the coming season.

Lien was the only one to follow her father into the rice paddy. He walked through each ditch, as if to confirm that every seedling had been uprooted, destroyed. Lien kept up as best she could, but the burnt rice stalks sliced deep into her bare feet, slowing her down. When she caught up to him near the edge of their property, he was staring at the ground. He sank his knees into the crusty, dry dirt and dug into the earth with both hands. He held it up to Lien. All their work, all those hours, weeks, and years. Now ash and gunpowder.

We can replant, Lien said. We can try again.

Her father shook his head. It's too late. We'll have to wait for next season.

But what are we going to eat? She could feel it creeping into her voice. She swallowed hard, wanting to will the fear away.

Since she was little, Lien had always been grateful to be born into her family. Unlike others in the village, their family valued daughters as highly as sons. Each child considered special and necessary. They looked down on other families who spoiled their sons and ignored their daughters, thought them to be old-fashioned, outdated, cruel.

Lien had always been treated like a firstborn son, with all the privileges and honors. Now she suddenly understood the responsibility that came with those benefits and, for the first time, wished she were a boy. Sons could go out and make money in place of the father and support the family. Daughters didn't have the same liberties.

The servant returned with it. Tiny. Wrinkly. Slippery. Smelling like sour milk and feces. Its eyes hadn't opened yet. Lien held it away from her, tilting and inspecting it like her fish at the market.

The baby looks strong, the girl said. It looks like you.

No it doesn't.

The servant said the infant had already been fed. Lien wordlessly handed it back to her.

Every patient's possessions lay beside her mat against the wall. On the girl's side were several bags neatly stuffed with clothes and toiletries. There was nothing on Lien's side. Lien was used to the look the girl gave her now: compassion, pity, a little smugness. She tried to ignore it.

You know, if you need money, the girl said, I know some people—

I already have a job.

What do you do?

I work on a fishing boat in Can Tho.

But you know you can make a lot more—

I'm not a whore. Lien didn't mean to sound rude. But she was tired. The walls were beginning to bend and wobble again.

The girl didn't seem to take offense. She even smiled. I wasn't either. And I won't be for much longer. But it's nice to eat. It's nice to provide for your family.

Later that evening, a servant arrived with their suppers. Rice porridge with chicken shreds. Lien savored every bite, even swallowing her pride to ask for another bowl. Part of her regretted that she'd be leaving tomorrow. She hadn't eaten this well since she was home. But she would be home soon.

She should have left immediately. Instead, waiting a week only served to divide the family even more. Lien's grandparents did not approve of her leaving for the city alone. Her parents felt there was no other choice. There was no money, and their food supplies were dwindling. Lien's father couldn't leave his young family and land unprotected. Her mother was expecting the baby in a few weeks. Lien's grandparents were too old. Her brothers and sisters were too young. Lien would go to Can Tho, the largest city in the Delta, to find work in the floating market. She would send money home and return after the next monsoon season in time for replanting the rice.

The night before she left, their family cooked a small chicken and the last of the wild sweet potatoes, giving the largest portion to Lien so she would have strength for her journey. Her brothers and sisters took turns sitting next to her while they ate, mostly in silence. She rubbed each of them roughly behind their ears, instructing them to be good for their parents.

Her grandfather reminded Lien of their country's long history of oppression and survival: first the Chinese, then the French, the Japanese, now each other. He'd been imprisoned and released from three regimes because it was his fate to survive. You will too, Miss Lien. You will because you are strong like me.

Her grandmother gave her several gold-plated necklaces and a jade bracelet, which she'd been saving as part of Lien's dowry. Her hands were cold when she held Lien's cheeks. Remember you are a good girl. Stay away from bad people. Do not do anything to shame us.

Her father dressed her in his warmest coat. Look how tall you are getting. Almost as tall as me. Your father is getting old now. He is not as smart as he once was. But you are, more than I ever was. You are my hope.

Her mother's eyes were wet, but she put on a bright smile for her daughter. She brushed Lien's long black hair and tied it into a knot on the top of her head. You should keep your hair up so people will know you come from a good family. I won't be able to do it for you anymore. You have to. You're an adult now.

Take care of yourself.

We are so proud of you.

Come home safe.

Do not let us down.

作品选读（二）

The Reeducation of Cherry Truong

(Family Tree)
By Aimee Phan

HALONGBAY, 2002

Minh Quang, the fishing junk they rented for the day tour through the caves, is large, with cabin seating for at least twenty passengers. Yet, they are only three. The family of crew members (two brothers, their wives, and four children) outnumber Cherry and her cousins. Once the junk pushes off from the dock, Xuan and Cam strip down to their swimsuits to sunbathe.

"Get out here," Cam barks from behind her sunglasses. "It's better if you lie down."

"Or I can wait for the Dramamine to kick in," Cherry says from the safety of the cabin.

"What kind of Vietnamese are you?" Xuan mocks. "It's a good thing you were born in America. You never would have survived the ride out."

Cherry checks her watch and realizes they still have nine hours before returning to land. The nausea weighs like a cloud in her chest and abdomen. She lies out on a row of seats, using her messenger bag as a pillow, listening to the chug chug of the boat engine. Cherry wishes her brother could have come with them, but there was no way he could leave Tham alone with the baby, even with the Trans' help. Small fingers tickle through her hair. Cherry turns and one of the children, the youngest girl, smiles at her, a dimple in her left cheek. The other kids stand behind her. When Cherry sits up, the older boy points to her bag, which she obligingly opens. They touch everything, her digital camera, her Dramamine, her journal, her purple leather wallet. Cherry asks them to be gentle with the bundles of letters. She lets them take pictures of each other with the camera and promises to mail them copies. Eventually, one of their mothers yells for the children to leave their customer alone.

The boat captain hollers that they are approaching the first isle of limestone caves. The morning fog has melted off, unveiling more fishing junks around them. Cherry steps out on the deck to join her cousins, who are waving at the tourists and locals passing by. The breeze feels soft and cool. One boat is full of fraternity boys who whistle at Cam, beckoning her to come on board. She shakes her head no, then flashes them.

Once the boat anchors, Cherry eagerly steps off to join the queue leading into the caves. Inside, she and her cousins shuffle through the line, gazing at the stalagmites and stalactites and the gaudy Christmas lights draped around them. The caves must have been beautiful once—they probably still are—but the rainbow neon lights and fake water fountains remind Cherry of a bad Vietnamese pop—music video. Empty beer bottles and stray trash litter the partitioned walkway and the corners of the caves.

When the second isle offers more of the same, they request that the captain scrap the caves for the rest of the day. The captain suggests taking them to a secluded bay that none of the other junks know about for kayaking and swimming. They stop at a floating fishing village, where the wives pick up some of the most colorful fish Cherry has ever seen to cook for lunch.

As promised, the captain takes them to an empty bay of lushly forested islands and islets surrounded and shaded by larger karsts. Some of the faraway limestone islets look like giant sea turtles bubbling to the water's surface, while others resemble stony skyscrapers. Cam and Xuan race each other to the closest isle, diving off the junk without hesitation. After pulling off her tank top and shorts, Cherry stands at the edge of the boat. She stares into the water, remembering all the gasoline and refuse floating in the harbor. The first time she tried swimming in the ocean was when her parents took them to Mexico for a vacation. While the rest of her family swam through the waves, she was repulsed at how the saltwater burned at her eyes and nostrils. For the rest of the afternoon, she sat on the shoreline, waiting for her parents and Lum to return. But that was many years ago. Behind her, she can hear the children laughing. Instead of looking, Cherry closes her eyes, bends her knees and jumps.

The bay feels seductively warm, the water gliding around her bare arms and legs like a silky blanket. Cherry blinks a few times and then stretches her arms into a lazy freestyle. Her cousins wave at her from the islet, and Cherry takes her time swimming toward them, enjoying her few minutes alone, yet still in the comfort of their watchful gazes.

While Cam tries to climb up the limestone's jagged edges, Cherry and Xuan find a smooth surface to sit and watch her. Occasionally, the water laps up, splashing their feet, trickling between their toes. Xuan and Cam had wanted to come to Ha Long Bay because of Grandmère's stories. Her ancestors were once fishermen in Ha Long Bay, long before their family migrated to the south.

"What was Grandpère's funeral like?" Cherry asks. She has always regretted not attending to support Grandmère.

"It didn't rain," Xuan says, "which he would have approved of. Most of our parish was there, and his friends from the community center. Even Ba Cuc and her family were there, though we didn't realize at the time who she really was."

"How do you think they met?" Cherry asks.

"I think they knew each other in Vietnam," Xuan says. "I guess he followed her to Paris."

"Or she followed him."

He squints, leaning back on his elbows. "I guess we'll never know."

Cherry falls silent. Although she hasn't opened Grandpère's letters, she doesn't trust having them away from her, afraid that if left in Saigon, the Trans will find them, or worse, Lum will throw them out. But perhaps there is another reason she brought them on this trip. Maybe she and her cousins are meant to read them together.

"I can't really judge him," he says, the water glittering off his hair. "Not now. People do really stupid things when they think it's for love."

Cam calls out for a hand. Cherry jumps up to help her cousin with a final, slippery step over two mossy boulders. Several nicks decorate her legs, but Cam proudly grins over her accomplishment.

"Nice view?" Xuan asks.

"There isn't a bad one," she says, collapsing onto the rock, folding her scratched up knees in front of her. She looks around them, happily exhaling. "Maybe we should move here. We'll get a houseboat and float around. I'll learn to fish and Xuan can operate the boat."

"What about Cherry?" Xuan asks.

"She'll be the house doctor," Cam says, turning to rest her head in Cherry's lap. "In case any of my cooking makes us sick."

"I can barely watch over myself," Cherry says

"You're being modest," Xuan says. "You survived one of the worst things that can happen to a person. They can't teach you that in medical school."

Cherry feels her face growing warm. "That doesn't mean I can take care of anyone."

"Yes, you can," Cam says. "Who's been holding our passports and getting us to our trains and boat rides on time? Who found the local pharmacy when Xuan got the runs in the middle of the night in Hue? You're like Grandmère. It's your nature."

"I knew it." Cherry beams at her cousins. "I should have grown up with you."

"Trust me," Cam says, closing her eyes. "It wasn't so great on our side of the ocean."

"But we could have been together."

"We're together now, right?"

"I'm going home next week. So are you."

"We don't have to," Xuan says.

"But you both have jobs," Cherry says. "I have school."

"They'll be there when we return," Cam says, opening her eyes and spotting Cherry's doubtful expression. "They will."

After they've had enough sun, they begin swimming back to the Minh Quang. There is no rush, so they float on their backs, admiring the bright blue of the cloudless, open sky. The children are out on the deck, and Cherry waves at them, thinking that lunch must be ready. They stand at the edge of the junk and one of the boys struggles with something in his arms. Cherry floats over on her stomach, treading water, trying to determine what it is. Then a flutter of papers drops from his arms and off the side of the boat. Another. And another. The children are yelling, and one of their mothers emerges on the deck. She roughly yanks at the boy's arm, pulling him back from the junk's edge. In his other hand is Cherry's camera. He was trying to take a picture of them.

The yellowed envelopes scatter across the top of the water, fanning out like schools of fish. For a brief moment, they stand out bright and clear in the jade-green bay. Xuan and Cam swim ahead of her toward the soaking letters. But Cherry can already feel them growing heavy, sinking, sinking to the bay floor.

21
(Ocean Vuong, 1988—)
王洋

作者简介

　　王洋（Ocean Vuong, 1988— ），美国越南裔诗人和小说家，出生于越南胡志明市（Ho Chi Minh City）。他的外祖母是一个普通的越南女性，嫁给了驻越美国海军，育有三个混血孩子。越南战争结束后，王洋的外祖父回到了美国。留在越南的外祖母因与美国人的关系而饱受新政府的压迫和排挤，生活举步维艰。迫于无奈，外祖母将三个孩子送到了孤儿院。王洋的母亲在孤儿院长大，后来生下王洋。1990年到美国后，王洋的父亲抛弃妻儿远走高飞。王洋幼年患有阅读障碍症，直到11岁才学会阅读。经过后天的努力，他从纽约城市大学（City University of New York）获得英语专业学士学位，从纽约大学（New York University）获得艺术硕士学位。他目前是马萨诸塞大学安姆斯特分校（University of Massachusetts Amherst）的助理教授。

　　他的作品有：诗集《燃烧》（Burnings, 2010）、《不》（No, 2013)与《子弹穿过的夜空》（Night Sky With Exit Wounds, 2016），小说《逆境中的短暂辉煌》（On Earth We're Briefly Gorgeous, 2019）。他荣获了露丝·丽莉与萨珍特罗森博格奖（Ruth Lilly/Sargent Rosenberg fellowship）、手推车奖（The Pushcart Prize）、伊丽莎白·乔治基金奖（The Elizabeth George Foundation Fellowship）、史丹利·库尼茨青年诗人奖（Stanley Kunitz Prize for Younger Poets）、怀丁诗歌奖（Whiting Award for Poetry）与T. S. 艾略特奖（T. S. Eliot Prize）等众多重要奖项。《逆境中的短暂辉煌》是王洋的第一部小说，入围2019年"美国国家图书小说奖"，登上《华盛顿邮报》（Washington Post）2019年"十佳图书"之榜，在2020年荣获

"福克纳小说奖"。

选段分别出自小说《逆境中的短暂辉煌》和诗集《子弹穿过的夜空》。前一选段讲述了主人公祖母疯癫的生活状态，表达了作者对战争创伤和历史记忆的反思。后一选段《对穿伤口的自画像》（"Self-Portrait as Exit Wounds"）讲述了难民在后创伤阴影下的苦苦挣扎，表达了战争对越南裔带来的不可磨灭的记忆。

作品选读（一）

On Earth We're Briefly Gorgeous
By Ocean Vuong

Memory is a choice. You said that once, with your back to me, the way a god would say it. But if you were a god you would see them. You would look down at this grove of pines, the fresh tips flared lucent at each treetop, tender-damp in their late autumn flush. You would look past the branches, past the rusted light splintered through the brambles, the needles falling, one by one, as you lay your god eyes on them. You'd trace the needles as they hurled themselves past the lowest bow, toward the cooling forest floor, to land on the two boys lying side by side, the blood already dry on their cheeks.

Although it covers both their faces, the blood belongs to the tall boy, the one with eyes the dark grey of a river beneath somebody's shadow. What's left of November seeps through their jeans, their thin knit sweaters. If you were god, you'd notice that they're staring up at you. They're clapping and singing "This Little Light of Mine," the Ralph Stanley version they'd listened to earlier in the afternoon on the tall boy's stereo. It was his old man's favorite song, the tall boy had said. And so now their heads sway side to side as their teeth glow between the notes, and the caked blood crumbles from their jaws, flecking their pale throats as the song leaves them in fistfuls of smoke.

"*This little light of mine, I'm gonna let it shine. This little light of mine, I'm gonna let it shine... All in my house, I'm gonna et it shine.*"

The pine needles spin and sputter around them in the minuscule wind made by their moving limbs. The cut under the tall boy's eye has reopened from his singing, and a black—red line now runs down his left ear, curving at his neck and vanishing in the ground. The small boy glances at his friend, the terrible bulb of an eye, and tries to forget.

If you were god you would tell them to stop clapping. You would tell them that the most useful thing one can do with empty hands is hold on. But you are not a...

You're a woman. A mother, and your son is lying under the pines while you sit at a kitchen table across town, waiting again. You have just reheated, for the third time, the pan of fried flat noodles and scallions. Your breath fogs the glass as you stare out the window, waiting for the boy's orange New York Knicks sweater to flash by, as he must be running, it being so late.

But your son is still under the trees beside the boy you will never meet. They are yards from the closed overpass, where a plastic bag thrashes against the chain link surrounded by hundreds of one-shot liquor bottles. The boys begin to shiver, their claps slow, nearly inaudible. Their voices subdued as the wind swarms hugely above them—needles clicking down like the hands of smashed watches.

There are times, late at night, when your son would wake believing a bullet is lodged inside him. He'd feel it floating on the right side of his chest, just between the ribs. The bullet was always here, the boy thinks, older even than himself—and his bones, tendons, and veins had merely wrapped around the metal shard, sealing it inside him. It wasn't me, the boy thinks, who was inside my mother's womb, but this bullet, this seed I bloomed around. Even now, as the cold creeps in around him, he feels it poking out from his chest, slightly tenting his sweater. He feels for the protrusion but, as usual, finds nothing. It's receded, he thinks. It wants to stay inside me. It is nothing without me. Because a bullet without a body is a song without ears.

Across town, facing the window, you consider reheating the noodles one more time. You sweep into your palm pieces of the paper napkin you had torn up, then get up to toss it out. You return to the chair, wait. That window, the same one your son had stopped at one night before coming in, the square of light falling across him as he watched your face, peering out at him. Evening had turned the glass into a mirror and you couldn't see him there, only the lines scored across your cheeks and brow, a face somehow ravaged by stillness. The boy, he watches his mother watch nothing, his entire self inside the phantom oval of her face, invisible.

The song long over, the cold a numbing sheath over their nerves. Under their clothes, goose bumps appear, making their thin, translucent hair rise, then bend against the fabric under their shirts.

"Hey Trev," your son says, his friend's blood crusted tight on his cheek. "Tell me a secret." Wind, pine needles, seconds.

"What kind?"

"Just—like... a normal secret. It doesn't have to suck."

"A normal one." The hush of thinking, steady breaths. The stars above them a vast smudge on a hastily-wiped chalkboard. "Can you go first?"

On the table across town, your fingers stop drumming the Formica.

"Okay. You ready?"

"Yeah."

You push back your chair, grab your keys, and walk out the door.

"I'm not scared of dying anymore."

(A pause, then laughter.)

The cold, like river water, rises to their throats.

Ma. You once told me that memory is a choice. But if you were god, you'd know it's a flood. Because I am your son, what I know of work I know equally of loss. And what I know of both I know of your hands. Their once supple contours I've never felt, the palms already callused and blistered long before I was born, then ruined further from three decades in factories and nail salons. Your hands are hideous—and I hate everything that made them that way. I hate how they are the wreck and reckoning of a dream. How you'd come home, night after night, plop down on the couch, and fall asleep inside a minute. I'd come back with your glass of water and you'd already be snoring, your hands in your lap like two partially scaled fish.

What I know is that the nail salon is more than a place of work and workshop for beauty, it is also a place where our children are raised—a number of whom, like cousin Victor, will get asthma from years of breathing the noxious fumes into their still-developing lungs. The salon is also a kitchen where, in the back rooms, our women squat on the floor over huge woks that pop and sizzle over electric burners, cauldrons of phở simmer and steam up the cramped spaces with aromas of cloves, cinnamon, ginger, mint, and cardamom mixing with formaldehyde, toluene, acetone, Pine-Sol, and bleach. A place where folklore, rumors, tall tales, and jokes from the old country are told, expanded, laughter erupting in back rooms the size of rich people's closets, then quickly lulled into an eerie, untouched quiet. It's a makeshift classroom where we arrive, fresh off the boat, the plane, the depths, hoping the salon would be a temporary stop—until we get on our feet, or rather, until our jaws soften around English syllables—bend over workbooks at manicure desks, finishing homework for nighttime ESL classes that cost a quarter of our wages.

I won't stay here long, we might say. I'll get a real job soon. But more often than not, sometimes within months, even weeks, we will walk back into the shop, heads lowered, our manicure drills inside paper bags tucked under our arms, and ask for our jobs back. And often the owner, out of pity or understanding or both, will simply nod at an empty desk—for there is always an empty desk. Because no one stays long enough and someone is always just-gone. Because there are no salaries, health care, or contracts, the body being the only material to work with and work from. Having nothing, it becomes its own contract, a testimony of presence. We will do this for decades—until our lungs can no longer breathe without swelling, our livers hardening with chemicals—our joints brittle and inflamed from arthritis—stringing together a kind of life. A new immigrant, within two years, will come to know that the salon is, in the end, a place where dreams become the calcified knowledge of what it means to be awake in American bones—with or without citizenship—aching, toxic, and underpaid.

作品选读（二）

Night Sky With Exit Wounds

(Self-Portrait as Exit Wounds)
By Ocean Vuong

Instead, let it be the echo to every footstep
drowned out by rain, cripple the air like a name
flung onto a sinking boat, splash the kapok's bark
through rot & iron of a city trying to forget
the bones beneath its sidewalks, then through
the refugee camp sick with smoke & half—sung
hymns, a shack rusted black & lit with Bà Ngoại's
last candle, the hogs' faces we held in our hands& mistook for
brothers, let it enter a room illuminated
with snow, furnished only with laughter, Wonder Bread
& mayonnaise raised to cracked lips as testament
to a triumph no one recalls, let it brush the newborn's
flushed cheek as he's lifted in his father's arms, wreathed
with fish gut & Marlboros, everyone cheering as another
brown gook crumbles under John Wayne's M16, Vietnam
burning on the screen, let it slide through their ears,
clean, like a promise, before piercing the poster
of Michael Jackson glistening over the couch, into
the supermarket where a Hapa woman is ready
to believe every white man possessing her nose
is her father, may it sing, briefly, inside her mouth,
before laying her down between jars of tomato
& blue boxes of pasta, the deep—red apple rolling

from her palm, then into the prison cell
where her husband sits staring at the moon
until he's convinced it's the last wafer
god refused him, let it hit his jaw like a kiss
we've forgotten how to give one another, hissing
back to '68, Ha Long Bay: the sky replaced
with fire, the sky only the dead
look up to, may it reach the grandfather fucking
the pregnant farm girl in the back of his army jeep,
his blond hair flickering in napalm—blasted wind, let it pin
him down to dust where his future daughters rise,
fingers blistered with salt & Agent Orange, let them
tear open his olive fatigues, clutch that name hanging
from his neck, that name they press to their tongues
to relearn the word live, live, live—but if
for nothing else, let me weave this death beam
the way a blind woman stitches a flap of skin back
to her daughter's ribs. Yes—let me believe I was born
to cock back this rifle, smooth & slick, like a true
Charlie, like the footsteps of ghosts misted through rain
as I lower myself between the sights—& pray
that nothing moves.

22

(Violet Kupersmith, 1989—)
维奥莱特·库伯史密斯

作者简介

维奥莱特·库伯史密斯（Violet Kupersmith, 1989—），美越混血作家，出生于宾夕法尼亚州。她的父亲是美国白人，母亲是越南人。1975年北越攻陷西贡（Saigon，今胡志明市）后，她母亲随同家人乘船逃离越南，定居在德克萨斯州的亚瑟港。2011年从霍利奥克山学院（Mount Holyoke College）毕业后，维奥莱特参加美国富布赖特项目，到越南茶荣（Tra Vinh）支教。2013年至2015年，她在越南大叻（Da Lat）和胡志明市居住，2015至2016年，她在英国诺里奇东英吉利大学（University of East Anglia in Norwich）担任创意写作研究员。

她的作品有，短篇小说集《素馨花宾馆》（*The Frangipani Hotel*, 2015）与最新的小说《围着我的躯体建你的房子》（*Build Your House Around My Body*, 2021）。

选段分别出自《素馨花宾馆》中的故事《素馨花宾馆》（"The Frangipani Hotel"）和《围着我的身体建你的房子》中的《西贡：失联三天后》（"Saigon: Three Days After the Disappearance"）。前一选段刻画了素馨花宾馆惨淡的经营与破旧的外表，体现了殖民历史对越南人文、社会与历史带来的摧残。后一选段以鬼魅隐晦的方式展现了悲惨的家族命运，烘托出残酷血腥的战争历史画面。

作品选读（一）

The Frangipani Hotel

(THE FRANGIPANI HOTEL)
By Violet Kupersmith

THE ONLY PHOTOGRAPH I have of my father doesn't show his face. He and his two brothers stand with their backs to the camera before their father's grave on a sunny day in April 1973. My grandfather was killed when a building collapsed during the bombings that December, and the incense on top of his tomb—just visible over my uncle's right shoulder—is almost all burned down. All three of the brothers are wearing their traditional silk jackets and trousers, but the trousers are white and don't show up well because of the brightness of the sun and the pale marble of the cemetery all around them. It tricks my eyes whenever I look at it—for a moment I always think they are floating.

    The picture hangs in the lobby of the hotel now, on the wall before you reach the stairs, and like everything else in the building, it's covered in a film of perma-grime. My family has owned the Frangipani Hotel on the corner of Hàng Bạc and Hàng Bè since the thirties, when it was L'Hôtel Frangipane. Swanky name, shitty place. It's in the Old Quarter, where all the buildings are narrow and crooked and falling apart, and some still have bullet holes from the sixties in their concrete sides. There's a karaoke bar across the street, a massage parlor of ill-repute next door, and the Red River's a couple of blocks east. The Frangi itself is a seven—story death trap, with four-footed things scurrying around inside the walls and tap water that runs brownish. If you slammed a door too hard the entire thing would collapse. It's painted a sickly pale pink on the outside, and lined with peeling brown-and-gold–striped wallpaper on the inside. The large sign that hangs on the front of the whole mess with "The Frangipani Hotel" painted on it is crooked.

    When Hanoi was bombed, the building was abandoned and five army officers and their concubines moved in. After the war, when what remained of our family began trickling back into the city, they found maps and diagrams scrawled in chalk on the walls and dusty boxes of ammo stacked in corners. I don't know how they managed to get the place back—the government was still repossessing property and evicting people left and right in the postwar years. Maybe we were lucky. Maybe the place was even too old and nasty for the communists. I don't know how we manage to stay in business now—Hanoi is full of newer hotels in less seamy parts of town, and why anyone would choose to stay at the Frangi instead is one of my favorite diverting mysteries to ponder while I'm working at this shithole.

I'm at the reception desk because I'm the only one who speaks passable English, and my cousins Thang and Loi are doormen or bellhops, depending on the situation. Thang is the good-looking one-high, chiseled cheekbones, long eyelashes, the kind of red-brown skin that looks warm and like it would smell slightly spicy, the kind of smile that makes women weak in the knees. Loi has the face and personality of a toad. However, he can be useful because his ubiquitous presence dissuades our female guests from trying to sleep with Thang, and because he makes even me seem handsome by comparison.

Their father—my uncle Hung—is legally the owner and manager of the hotel. He and my father and their brother Hai ran it together before the war, but then Uncle Hai drowned in an accident that no one ever talks about and my Ba went insane and offed himself a few years later, so now it's his. In his mind, Uncle Hung is a major player in what he refers to as the "Hospitality Industry," and not in charge of a half-star hotel. He's even started calling himself "Mr. Henry" in an attempt to better connect with the Western guests. However, he can't really pronounce "Henry," let alone "Frangipani," so watching him greet guests and introduce himself is endlessly amusing.

The other day, Mr. Henry decided to assemble the family for what he called a "staff meeting." It consisted of him, Thang and Loi, their mother and her sister, who are the housekeepers, me, my mother, who cooks the complimentary breakfasts, and my grandmother—my Ba Noi—who either sits upstairs in her room and raves all day or is dragged downstairs by Mr. Henry and positioned in the lobby with a cup of tea to give the hotel a homey feel.

We gathered in the first-floor room where Thang takes his girls and Loi and I take naps on slow days.

"Why are we here? What are we doing here?" Ba Noi said as she sat down.

"I agree," said my auntie Linh. "Why do we need a meeting, Hung? Couldn't whatever it is have waited a couple of hours until dinner?"

"I think Ba Noi is just being generally senile," I chimed in. "She probably doesn't even know we're having a meeting."

Thang and Loi at the same time: "You're a little shit, Phi, you know that? A real shit," and "Don't talk about Ba Noi when she's in the room!"

I looked over at Ba Noi. She was smiling beatifically at a decorative vase of plastic flowers. Mr. Henry—who was wearing only boxer shorts and rubber sandals to his own staff meeting—tried calling everyone to attention. He cleared his throat.

"Valued employees!" he began. He had obviously rehearsed this beforehand. My auntie Mai turned her snort of laughter into a cough when he shot her a look. "Valued employees, I have called this meeting because I have decided that we must change our entire marketing strategy …"

I hadn't realized we'd had a strategy, other than not to accidentally poison the guests, or, in Thang's case, accidentally get them pregnant.

"… We need to add a little more class to our establishment …"

Uh—oh. The last time Mr. Henry wanted to add more class to the Frangi, he sank us into debt by installing a heinous plaster tiered-basin fountain in the middle of the lobby that breaks down every month or so.

"… And we need to reach out to the international corporate community! It's the businessmen from Japan and Australia and Singapore and the USA who have all the money, and so we will convince them to come to the Frangipani Hotel! How will we do this?" Mr. Henry paused dramatically to stare around the room at us. "Easy!" He dragged a large plastic shopping bag from the closet and began to dole out its contents. With his drooping stomach, he looked like a budget Vietnamese Santa Claus. First he pulled out a large stack of loose leaf paper and handed it to Auntie Linh.

"What's this, Hung?"

"Put a little in every room—it's our new, monogrammed hotel stationery! I got it done cheap by a friend on Hàng Ma. Now, for the boys, something special …" He reached into the bag again, and as our eyes widened in horror, he slowly drew out two pairs of matching, mustard-colo red trousers and jackets with unraveling gold epaulets and tossed them to Thang and Loi. "New uniforms! There, aren't they smart?" Thang stared at the yellow atrocity, looking as if he might cry.

"Snazzy!" I whispered to him. "Imagine what a lady-killer you'll be in that!"

But Mr. Henry rounded on me next. "Phi, you've got English and a bit of French under your belt, right? Well, there should still be some room left up there," he said as he tapped my forehead with a chubby index finger. He dropped a heavy book in my lap. "You're learning Japanese now."

I looked down at the book's cover. Little cartoon children with purple hair smiled up at me. No way.

"Don't you think there's an easier way to do this?" I pleaded. "Maybe repainting the building a color that isn't pink?"

Mr. Henry pretended he hadn't heard me and added, "One more thing—I'm cutting down on your cigarette breaks. It's a filthy habit, and a customer could come in while you're not there. You're down to four a day now."

I'm still feeling sore about this—I've always taken as many cigarette breaks as I pleased, which is probably giving me a mélange of cancers, but it gets me away from the reception desk. During the day I'll just smoke on the corner curb with Thang, but at night I always go around the block to Hoan Kiem Lake. Nothing gives me greater pleasure than leaning against the splintering red bridge that spans it, flicking my cigarette butts into the filthy green water, and staring at people.

Tourists swarm the place even in low season, dutifully snapping photograph after photograph of the ancient tower in the middle of the lake, and giggling Vietnamese teenagers take pictures of themselves on their cellphones. Around the perimeter, couples wander, holding hands, and groups of old women do tai chi to a cassette player warbling bamboo flute music. It's the most crowded spot in the city, but it's where I go to be alone. The water is smeary with the reflections of yellow, green, and blue lanterns hanging from the trees at its edge. Sometimes kids will sit on the lower branches and try to fish, but everyone knows that there's nothing to catch in Hoan Kiem but empty Coca-Cola cans and used heroin needles. Legend says that centuries ago, a giant turtle lived at the bottom of the lake, and it once gave a magic sword to a general to help him defeat the Chinese invaders. I'm supposed to tell the story to all the tourists who stay at the Frangi.

They say that the lake is the soul of this city. I think they might be right.

作品选读（二）

Build Your House Around My Body

(Saigon: Three Days After the Disappearance)
By Violet Kupersmith

LONG WOKE IN THE MIDDLE of the night to Winnie standing over him. When he opened his mouth she clamped a hand over it. Shook her head. Long tried to speak her name into her palm anyway, and she pressed her hand down even harder on his lips, with a force that surprised him. She was wearing a motorbike face mask that he had never seen before. A Hello Kitty–patterned one. Winnie lifted her hand from his mouth but raised her index finger over her face mask. Shhh. Then she beckoned for him to follow her. Down the staircase, through the kitchen, over to his motorbike.

"Where are we going?" Long whispered in the darkness of his foyer. He didn't know why he hadn't attempted to embrace her, or demonstrate in some other way his relief at her return. It occurred to him that he might be dreaming, and he looked around his house for some sign of trees.

Winnie had pulled open the gate. "The beach." Her voice was muffled by the face mask. She handed Long a bag that he hadn't noticed her holding, and when he took it in his arms it wriggled, and he nearly dropped it in surprise. Long looked down and saw that there was a small, filthy dog inside the bag with its head poking out of the zipper flap at the top.

"Winnie, wha—"

She held her finger up to her face mask again. Shhh. —

WINNIE HAD BECOME A better driver, and Long didn't know how or when it had happened. She sailed smoothly down the highway to Vung Tau in the dark. Maybe this was what she had been doing for the past three days. He was still groggy, and he tightened his arms around her waist. For some reason, he did not want to ask her where she had been, or even where the dog had come from. None of it felt like it mattered. The dog was sitting obediently on his lap between them. They were one of only a handful of motorbikes traveling at this hour, but occasionally a truck or a bus would howl past and Long's baggy raincoat sleeves would flap noisily in its slipstream. Before they left, he had accidentally grabbed Winnie's jacket from the seat compartment instead of his own, but didn't notice until after he had already tugged it on. His hands were cold now, so he took them off of Winnie's waist and stuffed them into his pockets, where one of them brushed against something papery. Long passed the time by studying the shadows flashing by on the side of the road and trying to identify them: the dark, hulking outlines of tire factories and textile warehouses and packaging plants, the small apartments where the people who worked in them lived, the last of the spider-legged mangrove swamps this far north of the Mekong. And then finally, he smelled salt.

They reached Vung Tau just after dawn. It had already begun waking up, its eyes blinking in the morning light; motorbikes were being loaded with hot bread, the morning swimmers were already performing their calisthenics on the sands of Bãi Sau. But Winnie was not stopping yet; she drove them down the entire length of the spindle of a city, to the very tip of the peninsula, to the lonely beach that lay at its end. When there was no more road to follow, she parked the motorbike and they dismounted. In the daylight, Long could see now that Winnie was wearing new clothes in addition to the face mask. She was all in white.

She stared out at the sea in the milky new morning, and she did not blink or move or even breathe for what felt like two minutes. Long twisted his head all around, looking at a group of haggling fishermen, looking at the sky, looking at the rock formations by the water, their edges dizzyingly sharp. He turned to look at the sun-whitened façades of the hotels behind them, at the symmetry of their balconies, at the enormity of the shade cast by their awnings. Behind the hotels, the hills. Somewhere at their top, a lighthouse that the French had built a hundred years ago. Long put his hands into his pockets absently and reencountered the piece of paper inside one of them. He took it out and gave it a brief and indifferent examination—it was a blank slip of paper, the size of a bill or a receipt or a lottery ticket, but there was nothing written on it—before folding it back up and putting it away.

Winnie was moving again. She stepped onto the sand and began walking away from the cluster of fishmongers, taking the dog out of the bag and letting it trot alongside her. Her hair was blowing in the briny air, and Long could see, ruefully, that it had grown long again without his noticing. He hadn't been paying enough attention to her lately. All along, he thought to himself, he had been waiting for her to become someone else for him—to turn into Binh, probably—instead of loving the real Winnie in front of him. He was going to change, he decided. Why not move here? The sea would heal them. He could find a job at a different school, and Winnie would be happy by the beach. This was what they

It was low tide now, and the sand was glittering with all the unsellable things that the fishermen had drawn in with their nets and then discarded-jellyfish and already-dead slipmouths and old shoes and sea cucumbers and one pike eel that was still alive, but barely. As they passed, Winnie nudged the eel back within reach of the tide with a sneakered toe.

She led them to a sheltered spot by the rocks and then set down her bag. The dog was now entertaining itself by chasing a small crab it had found. Winnie looked out at the water again, and then at Long. There were tears in her eyes. Then she finally removed her face mask for the first time, and she smiled at him.

"Do you think you would recognize me anywhere?" she said.

Long frowned. "Winnie, what's wrong with your voice?"

Winnie held his gaze. "I mean, if you saw me, would you know it was me?"

Her timbre had completely changed. Her accent had completely changed. How could the face mask have done this? "Winnie," stammered Long, "what happened to you?"

She shook her head and she reached into the bag. From it she removed the two large dried squid that Long had purchased for her six years ago in Ia Kare, withered and brown and slightly larger than the length of her hands. Long could not put a name to what had transpired, but he felt the edges of the truth brushing up against each other. "No," he said softly, though he wasn't sure yet what he thought he was refuting. She whistled to the dog, who promptly dropped its crab and frisked over to her across the sand. She flicked one of the dried squid to it like a Frisbee, and the dog caught it in its mouth and quickly retreated to the rocks to gnaw on it before she could change her mind.

She paused at the water's edge before entering and took a deep, shaky breath. Then she took her arms and wrapped them around herself, embracing her own body tightly for a full minute. And then finally, she stepped in, Long two paces behind her. They waded through the shallow, foamy spittle to finally reach the point where the water came up to their knees. She crouched down. Long watched as she held her squid beneath the surface of the waves.

"It's dead, silly," he said with a smile. "What are you trying to do to it?"

She was rehydrating the squid. He still didn't understand why. Then Long frowned. The squid's body had grown bigger. Paler, too. That's not right, he thought. Its skin had expanded to the size of a very large plastic grocery bag.

The tide was starting to come in now. A wave knocked her off her feet, and Long sloshed over, hindered by his sodden pant legs, to help her back up.

But she was not trying to get up again, he realized, too late. She was lying back in the water, her hair floating all around her, and she had inserted her legs into the sack of the squid's body, which had now become the size of her own. She pulled its head over hers as a second wave came crashing in.

The skin of the creature glimmered momentarily beneath the surface of the water, and she was gone.

中国人民大学出版社外语出版分社读者信息反馈表

尊敬的读者：

  感谢您购买和使用中国人民大学出版社外语出版分社的 _____ 一书，我们希望通过这张小小的反馈卡来获得您更多的建议和意见，以改进我们的工作，加强我们双方的沟通和联系。我们期待着能为更多的读者提供更多的好书。
  请您填妥下表后，寄回或传真回复我们，对您的支持我们不胜感激！

1. 您是从何种途径得知本书的：
    □书店　　　□网上　　　□报纸杂志　　　□朋友推荐
2. 您为什么决定购买本书：
    □工作需要　□学习参考　□对本书主题感兴趣　□随便翻翻
3. 您对本书内容的评价是：
    □很好　　　□好　　　□一般　　　□差　　　□很差
4. 您在阅读本书的过程中有没有发现明显的专业及编校错误，如果有，它们是：
    _____
    _____
    _____

5. 您对哪些专业的图书信息比较感兴趣：
    _____
    _____
    _____

6. 如果方便，请提供您的个人信息，以便于我们和您联系（您的个人资料我们将严格保密）：
    您供职的单位：_____
    您教授的课程（教师填写）：_____
    您的通信地址：_____
    您的电子邮箱：_____

请联系我们：黄婷　程子殊　吴振良　王琼　鞠方安
电话：010-62512737，62513265，62515538，62515573，62515576
传真：010-62514961
E-mail：huangt@crup.com.cn　　chengzsh@crup.com.cn　　wuzl@crup.com.cn
　　　　crup_wy@163.com　　jufa@crup.com.cn
通信地址：北京市海淀区中关村大街甲 59 号文化大厦 15 层　　邮编：100872
中国人民大学出版社外语出版分社